ALIEN EMPRESS

ARGONAUTS

BOOK THREE

IRIDIUM

PUBLISHING
A DIVISION OF

HOOKE
PUBLICATIONS

BOOKS BY ISAAC HOOKE

Military Science Fiction

Argonauts
Bug Hunt
You Are Prey
Alien Empress

Alien War Trilogy
Hoplite
Zeus
Titan

The ATLAS Series
ATLAS
ATLAS 2
ATLAS 3

A Captain's Crucible Series
Flagship
Test of Mettle
Cradle of War
Planet Killer
Worlds at War

Science Fiction

The Forever Gate Series
The Dream
A Second Chance
The Mirror Breaks
They Have Wakened Death
I Have Seen Forever
Rebirth
Walls of Steel
The Pendulum Swings
The Last Stand

Thrillers

The Ethan Galaal Series
Clandestine
A Cold Day In Mosul
Terminal Phase

ALIEN EMPRESS

ARGONAUTS

BOOK THREE

Isaac Hooke

This is a work of fiction. All characters, names, organizations, places, events and incidents are the product of the author's imagination or used fictitiously.

Text copyright © Isaac Hooke 2017
Published March 2017. All rights reserved.

No part of this publication may be copied, reproduced in any format, by any means, electronic or otherwise, without prior consent from the copyright owner and publisher of this book.

www.IsaacHooke.com

ISBN-13: 978-1-5207711-5-1
ISBN-10: 1-5207-7115-0

Cover design by Isaac Hooke
Cover image by Shookooboo

contents

ONE 1
TWO 8
THREE 17
FOUR 30
FIVE 38
SIX 52
SEVEN 61
EIGHT 75
NINE 84
TEN 95
ELEVEN 105
TWELVE 114
THIRTEEN 124
FOURTEEN 135
FIFTEEN 141
SIXTEEN 148
SEVENTEEN 160
EIGHTEEN 167
NINETEEN 178

TWENTY	187
TWENTY-ONE	195
TWENTY-TWO	204
TWENTY-THREE	213
TWENTY-FOUR	224
TWENTY-FIVE	230
TWENTY-SIX	237
TWENTY-SEVEN	247
TWENTY-EIGHT	256
TWENTY-NINE	265
ACKNOWLEDGMENTS	279

*To my father, mother, brothers, and
most devoted fans.*

one

Rade aimed his targeting reticle over the distant mech. The unit had emerged from cover only a moment before, revealing its position. The other tangos were likely hidden nearby, ready to offer ancillary fire.

Rade resided near the top of a rocky escarpment, partially concealed behind a boulder. The camouflage skin of his Hoplite had changed to blend in with the surrounding terrain, hiding the rest of him, at least on the visual band.

He tracked the target as it raced across the grassy plain, hurrying toward a knoll. He was about to squeeze the trigger when a missile alarm went off.

The Raptor drone ten thousand meters above had detected his heat signature early: that could be the only explanation. The metallic hull of his mech absorbed heat much faster than the neighboring rock. He had hoped he would have a few more seconds.

Apparently not.

He had positioned his ballistic shield above him to protect against incoming laser fire; those in command of the Raptor obviously realized this, and had elected to fire a Hellfire instead to maximize the damage potential.

Rade activated his jumpjets and fired his Trench Coat antimissile countermeasures. Thirty-four pieces of seeking metal emerged from the nozzles surrounding his waist. He latched onto the rock face higher up and ascended rapidly with quick movements of his arms and legs. Before he had moved very far explosions rocked the area and he lost his footing.

Rade activated his jumpjets again, intending to make for a plateau higher up. He aimed his grenade launcher at the distant knoll below and released several frags. He also launched a few more grenades at potential hiding places the others might have been using.

But before he landed on the plateau, his screen turned black.

"Gotcha," Shaw said.

The inner cocoon of the cockpit retracted and Rade fell to the bottom of the chamber. He opened the hatch and emerged from the simulator pod.

Seven other pods were crammed into the storage facility adjacent to the combat room. From them, the other Argonauts emerged.

"Well that was fun," Bender said.

"Damn it," Rade said. "You guys got lucky. The Raptor found me early. A few more seconds and I would have had you."

"You would have had Bender, you mean," Tahoe said. "The only one of us who ran out into the open. The rest of us were still in hiding. And once you revealed your position by firing on Bender, we would have had you anyway."

"So you think," Rade said.

"You know," TJ said. "Standardized maps are the way to go. This randomized mission bull is a crapshoot. Either the odds lean heavily in your favor, or against."

"That's the way it is in real life," Lui said. "We never get to pick the odds."

"Still," TJ said. "Your starting position, and the respective positions of your hunters, can truly make or break the scenario."

"So this is what, the third time you've failed the qualification, boss?" Fret asked.

"Fourth," Rade said quietly.

The survival qualification was taken straight out of Rade's military background. As a MOTH, he had been required to retake the qualification once a year, and he enforced the same rule on each and every member of his crew. He used similar failure criteria as the military version, in that an unsuccessful applicant had to wait a week before trying again. But if this were an actual MOTH qualification, Rade would have been kicked out after the fourth time. The longest losing streak anyone had had so far was Fret, at six times in a row. The fact that Rade was closing on that number was more than embarrassing.

"Maybe it's time you hunkered down in the sim room with the rest of us," Tahoe said. "And shot out some tangos, like we used to do in the run-up to qualifications."

"Why not just cancel the qualification entirely?" Fret said. "Come on, let's be realistic. These types of scenarios never happen in real life. They're so contrived. Thrown onto a rock face in the middle of a barren landscape. A Raptor searching for you overhead. A hunter killer team hidden somewhere on the plains below. When does that ever happen? You'd see the hunter killer team coming in from a mile away, with ample time to prepare, or snipe them."

"I'm not going to cancel the qualification," Rade

said. "We need to maintain our finely-honed edge. But TJ is right, the simulation scenario might be overdue for some tweaking. I'll see if Harlequin can come up with something more realistic. In the meantime, I'm going to practice my ass off, as per Tahoe's suggestion."

"Ha!" Bender said. "Practice! Everything can be solved with *practice!* When are you going to admit that you're just too old, boss. You ain't cut out for this boots-on-the-ground stuff no more."

"I'm not too old," Rade replied. "As I said, I just need some more time in the sim."

"You know what the problem is, don't you?" Manic said. "Too many bedroom sessions between you and Shaw. That's where all your practice is these days."

"Hey, leave our bedroom out of this," Shaw said. "The only reason Rade is failing is because... well, actually, Bender's right. He's too old."

"Thank you," Bender said.

"Yeah, *thanks*," Rade said.

"Welcome, honey," Shaw said sweetly.

"When did my crew turn against me?" Rade said.

"When you started requiring us to pass MOTH qualifications every year..." Fret said.

"He's right," Tahoe said. "We're not MOTHs anymore, boss."

"We still need standards," Rade insisted.

"Maybe it's time to lower those standards," Lui said.

"Never," Rade replied. "I told you, we can't lose our finely-honed edge."

"But that's what our combat robots are for," Fret insisted.

"Is it?" Rade said. "And what happens when the

robots fail? Who fights for us then?"

Fret didn't have an answer.

Rade noticed a call request indicator in the lower right of his vision. It was from Surus.

Rade accepted. "Hello there, Surus, what can I do for you?"

"Rade, I need to see you in your office," Surus said.

"I'll be there shortly." Rade disconnected and turned toward Shaw. "The alien needs to see me in my office."

"You and her have been spending a lot of time together in that office of yours..." Shaw said.

"Come with me, then," Rade said.

"I think I will," Shaw replied.

The pair made their way to the bridge. When they arrived, they squeezed past that cramped series of curved stations to the adjacent office. Surus wasn't yet there.

Rade edged by the visitor's chair, and his desk, to take his customary seat. Shaw remained standing.

When Surus arrived, Rade gestured toward the visitor's chair. "Have a seat."

Surus glanced at Shaw uncertainly, then sat. "Thank you." The Artificial the alien inhabited always looked the same, the epitome of effortless beauty.

"I appreciate your seeing me on such short notice," Surus said.

"Of course," Rade said, leaning backward to rock his chair. "You're our client. You're paying for our time. So what do you have? You've found another Phant for us to track down?"

"I have to return to my homeworld," Surus said.

Rade stopped rocking in his chair. "Why, what's happened? Our mission is over, then?"

"Not over," Surus said. "Merely on hold. Our homeworld is under attack."

"Is it Phants?" Rade asked. "Motherships from another hive?"

"No," Surus said. "The Greens are mounting a desperate defense against an attack from another Tech Class IV race. I will call them the Hydra, though of course there is no translation for their true name in the human tongue. An aquatic species, the Hydra are one of the few species beside the Elder that the Phants could never conquer in their native region of space. The Phants did inflict great suffering upon them, however, and caused severe damage to their colonies. After repelling the involved Phant hives, the Hydra swore to hunt down every last one of our species, regardless of affiliation. They've had varying degrees of success in that regard, mostly tracking down those Phants that have chosen to nest away from the Motherships, subsisting upon the geronium deposits in the upper atmospheres of gas giants.

"The Hydra have developed a sophisticated method of detection. Specifically, they dispatch seekers to furtively scan the gas giants of systems in the region, and whenever they encounter any hives, they send in a special kill fleet to clean them up."

"I take it they don't discriminate between Greens and other Phants?" Rade asked.

"They do not," Surus said. "The Greens are grouped in with every other Phant in terms of their 'enemy' status. My homeworld was supposed to have a shielding system in place that would fool the scans of the seekers, but apparently the Hydra found a way around that."

"What can we do?" Rade asked.

"I am returning to defend my homeworld," Surus

said. "I cannot ask for your help in this matter. It is beyond the scope of our contract."

"You don't have to *ask*," Rade said. "Because we're helping without question. We owe the Greens. Without you, humanity would have fallen to the other Phants."

Surus nodded. "If you go, there is a good chance you will not return. In fact, there's a good chance *I* won't return."

"I understand," Rade said. "Just let me tell the men. I don't want to force any of them to come along."

"If you go, they'll follow you," Surus said.

"She's right," Shaw said. "We'll follow you to the ends of the galaxy."

Rade smiled fleetingly. "That's what I'm afraid of. I'll do my best to discourage them. None of them has to do this. *You* don't have to do this."

"Like you said, we owe the Greens," Shaw said.

two

When Rade relayed the news about the attack on the Green homeworld to his men, unsurprisingly everyone wanted to go.

"How do we get to their homeworld?" Manic said. "The Greens collapsed the last Slipstream leading to their region of space a good, what, twenty years ago?"

"I kept an Acceptor before our Mothership departed," Surus said. "It resides under 24/7 guard on my base."

"Your base?" Manic asked.

"Yes," Surus said. "My company, Green Systems, purchased a Franco-Italian moon shortly after incorporating. I contracted some of the best developers in the galaxy to construct a headquarters on that moon. My own private base of operations."

"Must be nice to have cashflow like that," Manic commented.

"Once we reach the homeworld, I don't suppose there's a chance we'll get some of those nice Tech Class IV mechs the Greens have?" Bender asked.

"I have purchased several Titan classes," Surus replied. "They are waiting at my base. You will all get one before we use the Acceptor to teleport to the homeworld."

"But Titans are not Tech Class IV," Bender whined.

"No, they are not," Surus said.

"Can we take the Titans back to the *Argonaut* when we're done the mission?" Fret said.

"Ha," Tahoe said. "Good luck fitting even one Titan in the hangar bay. Far too tall."

"Then let's get a new ship?" Fret asked.

"We've been through this before," Rade said. "The *Argonaut* suits our needs just fine for the moment."

"The Titans are for this mission alone," Surus agreed. "Additionally, I am uncertain how long we will use them once we cross to the Green homeworld."

"What do you mean?" TJ asked.

"The situation on the homeworld is grim," Surus replied. "The siege has been ongoing for the past six months. I am not sure how much longer the defenses will last. When we arrive, it might be to a destroyed world. Or a world on the brink of destruction."

"So this 'homeworld' of yours is really just a Phant hive in the upper atmosphere of a gas giant, right?" Bender said.

"That is correct. Or rather, several individual sub-hives, scattered throughout the atmosphere."

"What happened to that big skull-shaped ship of yours you used to drive around the galaxy?" Bender asked.

"We still have it, of course," Surus said. "Unfortunately, the ship is tied up in the war against the remaining Phants, and won't be able to reach the homeworld for another six years."

"Ah."

There were a few more questions and comments, and when the crew had no more, Rade dismissed the men.

Shaw lingered in the combat room, which also served as the mission briefing area aboard the *Argonaut*. Tahoe stayed behind, too, not moving from where he sat cross-legged on the mat.

"I don't suppose we can continue toward our original stop of Bharat Station?" Tahoe asked.

Rade checked the galactic maps on his Implant. "No, I'm afraid not. From our current location, if we continue to Bharat now, it'll take us an extra three weeks to reach Taurus 62." That was the moon where the Green Systems base resided. "I know you arranged to meet Tepin and the kids at Bharat. I'm sorry."

Tahoe hid his disappointment well. "Not a big deal. I mean come on, I'd much rather be fighting for my life on some alien homeworld on the far side of the galaxy, than spending time with my nagging wife while our kids run around out of control on the station. Who wouldn't, right?"

"I can't actually tell if he's being sarcastic or not," Shaw said. "Considering how old his 'kids' are."

"It sounds like he's not really looking forward to either option," Rade said. "And I don't blame him. Did Tepin already buy the tickets to Bharat?"

"Yeah," Tahoe said. "But it's not a big thing to cancel. She'll be happy to stay on Earth."

Rade rested a hand on Tahoe's shoulder. "I know it's been a long time since you were able to see your family. I'll make it up to you when the current mission is done."

"It's always when the current mission is done," Tahoe said. "But when the current mission is done, we always have another mission. Sometimes it seems like we never have a break. I like to work like the next man, but sometimes I feel we're headed toward burnout. And I'm not just talking about myself."

"I'm not quite sure what you mean," Rade said. "We have lots of breaks between missions. A ton of free time. It usually takes anywhere from three to eight weeks to reach a given planet involved in an op. Look at our current mission: we have two weeks until we reach the Green Systems base."

"Well sure," Tahoe said. "Except that we're cooped up aboard the *Argonaut* the whole way, feeling the simmering tension of expectation as we await our arrival. It's not really a break if you ask me. Getting aboard a roomy station, or even better, visiting a terraformed planet, with no future missions in sight, no cares in the galaxy, now that's what I call proper shore leave."

"There is always immersive VR," Rade said.

"The mind might sometimes believe it," Tahoe said. "But not the body."

"All right," Rade said. "I'm not going to argue with you on this because I know I'm right. And as I said at the beginning of the briefing, it's not required of any of you that you come. If you don't think you can handle it, then please do tell me and I'll drop you off at the nearest base."

"I already told you I can handle it," Tahoe said. "I'm just a bit pissed at the timing is all. And a little worried about you."

"Worry about yourself, not me," Rade said. "I'm better than I've ever been. Just ask Shaw."

Smiling, he rubbed her on the back.

She shook her head and half rolled her eyes in exasperation.

"How's your PTSD?" Tahoe said.

Rade stiffened and the smile fled his face. He purposely kept his voice very calm as he said: "What PTSD?"

"Well," Shaw said, raising her hands. "I think it's time for me to excuse myself." She gave Rade a kiss on the cheek. "I'll see you later."

She started to go.

"No," Rade said. "You stay. I want you to hear this. What PTSD, Tahoe? If I had post traumatic stress disorder, do you think I'd be able to do what I do? Lead you guys on life or death missions across the galaxy, and still function at the high levels of performance you've all come to expect from me?"

"You're very good at hiding the symptoms," Tahoe said. "But you can't fool me, nor the others, really. We know what's wrong. After a fight, you go and hide away, and just sit there, staring into space for hours on end. It's not normal, brother."

"He's been taking counseling sessions with Bax," Shaw said. "He—"

Rade raised a quick hand to silence her.

"I have some lingering combat issues, yes," Rade said. "But it's nothing I can't deal with."

"Are you sure you don't want to talk about it?" Tahoe asked.

Rade hesitated. Finally: "No, my brother." Anything he told Tahoe would only serve to burden the man.

Tahoe nodded. "I'm here for you whenever you need me."

With that, his friend left.

"You don't understand," Shaw said. "We want to help you, Rade. But you won't let us in. Why don't you let Bax record your session sometime, so I can watch it afterward?"

"You don't want to see that," Rade said. "You don't want to hear."

"I do."

Rade shook his head adamantly.

Shaw sighed. "You have this pain trapped inside you that you don't want to let any of us see, like a piece of grit trapped in your shell, constantly irritating you. Let us help you form a protective shield around that grit. Let us help you turn it into a pearl."

"It's actually a myth that oysters form pearls around pieces of grit or sand," Rade said. "The pearls actually form around parasites like sea worms. Those are the irritants."

"Well that's even more apt," Shaw said. "Let us help you form a pearl around the parasite that won't give you peace."

"It's not going to be as easy as that," Rade said. "This is only something I can deal with on my own."

"There's holistic treatments we can try..." Shaw suggested.

"No," Rade said. "I don't need it. I can handle this. Trust me. Shaw. Baby. Trust me."

But Shaw only shook her head. "Tahoe was right. If you keep this up, you're going to burn yourself out. You've built up a house of cards. The stress, combined with the lingering combat issues as you call them, are going to lead to the collapse of that house if you're not careful."

"It will never collapse," Rade said. "Because it's a house of cards glued together by you."

Shaw smiled. "That's sweet. But unfortunately, I'm not sure even I will be enough to stop the collapse."

She left the combat room, too.

Rade lowered himself to the mat when she was gone and he stared unblinking at the overhead.

"Are you all right, boss?" Bax asked.

"Yes," Rade told the *Argonaut's* AI.

He tried to keep the scenes of battle away. He tried

to keep the sounds at bay. But they came then, flooding in, and he found himself buried in the sand once more, with dark shapes closing in on all sides...

DURING THE JOURNEY to the moon base, the crew took turns exercising in the cramped gym. Rade and the others had pushed themselves since returning from the Xaranth mission, aiming to acquire all the muscle mass they had lost due to radiation and starvation. The natural members of the crew found their gains plateauing already, and Rade was no exception. He elected not to use any gear—the steroid kind—even though Bender offered to share his supply. In all honesty, Rade didn't feel the need to get bigger than he was at the moment.

The sheer volume of food required to maintain that weight seemed wasteful. Not to mention the huge strain on the body all that muscle mass imparted. In the past, he wanted to be the biggest, baddest, meanest mofo around, if only to command the respect of his men. But he soon realized that that same respect could be garnered from force of will alone, as he had learned from past commanding officers such as Lieutenant Commander Braggs and Chief Bourbonjack. Both had been mere sticks relative to the other MOTHs, though they were hard and lean, and usually bested most of the men on all the calisthenics training, especially the long distance running evolutions. When you were carrying around an extra hundred pounds of body weight, muscle or no, you were going to run a slower kilometer. Of course, jumpsuits made up for all of that. Jumpsuits and their strength-enhancing exoskeletons: the great equalizers.

Rade finally passed the survival qualification simulation on his fifth try. It was a relief, and told him that he hadn't lost his touch after all. He was just about ready to cancel the yearly test, because there was no point in making the others do it if he couldn't pass it himself. He decided that when next year rolled around, he would think very carefully about repealing that qualification. Like Bender had said, Rade was getting up there in age, and since he couldn't afford the yearly rejuvenations that the military offered its older recruits, he would have to seriously consider changing certain things. Still, he had meant it when he told his men they needed to maintain their finely-honed edge. If he dropped the qualification, he'd have to find some other way for them to do that, and until he could come up with something the test would simply have to stay.

He issued disciplinary action against some of the crew during the journey. Bender and Manic got into a fight: something about Bender's sister's pussy. Fret and Lui fought because Lui apparently ate a cake Fret had baked and decorated. Rade had docked their pay. That was all he could do, really. He used to cut their food rations as punishment, but he had learned right away that when you reduced the calories of big men like these it only made them more prone to anger.

Ordinarily he wouldn't have paid much attention to those incidents, as fights like those came hand in hand with a crew filled with so much testosterone. But there were other weird behaviors that bothered him. The most glaring was Shaw's: she was becoming increasingly self-conscious around Surus. At first Shaw had been so congratulatory whenever she and Surus met in private: complimenting Surus on her nails, or how she had done her hair, and so forth. Surus always returned the praise. But Shaw had stopped the compliments lately, and seemed strangely nervous around Surus, always looking at everyone else when the Artificial entered for example, to see what their reactions were. In the evenings, Shaw would examine her face closely in the mirror and complain about any fine line she thought she saw, saying she needed to see the rejuvenation specialist soon. Rade supposed it was hard to measure up to the perfection of a machine, but still, he thought she was overdoing it.

When considering all this odd behavior—the fighting over cakes, the self-consciousness—Rade began to realize that Tahoe might have been on to something when he said that they really needed a real shore leave. Perhaps the crew truly had been cooped up aboard the *Argonaut* for too long.

After this mission I'll order some liberty time for sure, Rade promised himself.

But he had made such promises before, he realized. And broken them.

Then again, maybe he was being too hard on himself. Before accepting Ms. Bounty as a client, he had in fact given the crew liberty time on Etalon Station. And also after successfully trapping the first Phant in the core of a star.

But that was eight months ago.

Yes, maybe it's been a little too long.

three

The *Argonaut* was on final approach with Taurus 62. Rade sat at the head of the circular series of stations known as the Sphinx on the bridge. The video feed from the nose camera resided in the upper right of his vision. The moon filled half the view. Two Franco-Italian corvettes orbited nearby.

Rade tapped in Surus, who resided in her guest quarters in the cargo hold.

"Should we be worried about those corvettes, Surus?" Rade said.

"They're mine," Surus replied.

"Thank you." Rade disconnected. He turned toward Fret. "Have we been given permission to orbit?"

"We have," Fret confirmed. "I've received the orbital information. I'm forwarding it to Lui."

"How's it look, Lui?" Rade asked.

"They want us in a geosynchronous orbit about one hundred and twenty kilometers above the base," Lui replied.

"That's fine with me." Rade turned toward his astrogator. "Shaw, put us into orbit."

"Aye, boss," Shaw replied.

A few minutes later, when they had moved into

place, Rade told Fret: "Request permission to land."

Fret's lips moved soundlessly as he communicated with the base on the moon below: he had raised a noise canceler around himself so that he wouldn't disturb the other members of the bridge crew while he talked.

In a moment Fret looked up: "We have permission."

"All right," Rade said. "Let's get to the Dragonfly. Bax, you have the conn. Take good care of my ship while we're away, you hear?"

"She will not have a scratch," Bax promised. "Even should the star nova, or the moon explode."

"That's a bit melodramatic, isn't it?" Rade said as the crew exited the bridge and made its way through the corridors.

"I suppose," Bax replied. "Though I wanted to show you the extent of my dedication."

Bender interjected: "Yeah but, AI bitch, if the star goes nova, no way you're going to escape."

"Perhaps," Bax said. "But perhaps not. It all depends on the strength of the explosion. If it is a hyper nova, then of course I would not survive. But a mere surface ejection event? I think I can survive the expulsion of some interstellar matter."

"*Superheated* interstellar matter," Bender corrected.

"I am confident I could use the moon as a shield if the star blows," Bax countered.

"Ah, whatever, pussy AI," Bender said. "I got some real work to do. You enjoy your imaginary scenarios. Have fun babysitting an empty ship."

"I certainly shall," Bax replied. "I will compose a poem for you in your absence. I plan to title it, The Short Life of Bender, Who Was Accidentally Spaced From the Cargo Bay After He Offended the AI of His

Ship."

"*What?*" Bender said. "You go ahead and try that shit. We'll see what happens to your AI core when I'm done with you. Did you hear that crap, boss? The ship's AI was threatening me. *Threatening!*"

"Nah," Rade said. "He was just joking around. Isn't that right, Bax?"

The *Argonaut's* AI didn't answer.

"Bax..." Rade said.

"Oh yes, of course," Bax said. "I was completely joking, Bender. Have a nice trip!"

"Damn it," Bender said. "To compound my problems, now I got to watch my back against the vindictive AI of my own ship. Ridiculous."

The crew joined Surus in the shuttle hangar bay. Rade had decided not to bring any combat robots along for the mission. The only mechanical presences would be in the form of Harlequin, and Surus' host Emilia Bounty.

The crew went to their lockers and suited up. Shaw hid behind the door of her locker while she dressed, as usual. Rade thought that was cute, because no one would dare cast a glance her way while she changed, not anymore. They had gotten too many black eyes from Shaw, and not to mention Rade.

After suiting up, he felt the sting in his arm from the accelerant that would allow him to adapt to the inner environment of the suit, then he boarded the ramp of the shuttle. It was called a Dragonfly because of the four equal-sized wings protruding from the front area that were vaguely reminiscent of the insect.

Rade took his seat and the clamps telescoped in from the sides and secured him in place. Bender sat on his right. Tahoe his left. In the seats directly across from him were Harlequin and Surus. The two

Artificials usually stayed close together, and hung out in off hours. Like attracts like, Rade supposed.

Shaw was in the pilot seat.

When everyone was aboard and clamped in, Rade ordered: "Take us down, Shaw."

"Aye, boss," Shaw replied.

That never gets old, he thought.

He ran his gaze across his men.

I'm their boss. And damn proud of it.

While it felt good to be in command, it was also a great burden of responsibility. He didn't take the duty lightly. These were his men to lead, and if he messed up, some of them would die.

The shuttle pulled outside and the zero gravity took hold. He always found that design a bit odd, how the inertial dampeners would prevent him from feeling many G forces and yet the engineers hadn't bothered to implement artificial gravity while they were at it. He thought it shouldn't have been too much of an effort to extend the dampeners to provide that gravity, but hey, what did he know about engineering design? Maybe it was something that violated power cost rules or whatever they called it.

His eyes lingered on Harlequin directly across from him. The Artificial was wearing a strange expression. It looked... wistful?

Rade tapped him in. "So how have you been feeling lately?"

"I'm an Artificial," Harlequin replied. "Therefore, I am always feeling fine. Why do you ask?"

"You were possessed by two Phants now," Rade said. "I was just wondering if there were any lingering aftereffects to your programming all these weeks later."

"The Black did successfully reprogram some of my

inner workings, yes," Harlequin replied. "But my antivirus subroutines hunted down the changes and reverted them all. I've also reapplied several manufacturers patches since then, which overwrote much of the code the Phant tampered with. So as far as lingering aftereffects go, there should be none."

"Well that's somewhat reassuring," Rade said. "How was the Phant able to reprogram you anyway? While inside your AI core? I'm not sure I understand how that's possible. Unless it was something done psychically, like the Black did with me. Though again, I'm not sure how that would be possible."

"As AIs, we are capable of learning," Harlequin explained. "This is done via something called self-modifying code. When our neural networks learn something new, we modify that code in realtime, and it executes without requiring a shutdown. Unfortunately, it is also a way to introduce viruses and Trojans. But as I said, my antivirus software inoculated me against the worst of it, and I installed patches to eliminate all other tampered code."

"Good," Rade said. "Though I suppose, what I was more hinting at, was how the ordeal affected your personality."

"My personality is unchanged," Harlequin said. "Although, I have to admit, I have developed quite an odd predilection for violence against Phants. I'm looking forward to the day when we hunt them again."

Rade pursed his lips. "You're okay with this mission, then? We'll be helping a lot of Phants. I know you're friendly with Surus and all, but still..."

"I am completely fine with helping the Greens," Harlequin said. "They are not our enemies."

"True enough," Rade said.

"But how are you, may I ask, boss?"

"Good," Rade said. He disconnected from Harlequin immediately after. It was a bit rude, but it helped forestall any other questions.

He tapped in the external camera so he could view the moon during the approach.

He saw a hemisphere that looked very similar to Earth's moon with that white, gray surface pocked with craters. The base itself was composed of three glass-paneled geodesic domes placed in a triangular pattern. The lower right dome was filled with green foliage, reminding him a little of a jungle—it was obviously a hydroponics farm of some kind that made the base self-sustaining. The topmost and left domes composing the triangle had smaller, more traditional buildings inside them. These were low rise structures made of concrete, and a few taller buildings of metal and glass that looked like medium-rise office buildings.

The shuttle was headed toward the base of the central dome, where a metal rim capped the underside. He could see the outline of what looked like a few double doors along that rim. The hangar bays, no doubt.

He wondered at first how safe those geodesic domes were, seemingly exposed to passing meteors and comets as they were. The atmosphere-less moon obviously was no stranger to meteor impacts, given all the craters that pocked the surface.

But then Rade noticed the large, nasty-looking turrets on either side of the base, and he realized no meteor had a chance in hell of arriving intact. Then again, even a pulverized meteor could cause damage. Perhaps the two corvettes he had seen in orbit would drag the bigger meteors and stray asteroids out of the way.

"Yup, that's a moon all right," Lui said.

"Looks like Bender's zit-covered ass," Manic said.

"My ass ain't white," Bender said. "That's your ass, bitch."

"My ass doesn't have acne scars on it like yours," Manic said.

"Who says those are acne scars I'm talking about on your ass?" Bender retorted. "Those are stains from all the times Fret sprayed you after pulling out."

"Spec ops people don't talk like that," Fret mocked. It was an oft-used refrain on his part, based on something Fret had read on the comment section of the InterGalNet site Rade had set up for the business.

"Like I give a shit what the general public thinks MOTHs are supposed to talk like," Bender said. "Some InterGalNet troll thinks spec-ops is all about stone-faced men who say one or two words, grunt a few times and stare down everyone who tries to talk to them like some brainless moron. That shit pisses me off to no end. Almost as bad as those shitwads claiming to be ex-MOTHs we sometimes find hanging around the station dive bars. You know the kind: those lowliest of scumbags whose asses get kicked the moment I realize them for the posers they are. I tell you, this right here—" He slapped his gloved fist against the chest of his jumpsuit. "This is how the true spec-ops people talk, baby."

"He really likes the sound of his voice today," Tahoe commented.

"He's just trying to impress Surus," Shaw said.

"Humph," Bender said. "I'm muting y'all now. Good-bye."

The hangar bay doors at the metal base of the geodesic dome parted as the shuttle approached, and Shaw piloted the Dragonfly toward the opening.

"You're coming in too fast," Surus said.

"Backseat driver," Manic commented.

Artificial gravity returned as the shuttle entered the bay, and Rade felt the deck shudder as Shaw issued a rapid burst of countering thrust to slow both their forward motion and descent at the same time. The craft dropped down hard on the landing pad and Rade was jerked violently in his seat, along with everyone else.

"Sorry about that," Shaw said. "Surus was right: I came in a bit too fast."

"Bender's comment about Fret spraying Manic's ass must have excited her," Lui said.

"Yeah, that's it," Shaw said.

"Cut her some slack, guys," TJ said. "I'd like to see you all land a shuttle at speed. No one's perfect."

"Except an Artificial," Harlequin replied.

"I'd rather have Shaw pilot any day over *you*," Bender said. "You AIs with your damn bragging tongues. 'We're the best at everything! You humans suck at everything and can kiss our tin can asses.' Why don't you go kiss up to Surus some more. Tell her about your man problems."

Harlequin cocked an eyebrow behind his faceplate. "My man problems?"

"Yeah, how you wish you were a real man like us MOTHs."

"*Ex*-MOTHs," Lui clarified.

"Once a MOTH, always a MOTH," Bender said.

"Just the other day you were the one clarifying that you weren't a MOTH anymore," Lui said.

"Well I changed my mind," Bender said.

"Harlequin is like Pinocchio, he wants to be a real boy," TJ said.

"The hangar atmosphere has pressurized," Shaw

announced.

"Okay, everyone out," Rade said. He was glad for a chance to get moving. As were the others, no doubt. Their crude banter typically increased in the moments before a deployment actually began. That they were trading jibes so heavily told him the Argonauts were more antsy than usual about what awaited. And the lack of response to those jibes was telling. Neither Bender nor Manic had threatened violence in reply to some of the cruder comments, as they would have if they were on the ship. Because the words were not truly meant to insult, but to distract their minds from the terror that was slowly creeping in around the edges.

Rade didn't blame them. He felt that faceless terror too. If he pondered it for too long, or faced it head-on, it would engulf him. Better to let it linger at the periphery of his awareness, not truly acknowledged, but not forgotten either. Traveling across the galaxy to an alien homeworld under siege, hoping to offer what assistance they could to an alien race a full tech class ahead of humanity... Rade didn't have high hopes for the mission.

When we walk onto the Acceptor, we might never return.

To be honest, he wasn't even sure why Surus was letting them come. She had to think the Argonauts could make some sort of a difference, otherwise she wouldn't have allowed Rade and his team to join her. But at the moment, he couldn't quite fathom what aid his team could offer the Greens.

Then again, if the Greens truly were stretched to their breaking point as Surus had suggested, then they could probably use all the help they could get.

The ramp lowered, and the clamps securing them to the seats retracted. The group marched into the hangar, unsure of what sort of welcoming party they would find.

Outside, there were different Dragonfly models scattered throughout the hangar, but otherwise there was no one there to greet them at all.

Scratch that: a golden robot owl flew forward from where it had perched on a railing near the exit.

"What the eff?" Bender said.

"Hello, Little Noctua," Surus said, extending her hand. The owl landed on the wrist area of her jumpsuit, its claws retracting so as not to perforate the gloves.

"Welcome back, sweet master," Noctua said in a high pitched, loving voice. "I missed you."

"And I missed you, little one," Surus told it.

"*What the eff?*" Bender repeated.

"These are my friends, Noctua," Surus said, gesturing to the party. "Shaw. Rade. Tahoe. Bender. Lui. TJ. Manic. Fret. Harlequin."

Noctua tilted its little head toward them. "Hello there."

"My friends, meet Noctua," Surus said.

"Noctua?" Shaw asked.

"My assistant," Surus said. "Within her is contained all the wisdom, perspicacity, knowledge, and erudition of a thousand races. She is the archive of archives. Humanity relies upon special analytical programs to sift through those immensely large sets you call 'big data.' I rely upon Noctua. Come, little one, take us to the homeworld Acceptor."

"Are we going home?" Noctua said excitedly.

"No," Surus said.

"That makes me sad, master." Noctua took flight and swooped underneath an open hatch on the far side of the hangar.

"Is it just me, or is that thing creepy as hell," Bender said.

"The way it flies is kind of disturbing," TJ said. "It falls a half a meter, then flaps its wings like a hummingbird to get back up again, then pretends to flap them slower like a normal bird while it falls again before repeating the process. Brings new meaning to the phrase uncanny valley."

"Except Noctua was never meant to depict a real bird," Surus said.

"Really?" Manic said. "Then why give it the form of an owl?"

"I happen to like owls," Surus replied.

"You just contradicted yourself," Manic said.

Surus ignored him, continuing to lead the way, and Rade and the others followed. They took an escalator to a small terminal and then emerged inside the geodesic dome. The stars peered through the glass above; the points of light were blue shifted, as was common in glass coated with an anti-rad layer. The base probably also had a field generator that would simulate a small magnetosphere, deflecting most gamma and cosmic rays.

The one and two story concrete buildings around them looked similar to what one would find inside other geodesic domes that contained traditionally architected cities. None of the buildings were externally labeled in any way, Rade noted. Likely there were augmented reality indicators for each of them that he didn't have access to on his Implant.

"You might as well take off your helmets while you can," Surus said. "This is the last time you'll be breathing fresh air in a while."

"It's not recycled?" Fret asked.

"No," Surus said. "You did see the plants in the

hydroponic dome on the way in, didn't you?"

Rade unlatched his helmet and removed it. The air felt crisp on his face. He inhaled. It was indeed fresh, and smelled slightly of pine needles.

"Well I'll be damned," Bender said. "That air *is* good."

"Feels almost like we've landed on a terraformed world," Tahoe said.

"That's the idea," Surus said.

Rade attached the helmet to his harness and let it hang, then he followed Surus forward. Ahead, Noctua was circling near a wide hatch that connected to the northernmost geodesic dome, waiting for them.

Occasionally someone walked out of a building and headed toward another nearby. Dressed in blue fatigues, like the kind military personnel wore aboard starships, their faces all looked perfect. Artificials like Surus, no doubt.

One passing woman, carrying a bunch of vials on a tray, looked the spitting image of Emilia Bounty. She had to be the same make and model.

"Well hello," Bender told the woman as she passed.

The Artificial person ignored him and continued on her way.

"That's typical of all the approaches Bender makes," Manic said. "He can never get them to stop."

"Yeah whatever," Bender said. "I never see you stopping the ladies."

"I stop them all the time," Manic said.

"You're so full of it," Bender said.

"Ask Fret," Manic said. "He saw me pick up two chicks at Etalon station that time."

"Yeah you paid for them," Bender said.

"Actually, he didn't," Fret said. "He spouted some

mad game, my friend."

"Ha!" Bender said. "Mad game. Like Manic knows the meaning of the word. The only 'game' he knows is the video game kind."

"I'll show you," Manic said. "I'll pick up any chick in this facility. Just point her out."

"Okay, pick up the chick I just said hello to back there," Bender said.

"Um, real women only," Manic said.

"That will be kind of difficult," Surus said. "Considering that all of my personnel are Artificials."

"Oh well, guess I can't prove myself to you, Bender," Manic said.

"Yeah, figures," Bender said. "Video game player."

The team neared the hatch where the golden owl lingered, and Noctua dove through. Rade and the others followed Surus underneath that hatch and into the next dome, where the buildings were much the same as the last.

Ahead, the golden owl circled above a larger building than the others. It was more like a warehouse, and had a wide garage door to match.

Noctua landed on a small perch near that garage door.

"We've reached out destination," Surus said when they arrived.

"The mechs have been fueled," Noctua said as the garage door opened. "And they've passed the bootup checklist. I hope you are pleased, sweet master."

"I'm sure I will be," Surus said, walking inside.

"Mechs?" Bender said. "Man, I hope these are the Titans we were promised."

Rade and the others entered.

four

Inside awaited ten Titans, one for each of them, including Surus herself. There would be no passengers on this mission. The humanoid-shaped mechs stood three and a half meters tall, a full meter taller than the Hoplite models. The torsos weren't as bulky as previous Titans he had used in the past—Rade guessed because there wasn't the need for as much radiation armor on these units. The silvery color of the skin reflected the different members of the squad, the camouflage feature currently inactive. He recognized the different armament choices right away: the right arm could alternate between a "zodiac" electrolaser and a grenade launcher, while the left could switch between an ordinary "cobra" laser and an incendiary thrower. Those swivel mounts could also rotate aside entirely, allowing the mech to manipulate objects when the hands weren't needed; this allowed the Titan to scale walls, etc., without the weapons getting in the way. It also meant the Titan couldn't use those weapons during such activities.

A missile launcher was attached to each shoulder, holding seven rockets per launcher: Hellfire H-8A minis. These rockets were the same size as the H-7B minis, but had corrected the fatal flaw found in the latter versions: proximity fuses aboard the rockets rendered the warheads inactive when the Hellfire's were close to the launching mech. This prevented an enemy from detonating any of the rockets while the weapons were still racked in the launcher; in the past, it was possible to target those missiles, and a lucky shot could see the entire set of Hellfires detonate, causing major damage to the host mech. Rade had lost a man when that very thing had happened in the past, so he was glad to see the problem corrected, even if it was a little too late.

"These are special Titans," Surus said. "Their armor hardened to protect against the powerful laser weapons employed by the Hydra. My team has been working on modifying these units during our entire journey here, and only just finished the day before we arrived. Needless to say, this technology must never leave this moon. If these things ever got into the hands of the United Systems, your government could potentially become unstoppable in this region of the galaxy."

Rade had modified the simulation pods to emulate Titan models when Surus had first informed them about the mechs. He had used the updated weight specs she had provided for the armor, and he and his Argonauts had been practicing their war games ceaselessly since then. He had taken the men through several different scenarios, including a few underwater campaigns, at the suggestion of Surus. Apparently, the Hydra lived in atmospheres of liquid methane. During the simulations, the team had used different Titans for the land and underwater missions; in the latter, the mechs were equipped with fins and turbines. He didn't see any of those underwater Titan variants here. Rade assumed the team would be given new mechs later at some point.

Rade approached the mech assigned to him, as indicated by the green highlight Surus had outlined his Titan with. He donned his helmet, then clambered the leg rungs and swung inside the cockpit. The hatch sealed, the inner actuators enveloped him, and the feed from the head cameras piped into his vision.

"Welcome aboard, boss," came a voice that sounded suspiciously like Electron.

"Is it you, Electron?" Rade said.

"In the flesh," Electron replied. "Or rather, in the mech."

He glanced at the Titans Shaw and Bender had boarded, and saw the callsigns of their usual mechs displayed above their names: Nemesis and Juggernaut, respectively. The callsigns of the others were similarly familiar.

"Surus, what's up with the AIs?" Tahoe said over the main comm, asking the question that was on Rade's mind.

"I took the liberty of backing up your AI cores and downloading a copy into these mechs," Surus said.

"That's illegal you know," TJ said. "Overriding an existing AIs personality like that."

"I am well aware of the legal and moral issues," Surus said. "Which is why I purchased blank AI cores. There were not yet any engramic imprints for memories or personalities."

"Is that true, Harlequin?" Manic asked. "I mean, I know we bought you as a blank, but I thought that was only possible for smaller robots, like Artificials."

"It is very possible to procure mechs with blank AI cores," Harlequin said. "Though they have to be ordered specifically as such directly from the manufacturer. I am confident that no AIs were killed in the making of these mechs."

"Oh," TJ said. "Well, as long as Harlequin says it's okay I suppose it's all right then."

"Yeah, that Harlequin, he knows best," Bender said in a mocking voice.

Rade accessed the defenses of his Titan and noted that the Trench Coat anti-missile system had enough charges for eight uses, and that each arm had fully retractable ballistic / anti-laser shields, which could rotate in and out with the other weapons.

"No Lighters in these ones?" TJ asked.

That was a feature that allowed a million volts of electricity to flow through the external hull, blasting anything that foolishly attempted to attach to the mech. It was a feature inherent to the Titan class.

"The Lighters are there," Surus said. "But I have attached an extra safety access to them, as they will be more dangerous in the environments where we may be using them."

Rade knew what she was talking about. In the simulations, the range of the shock produced during the liquid methane scenarios was about twenty meters, though of course the voltage level was significantly reduced, as the current dispersed from the hull in all directions thanks to the surface area of the touching liquid. And while the hulls of their mechs were insulated, protecting the pilots in the cockpits from any external shocks, if they activated their Lighters too close to one another, there was a chance of shorting out some of the circuits in the extremities of their neighbors, such as those running the servomotors in the hands and feet for example.

"So how do we activate them?" TJ said.

"Navigate to the unlock menu on your HUD," Surus said. "And then the mechanism is the same as before."

"I got ya," TJ said.

Rade followed her instructions and familiarized himself with the interface.

"Please meet me outside when you are ready," Surus said. She approached the exit of the warehouse in her Titan, which was labeled Swift. Its feet stamped loudly on the burnished steel floor with each step.

"It's war time," Rade said. "Send your final messages to your friends and families. Because in a few minutes we're going to kiss the InterGalNet, and this entire side of the galaxy, goodbye."

Rade marched outside. He had no one to say goodbye to. His whole family was here already.

The others followed in a cacophony of humming servomotors and clanging steel.

Noctua landed on Swift and perched on the shoulder region.

"That ugly thing's not coming with us, is it?" Bender asked over the comm.

"Noctua will not be coming, no," Surus replied. "Her place is here, on this base."

"If I 'accidentally' shoot it down along the way," Bender said. "You're not going to cry are you?"

"If you shoot down Noctua," Surus stated quietly. "You will not live very long afterward."

"Oh-ho!" Manic said. "Better watch yourself Bender."

"Geez," Bender said. "She's a touchy one. I was joking."

Surus led them to a smaller building, this one made entirely of metal—no windows. It was guarded by two fierce looking walker robots. The walkers had no arms, but on either side of the box that formed their upper bodies were several laser and missile turrets. Gunships on legs.

The walkers stiffened as the Titan party approached, and all of their weapons pointed at the lead mech, Swift.

A moment later the robots stood down, their turrets swiveling downward once more.

A four meter tall door opened in the building and Swift entered. Rade followed, along with the others.

Within, two more of the walkers waited in the wide hallway just inside, and these parted to let the party pass.

The hallway opened into a circular chamber. At the center resided a wide disk engraved with Fibonacci swirls. Standing along the periphery of the disk were about twenty Centurion combat robots, facing outward with rifles in hand, the weapons currently lowered.

As the Titans entered, the Centurions moved away from the disk, gathering along the far wall.

"Enough security for you?" Tahoe commented.

"I take the defense of my homeworld seriously," Surus said. "If the United Systems, or any other governments of humanity attempted to forcibly take the disk, these robots would fight to the death, with instructions to destroy the Acceptor rather than allow it to fall into enemy hands."

"Probably a good idea," Rade said. "Considering the behavior of our governments in the past."

"What, you're trying to say the United Systems is warlike?" Lui said. "Nooooo."

"The United Systems wouldn't harm a fly," Fret commented. "Nuking an alien homeworld, well hey, that's not an issue. But a fly, no."

"You really think the United Systems would ever try to destroy the Green homeworld?" Shaw said.

"I'm not sure what to think of your government any more," Surus said. "There could come a day when all Greens are distrusted. A warmonger among your military could press for a surprise attack, saying that we are planning to subvert humanity in some way. While it sounds farfetched now, mark my words, there is very likely such a warmonger whispering lies into the ears of whoever will listen at this very moment. Yes, it is a very good idea to keep this Acceptor secure."

Swift approached the teleportation disk. Surus transmitted: "I will go first, and report back."

Noctua took flight and landed upon a special T-shaped perch that had obviously been set aside for the robot.

The mech stepped onto the device and vanished.

Rade stared at the lingering robots. He knew that Noctua was all that was preventing those robots from attacking them. He hoped Bender didn't say something to piss off the owl.

A persistent whining of servomotors filled the chamber. Fret was shifting his weight back and forth between his left and right foot, a nervous habit of his.

"Can you stop that!" TJ said.

"Sorry," Fret said. He ceased. A few moments later he started up again.

Swift reappeared on the Acceptor.

"The target zone is clear," Surus said. "But we're in the process of staving off yet another attack. The current hive's defenses have been devastated. Prepare to join battle when you pass through. I will stay here and activate the Acceptor for each of you in turn. Now go."

"Form defensive pattern cigar two on the other side!" Rade said. "Tahoe, TJ, go!"

This particular disk was wide enough to fit two

Titans at once, allowing the Argonauts to teleport in pairs. Tahoe and TJ stepped onto the disk, and vanished.

Rade called out the next pair and they too vanished. He continued until only he and Surus were left.

"Let's go," Rade told her.

She stepped onto the Acceptor with Rade.

"Goodbye sweet master," Noctua transmitted.

"Goodbye little one," Surus replied. "Watch my base well. If I do not return in one hundred and twenty days, you know what to do."

"Yes," Noctua said. "But you will return. You *will!*"

The warehouse blinked out.

five

Rade stood on a disk that was the twin to the one on the other side of the galaxy. It was placed on a platform composed of some kind of yellowish resin. The Titans had assumed defensive positions along the edges of that platform, their weapons aimed out into the swirling red and orange clouds around them. Bolts of sheet lightning flashed amid those clouds.

From the briefing, he knew he resided in the upper atmosphere of a gas giant. Artificial gravity countered the immense pull from the giant, bringing the gravity closer to Earth levels. In the distance, he saw the outline of the translucent sphere of energy that surrounded the Green hive, protecting it from the incredible winds and lightning of the ceaseless planet-wide storm. The outline shimmered with varying hues of yellow, the color strongest where the red and orange clouds seemed to flow the fastest—Rade guessed the hue meant how much energy moved into that particular section of the sphere to reinforce the shield and keep the storm outside at bay.

Directly above, far beyond the limits of the energy sphere, he saw a massive monolithic shape in orbit. It was pure black, with an elongated body and three prongs emerging from the front like talons or tentacles. It reminded him somewhat of a squid. It could be only the alien attacker.

From that ship emerged several smaller shapes streaking toward the roof of the energy sphere. They were skirmishers of some kind, Rade thought.

"Come!" Surus said from her position beside him. "Grav elevators run throughout the hive and will provide lift! I am sending markers to denote the flows of the gravity currents on your overhead map. Apply gentle bursts of thrust to switch between the flows."

Several color-coded arrow indicators appeared. Tunnels of upward gravity currents were indicated in green. Tunnels of downward currents were red. Sideways were yellow. And those that moved at angles through the rest were greenish-blue if they slanted upward, or yellowish-red if they slanted downward.

"Wait!" Rade said. "Wouldn't it be better to dig in here and fight?"

"No!" Surus said. "They will destroy the platform. You cannot dig in!"

"But how can we be sure the enemies won't use the Acceptor to reach human space?" Lui said.

"They can't access it," Surus said. "But as a precaution, I've changed the destination coordinates. Now come... we fight!"

Surus sprinted forward and took a running leap off the platform with her mech; she landed directly inside a tunnel filled with upward pointing arrows. Swift was rapidly lifted from view.

"Dorothy, we ain't in wonderland no more," Bender said.

Ordinarily, as their leader, Rade wouldn't have taken the point man position. But given that they would be visible on all sides out there, with no cover whatsoever, it wouldn't matter anyway.

"Let's go, people!" Rade leaped off, following Surus. The gravity current took him immediately, and his mech quickly traveled upward.

He glanced downward and saw the Phant city. Shaw had come to this place once years ago—during the First Alien War—and she had described it to him in detail. Even so, it was nothing like he had imagined.

He saw hundreds of tall, parallel plates placed equidistant apart. He zoomed in for a moment, and discerned the thousands of decagonal cells the plates contained. Green mist floated between some of them—those were the Phants themselves, which would assume a gaseous state in the absence of an atmosphere. There were other aquatic-like beings that reminded him of jellyfish. Shaw had called the latter the Keepers of the Hive, and their role was apparently similar to workers in a bee hive, though their consciousnesses could be commandeered by the Greens at will.

Along the edges, where the plates abutted against the energy sphere, long metal bars protruded, perhaps to act as lightning rods. Two bolts from the storm struck them as he watched. There were also several massive wind turbines jutting from the periphery of the city and into the storm. The rods and turbines had to be power generators.

He zoomed out and glanced at his overhead map, which showed the positions of various other platforms similar to the one he had started on, floating in seemingly random positions throughout the inside of the energy sphere. He passed a few of them, but they always appeared empty, so he wasn't sure what their purpose was. Perhaps the platforms were involved in regulating the grav channels in some way.

Unfortunately, the invisible currents themselves weren't shown on the map. He had to rely on his main vision to see the overlay markers Surus provided.

Rade returned his attention to her mech, Swift, which was continuing upward toward the monolith of the alien ship, and those fast approaching black skirmishers.

"Should we be worried about incoming fire from that ship?" Shaw asked. "Like say, lasers?"

"Their laser and plasma weapons cannot penetrate our defensive energy sphere," Surus replied. "They rely upon their weaponized battle suits to do that. And we definitely need to worry about those."

"You talking about those incoming skirmishers?" Bender asked.

Good to know that Rade wasn't the only one who thought of them as skirmishers.

"Yes," Surus answered.

As Surus continued her flight upward, he wondered if she intended to fly right through the energy sphere. But that didn't make much sense, because the Titans wouldn't be able to navigate in the storm outside, let alone counter the massive gravitational forces that awaited out there. Flying past the energy sphere would be a death sentence.

About a kilometer from the outskirts of the sphere, Surus jetted into an adjacent stream that carried her sideways. So she wasn't leaving the sphere after all.

Good.

When Rade reached that same area, he thrusted, attempting to follow her. Whoops. He had applied too much force: the thrust sent him into the current beyond it, which pulled him back downward again.

"This is going to take some getting use to," Lui

said. "You'd think she would have given us access to this scenario for the simulators."

"I considered doing so," Surus sent. "But at the time I did not believe we would do any actual fighting here. I did not expect our own defenses to have grown so weak. I apologize. Do your best."

Rade tapped in Surus directly.

"This is why you always consult with me on every matter regarding the mission at hand," Rade said. "And you don't make decisions based on what you *think* is best for the team by yourself. Because more often than not, your decisions will be wrong. You're wasting your money, otherwise. Not to mention putting all of our lives at risk."

"As I said, I apologize," Surus responded.

Rade thrusted again, this time more gently, and steered into another sideways-trending channel. He was quickly moving away from Surus. He noticed that the other party members weren't doing much better—the entire group was scattering throughout the energy sphere.

Rade could only shake his head, silently cursing Surus.

Shaw tapped in Rade. "Where the hell did you go?"

"I could ask the same question of you," he replied. He glanced at his overhead map. She was on the far side of the energy sphere.

"Shit," Shaw said. "Guess we're fighting this one alone."

"I'll do my best to get to you," Rade said.

"No," Shaw said. "Do your best to survive. I promise to do the same."

She disconnected.

Rade suppressed the urge to go to her as quickly as

possible. While it wasn't feasible, given the current network of grav currents, it also wasn't necessary. He knew she could take care of herself. It was why he had allowed her to come along in the first place.

"Get ready," Surus transmitted. "Target whichever of them you can."

Rade glanced upward. He saw that the dark streaks in the enemy vanguard had nearly reached the outskirts of the energy sphere.

He applied a slight burst of aft thrust and steered into an upward moving channel to intercept. He was slowly getting the hang of the grav currents.

The first of the enemy tangos penetrated the energy sphere. It passed right through, bringing with it a plume of gas from the storm outside before the section resealed.

Rade folded the anti-laser shield into his left hand and held it between himself and the target. Meanwhile, he switched to the zodiac in his right hand, and aimed it past the shield, switching his viewpoint to the scope.

"I would advise closing to within a hundred meters," Surus transmitted. "Our lasers and electrolasers will have the greatest impact at that range. And refrain from missile or grenade launches: they aren't designed to navigate the grav currents, and you will merely waste them."

"We just took a laser hit," Electron announced. "The intensity was immense—equivalent to the Vipers found aboard United Systems warships. If we were operating an ordinary Titan, that beam would have easily penetrated your shield, and possibly the hull armor of your mech underneath. As it was, we now have a centimeter-deep bore hole in our shield, directly above your head."

"Nice," Rade said. "Was it fired by the ship in

orbit?" He wondered if Surus was wrong about the lasers of the enemy warship, in terms of not being able to penetrate the energy sphere.

"No," Electron said. "The beam was sourced from your current target."

So not wrong, then.

Rade moved between grav channels, slowly making his way toward the tango. The target moved as if accustomed to the different currents already. If the Hydra had been involved in a long siege, which Surus had intimated, they would have definitely grown familiar with the grav channels by now, and had likely already replicated the exact currents in their own simulations.

All of a sudden the arrows in his current channel flipped, and Rade was proceeding in the opposite direction, away from the Hydra.

"I forgot to mention," Surus said. "The currents randomly change every ten minutes."

That ruled out the tangos knowing what channels to take in advance, then.

Rade jetted into another tunnel and set himself back on course toward the dark shape, which seemed to be making its way toward the plates of the hive below, threading between the different-sized platforms that floated throughout the inside of the energy sphere.

Rade zoomed in on his scope and saw a dark, ovule form. From the nose section several rods of different sizes protruded—likely weapon turrets. From the aft portion, four or five segmented tentacles were dragged along behind. It was like a smaller version of the warship he'd seen in orbit, but with trailing tentacles.

Above, several more of the Hydra craft penetrated

the energy sphere.

"We just took another laser hit," Electron said. "This one in the lower back, well away from the protective shield. It nearly bored all the way through the enhanced armored on your hull. If we take another hit there, the laser will penetrate through into the cockpit, and likely your suit."

Rade retracted the zodiac and positioned his right arm over his back, activating the shield instead. He held it so that his back was defended against the incoming enemies; he kept the other shield in front of him to protect against any shots from his target.

"The skirmisher we follow is concentrating its fire on the plates below," Electron said. "And ignoring us, for the time being."

"What are you trying to say, it's safe to retract my frontal shield?" Rade asked.

"Something along those lines, yes," Electron replied.

"When we're in range I'll think about it," Rade told the AI.

He continued switching between those grav channels, slowly closing the distance with his opponent. The target had reached a distance of a kilometer from the hive city below, and it selected grav currents that allowed it to repeatedly swoop past the parallel plates. According to Electron, it fired down at those plates every ten seconds without fail.

Rade glanced at his fuel indicator, but since so little fuel was required to change grav channels, he had only used up around twenty percent so far.

"We've taken a few more hits on the second shield you're holding behind you," Electron said. "But the enemy seems to be concentrating its attack on the hive structure below."

Tahoe's mech appeared beside Rade in another sideways-trending grav channel twenty meters away. He held his shields similar to Rade, with one in front of his mech, and another protecting his back quarter.

"Hey boss," Tahoe said. "Just like old times, huh? The two of us fighting side by side against alien aggressors. Bet you thought I forgot about you."

"Not at all," Rade said. "I just figured you were a little occupied like the rest of us."

"Oh I am," Tahoe said. "But it looks like we've been tracking the same bug. Let's see if we can take it out."

Rade glanced at the overhead map; Tahoe was the closest to him. The other Titans were busy engaging the remaining attackers, and dispersed throughout the inside of the sphere. Shaw was still out there, her vitals a bright green. She seemed to be coordinating with Surus and Harlequin.

Rade waited until he reached a distance of a hundred meters, as per the advice of Surus, then he swiveled the leftmost shield away and replaced it with the cobra.

Tahoe was about a hundred and twenty meters from the target. Rade considered holding off until Tahoe was within range as well, but figured that an extra twenty meters wouldn't matter too much for Tahoe, especially if they combined their beams.

"Tahoe, sync your cobra to mine," Rade said. "I want to target the same spot area."

"Just a second," Tahoe responded. He would be retracting the shield he held in front of him and replacing it with the cobra, as Rade had already done. "We're synced."

Rade saw the green sync indicator activate beside Tahoe's name. That meant even if Tahoe was swept away by another grav current, the laser would remain pointed at the same spot for as long as Tahoe's mech could maintain line of sight.

Rade attempted to align the targeting reticule of his cobra over the Hydra craft, but the tango kept sliding from view. It was constantly switching to other grav channels, forcing Rade to do the same.

Finally, Rade said: "Electron, I'm going to need a little help here."

"Where would you like me to target?" Electron asked.

"At the base of the tentacles on its aft quarter," Rade said. "That's the best spot, as far as I'm concerned. Fire when you acquire."

Rade kept control of the jumpjets and continued to leap between channels. His arm shifted constantly as the reticle attempted to get a lock on the requested spot. Finally the crosshairs touched the base and the laser engaged, firing Tahoe's at the same time.

The target swerved aside immediately.

"Looks like he didn't like that," Tahoe said.

"It's turning around," Electron said. "Toward us."

Keeping the laser active, Rade immediately swiveled his second protective shield into place to cover his forward quarter, leaving his aft quarter undefended. Tahoe did the same, but then jumped into a grav channel that swept him back and away.

"Damn it," Tahoe said. "Messed up, boss. Looks like you're on your own."

Rade remained on his current course, heading directly toward the tango. It was located in an adjacent flow that would bring it directly past Rade.

"We're taking repeated hits," Electron said. "It's concentrating its fire on the same spot area on the forward shield."

"How long will it hold up?" Rade said.

"Long enough to make a flyby," Electron said.

"That's all I need."

As the enemy tore past, Rade fired lateral thrust, transferring into the same grav flow as the robot skirmisher, and retracted his lefthand shield to latch onto its hull. He grabbed on just behind the forward laser turrets.

Those weapons attempted to swivel backward, but reached the limitation of their motion—he was still out of their line of sight.

With his other arm, he had moved his second shield behind him to defend his aft portion. He was getting ready to retract it to fire at point blank range at the skirmisher, when Electron spoke.

"The Hydra must have alerted its friends to its difficulties," Electron said. "Because I'm detecting an uptick in laser impacts on the rear shield."

"Surus, can the armor you added to these mechs withstand a missile detonation at close range?" Rade transmitted.

"I wouldn't recommend it," Surus replied.

Too bad, because Rade couldn't swivel his cobra laser into place while he held on with his fingers. Nor could he use the zodiac in his other arm, not when he needed to keep the shield in place to protect himself from attackers.

All he could do was hang on.

The segmented metal tentacles from the aft of the skirmisher wrapped around Rade's arm, attempting to tear him off. He refused to let go.

The Hydra robot leaped frantically from grav current to grav current, so that Rade had no idea what direction he was traveling in. The hive seemed to spin around him.

Rade activated his Lighter. At first he thought it had no effect on the Hydra, but then he realized that the mech was no longer leaping between grav channels, and was instead allowing the current to bring it closer to the city. The pair were hurtling directly for the edge of one of those plates.

"Uh," Rade said. He tried to activate his jumpjets and transfer to a different channel, but the Hydra countered no matter what direction he attempted—one of its automated subsystems was still online, he guessed.

He released his hold and attempted to pry himself from the body, but the tentacles held him in fast. He couldn't swivel the cobra into place because those metal appendages blocked the motion of the mounts.

He crashed into the outer portion of the resinous substance, breaking away the plate segment along with the cells it contained. Jellyfish were ripped away, plunging into the grav current with him. He continued falling directly toward the outer limits of the energy sphere.

"Uh," Rade said.

He passed through the energy field and into the atmosphere of the gas giant.

Rade felt the crushing gravity immediately. He would have blacked out, but Electron injected something into his right arm. The hull should have probably caved from the pressure as well, but the reinforcements Surus had made withstood the immense force. For the moment.

Barely conscious, he was aware of Electron's voice: "The main AI or pilot of the skirmisher appears to have come back online, as it is now adjusting course. It's heading back to the sphere. I've taken control of your arms and legs to ensure you don't release the enemy, just in case it attempts to relieve itself of its burden. I would advise not firing the Lighter again, for the time being."

Long minutes passed. Rade fell into and out of consciousness. Finally the craft broke through the sphere once more, and it was as if a massive weight lifted from Rade's chest as Earth-strength gravity returned.

The target swerved between two of the plates and, while keeping Rade pinned with one of its tentacles, it extended the remainder and ripped long scars through the decagonal cells. It also fired its lasers randomly, killing enemy jellyfish that attempted to block its path.

The Hydra passed right through the mist of a Phant, but the Green was apparently repelled, and could not penetrate to gain control of the craft. Rade didn't know if any Phant-repelling EM emitters were installed in the Titan. Well, even if a Phant did penetrate, Rade had an EM emitter in his jumpsuit, so he was safe in that regard, regardless of the status of the mech's AI core.

Rade pulled upward while jetting at the same time; the skirmisher didn't counter, allowing him to bring himself and the tango out of the plates and into another grav channel that swept them away from the hive.

The Hydra robot managed to lodge more of its tentacles underneath Electron's chest, and it lifted the body free. Still hanging onto him, it spun about, bringing its turrets to bear. Rade's left arm was tied up by the tentacles, but his other was still free...

Rade attempted to bring the shield on that arm forward to block the point-range laser attack, but another tentacle slammed upward, halting the motion of his limb.

The turrets aimed directly at his chest.

six

An energy beam tore into the dark, ovule body from the side, and those tentacles went limp.

Rade ripped the robotic appendages off of him and glanced toward his rescuer.

It wasn't one of his own men, but rather a large, golden mech, twice the size of a Titan.

As the mech jetted away into a different grav current, Rade realized there were other golden mechs out there fighting against the Hydra skirmishers as well. Piloted by the Greens, no doubt.

"I could use some help here," Shaw sent.

Rade glanced at his overhead map and zoomed in. Two of the Hydra flanked her Titan, Nemesis, and had wrapped their metal tentacles around her cockpit. It seemed they were trying to rip her apart.

Rade activated his jumpjets and hastily vaulted between the grav flows, making his way toward Shaw. He folded his left shield in front of him and aimed his electrolaser at the rightmost flanking unit, and with Electron's help fired the weapon. It made no sound in the void.

Rade struck the unit, but it remained gripping Shaw. He suspected he had disabled it, because it seemed to be dragging on her mech, no longer applying motive force to steer like it had moments ago.

Rade aimed at the second unit and fired again. That unit slumped, but once more didn't release her.

He calculated the trajectory of the current grav channel she was stuck inside, and realized she was on course to pass through the side of the energy sphere, just as he had.

"Can you jump to a different flow?" Rade asked her.

"Can't!" Shaw answered. "Every time I fire my jumpjets, these robots issue canceling thrust. It's the only part of them that's still active... there must be a few automated subsystems still running the engines."

Rade supposed he shouldn't have been surprised, as the same thing had happened to him only moments ago.

Perhaps it had been a bad idea to disable the skirmishers that held her.

"We're going to have to pry those tentacles free manually," Rade said. "And quickly! I'm coming for you."

"Hurry!" she sent.

Rade continued leaping between grav flows, and was two jumps away from her when his mech abruptly swung to the side, redirecting into a different current.

"Did you do that?" Rade asked his AI.

"One of the skirmishers just smashed into us," Electron said. "It's wrapped its tentacles around our ankle, and is dragging us away. I would recommend swiveling your shield downward."

Rade did so, barely blocking the near point-blank laser attack the robot Hydra unleashed. He bashed the gripping tentacle with his other foot, but was unable to kick the appendage free. Whenever he attempted to jet toward Shaw, the Hydra that held him issued countering thrust. He was forced to hold both of his shields toward the robot to defend himself.

He glanced toward her mech. The jets of the two Hydra that held her were still firing, preventing her from changing course—she continued hurtling unabated toward the outer limits of the sphere. Those partially offline Hydra were unknowingly dooming themselves along with her.

"Damn it," Rade said. "I'm going to have to spacewalk to her in my jumpsuit."

"Are you sure that's a wise idea?" Electron asked.

"Never said it was wise," Rade responded. "Open her up!"

The video feed winked out and Rade found himself in darkness. Then the actuators retracted and the cockpit hatch fell open. The two shields currently protected him from the skirmisher below.

Rade crawled to the aft quarter of the Titan, away from the tango that held the mech, and then shoved off. He fell in the same direction as the augmented reality arrows around him.

"As soon as you break free, join me," he told Electron.

"Shouldn't be long," Electron replied. The Titan repeatedly bashed the edge of one of its shields into the tentacle that gripped its ankle.

Rade activated his personal jetpack and vaulted between the grav flows. He felt extremely exposed out there without hull armor or the anti-laser shields. All it would take was one shot and he was gone. On the plus side, he made a much smaller target. But would it matter to the targeting systems of these skirmishers? He just hoped he would be too insignificant to attract their attention, and that the Titans would keep them well occupied.

"Electron, mark the golden mechs as friendlies," Rade said. "Then launch a few Hellfires. Let's give the Hydra some other small targets to fire at other than me."

Rade watched a couple of those rockets fire from Electron; the missiles moved in a haphazard fashion, their tracking mechanisms messed up by the constantly changing grav flows they flew into. If the missiles accidentally struck any other Titans or golden mechs, the proximity fuses wouldn't detonate since they were all marked as friendlies, so he didn't have to worry in that regard.

Rade closed with Shaw and landed on her mech. She was about thirty seconds from reaching the edge of the energy sphere.

"I got you," he told her. "I got you."

"*Where's your mech?*" Shaw said.

"Hey babe. It's coming." He drew the blaster from his utility belt and fired at one of the tentacles that held her, then was able to kick it away.

He shot another appendage. It didn't release right away like the first one. He aimed at a small bulge near the joint that he guessed was the equivalent of a servomotor and fired again. That did it: the limb released its grip on her, and he booted it aside. Two down. Six more to go.

He moved methodically between the tentacles until he had removed all except two. As he clambered toward one of them, a damaged rung on the surface of Shaw's Titan broke away; he clawed at the surface of her hull, trying to grip the next rung. The grav flow ensured that he was drawn along with her of course, but he was still forced to fire his jetpack to reattach.

"Rade, now would be a good time..." Shaw said.

Rade hurried up to the second last appendage,

plunged his blaster into it, and fired. He tore it away, freeing her right arm. The Hydra on that side fell away.

She reached across with the freed arm and tore away the final limb, releasing the second Hydra. She jetted into a different grav current just as the two Hydras were hurled outside, vanishing into the perpetual storm.

She thrusted again, jumping into a different flow, and Rade was nearly ripped away. He tightened his grip on the rung he held.

"Thanks hun," Shaw said, cradling him protectively with her shield arm.

"No problem," Rade lied.

Shaw switched between currents, slowly carrying him back toward Electron. Rade felt a little like a baby monkey hanging onto its mother's side for dear life as the adult leaped from tree to tree.

Electron was also making its way toward Rade. Apparently it had finally shed its burden.

Electron and Shaw joined the same grav flow and jetted toward one another.

Rade released Nemesis and pushed off toward Electron. The Titan grabbed him and shoved him into its cockpit.

"Welcome back, boss," Electron said when Rade was back in control.

"Good to be back," Rade replied. "Shaw, how would you feel about teaming up?"

"Thought you'd never ask."

Rade positioned Electron behind Shaw's mech and she synced her jumpjets to his own so that she would follow his movements, and together they jetted from grav flow to grav flow, fighting back to back. They used their shields to protect their front areas; Rade aimed his cobra at enemies, Shaw her electrolaser, and together they rained havoc down upon any Hydra skirmisher that flew past.

"We should have done this from the start," Shaw said. "This is where I belong, at your side. I just wish we would have had a chance to practice in an environment like this in the simulator."

"Once again Surus thinks she knows best," Rade said. "When in truth, the alien knows nothing."

The skirmishers continued to come for the better part of an hour, but finally, after several close calls, the Titans, with the golden mechs at their sides, managed to repel the last of them.

When the battle was done, the Titans regrouped on a platform midway between the hive below and the upper portions of the energy dome. The hulls of the mechs were riddled with laser bores, and Fret and Bender had shields whose top portions were eaten away entirely. Several of the Titans walked with obvious limps, the servomotors moaning in complaint. Rade checked the vital signs of the pilots and quickly determined that no one had sustained any serious injuries.

Above, the black monolith of the enemy starship continued to loom ominously, apparently locked in a geosynchronous orbit with the hive.

"Well that was fun," Bender said.

"Thank you for what you did back there," Surus said, walking her Titan toward Bender's. "You saved my host. Words cannot express my thanks."

"Was nothing," Bender said gruffly.

"What did he do?" Harlequin asked. Was that a hint of jealousy Rade detected in the Artificial's voice?

"It was masterful," Fret said. "I'll show you my recordings later. Basically, four of those robot bugs wrapped their metal tentacles around her Titan, see?

They were trying to drag her out of the energy sphere. So Surus emerged from the mech as this Green mist and moved like a madwoman between the robots, trying to possess them I guess, but they wouldn't let her in. They use EM emitters similar to the ones we have, probably. So Bender comes along, fires his cobra and zodiac in rapid succession, and sprays the final two with jellied gasoline. Surus flows inside her mech, and then Bender rips Sprint free and jets into another grav channel just as the four Hydras are sucked out. It was a work of art, I tell ya."

"As I said, nothing," Bender commented.

"You should let me tell them what you did for me," Shaw sent Rade directly.

"That's for me and you alone," Rade told her.

She sighed. "My humble warrior."

"There were many acts of valor performed today," Rade said. "We'll never know them all unless we pore over the video feeds with a fine-toothed comb."

"True enough," Shaw told him. "Still, I'm proud of you."

Now that the battle was over, Rade found himself wanting to be alone. The urge was nearly overwhelming, and it was all he could do to keep his feed online.

But when one of the towering golden mechs landed on the platform, his battle instincts came to the fore again, and the urge subsided. He was prepared to order his men to attack, if it came to it.

A relatively small cockpit opened in the center and an Artificial with Asian features emerged.

"Azen!" Shaw said.

"Greetings, my Shaw," Azen said.

"*My* Shaw?" Rade said.

"It's just how he greets me," Shaw said.

"And I would give you a kiss if we were in the flesh," Azen said. "Alas."

Rade felt his brow furrow, and he resisted the urge to smash the little Artificial with his Titan's fist.

"I never thought I'd see you again," Shaw said.

"Nor I, you," Azen replied.

"Yeah man, long time no see, bro," Lui said. "Last I saw you, you were returning through the Slipstream in your Mothership to wage war against the other Phants. How did that go?"

"The war still progresses," Azen said. "And will likely continue for the next seven hundred years until the enemy reaches human space, at which point it will spill into your territory."

"Maybe we can help you?" Tahoe said.

"Alas, the war against the Phants is not something that humanity can assist us with," Azen said. "Not yet, anyway. Perhaps in five hundred years maybe, when your technology has advanced a little further."

"So yeah, that was great and all," Fret said. "So can we go home now?"

"Of course." Azen sounded puzzled. "But why did you come, if you wish to leave so soon?"

"We're not leaving just yet," Rade said. "We're here to help."

"Damn," Fret said. "Had to try."

"I must thank you for your assistance back there," Azen said. "The Hydra deceived us. We have been attempting to broker a peace between our two races since their arrival, and the Hydra refused until a few days ago, when they finally agreed to begin initial talks. We chose to meet at a neutral location—the surface of a nearby moon. We brought nearly all of the mechs from this particular sub-hive with us to act as guards. But when we got to the moon, we discovered only a bomb waiting for us. Only half of us escaped, and we hurried back here to discover the sub-hive under attack, with mostly only you defending it. If you hadn't come, the damage would have been far more severe."

Azen glanced at the ship far above them. "The next attack won't be for several hours. They will need to regroup. Please, come down to the city with me. I have prepared quarters for you. While you rest, I will assign units to repair your mechs. We have 3D printers compatible with your technology. And when you are rested, and your Titans repaired, we can discuss a potential mission that might be of interest to you."

seven

Rade and Shaw were "quartered" in one of the thousands of decagonal cells that lined the parallel plates. It was really just a small alcove of about three meters in depth, made of the same resin as the platform they had arrived on. A soft mattress inside, covered in bedsheets, was the only furniture. It was too bad they couldn't properly use that mattress, not while stuck inside their jumpsuits.

Rade immediately flopped down on that bed, exhausted.

"Have a good cave out," Shaw told him.

Rade nodded slowly. "Thank you."

He stared at the bare ceiling. An internal light source lit the orange resin to the level of an overcast day.

He waited, expecting the scenes of battle to come. The noises of the dying. But instead, there was nothing. He was somewhat grateful. He repealed the internal noise canceler and listened to his own breathing as it echoed from the inside of the helmet. In and out. In. Out.

Thirty minutes passed, but sleep wouldn't come. Finally, he sat up.

"Did you experience lost time again?" Shaw asked

from where she was seated on the bed beside him. Her hands were open, and held in such a way that he thought she was reading a virtual book of some kind. Apparently she couldn't sleep either. He hadn't noticed when she had sat up. He blamed that on the jumpsuit.

"No," Rade said. "I felt every minute of the past thirty."

"Well that's good, isn't it?" Shaw asked.

"It's very good," Rade replied.

Shaw nodded slowly, apparently uncertain whether it really was or not.

"What are you reading?" Rade asked.

"Just a treatise written by a general during the Third Alien War," Shaw replied.

"A general?" Rade said. "Must be pretty dry."

"On the contrary," Shaw said. "He writes with wry humor. And there are quite a few sex scenes involving him and his female Artificial. He seems to employ her the most when the fighting becomes the worst."

"Sort of how I turn you into my sex doll before battle?" Rade said.

"Ha," Shaw said. "I think it's me who turns you into the sex doll before battle, hun. You're basically my stallion, and I ride you into the sunset."

"So that's what you think of me," Rade said. "I'm just a sex object to you."

"A very fine sex object at that," Shaw said. "Worth your weight in gold."

"Well then, that's a lot of gold."

She slid near him and pressed her side against his. How he wished he wasn't wearing a jumpsuit at the moment. "Thank you for what you did out there. Seriously. I almost died."

"You would have done the same for me," Rade said. He didn't want to tell her about his own brush with death. She would have felt immense guilt about not noticing, nor coming to his aid. "And in fact, you already have. You don't need to thank me, because you've saved me ten times over, and not just in battle."

She grabbed his gloved hand in hers and pressed the dome of her helmet against his. "And you've saved me, my love."

ELECTRON AND NEMESIS latched on to the resin outside the decagonal cell a few hours later. There wasn't a single dent on either one of them as far as he could tell. Not like earlier.

"Surus and Azen request your presence at Platform 5-D-iii," Electron transmitted.

"5-D what?" Rade asked.

"5-D-iii," Electron said. "They operate on a three-dimensional grid system of sorts. 5 stands for the x axis locator, D the y, and iii the z."

"All right," Rade said. "Add the info to my map and take us there."

"It's already on your map," Electron replied. The mech's cockpit hatch opened wide.

Rade crawled out of the alcove and clambered in. Shaw did the same with Nemesis on the opposite side of the cell.

The inner actuators enveloped him, the video feed filled his vision, and the mech HUD appeared. Rade checked the operational status of the unit. The jumpjet fuel supplies had been topped up. His servomotors were functioning optimally. And all laser damage had been repaired.

"These Greens have sure done a bang-up job on

the units," Shaw transmitted.

"I'll say," Rade replied.

Electron released the cell and allowed the grav currents to carry the Titan upward between the parallel plates that composed that area of the city, toward the empty space above. When they emerged, Electron and Nemesis leaped between grav currents, weaving between the various platforms, finally landing atop a wider one where the rest of the platoon had gathered.

Surus stood at the front near the golden mech Azen used. Her Titan looked like a child compared to the alien unit.

Around him, Rade noticed that none of the mechs limped, and no servomotors moaned. Like his own Titan, the laser holes in shields and armor had been plugged. Azen hadn't been kidding when he said he would repair them all. That Azen could do so in such a quick time frame impressed Rade, and he had to wonder how dire the situation of the Greens truly was. If they could repair human technology so quickly, it probably wouldn't take them long to build more golden mechs.

Then again, human tech was only class III, and likely needed far less energy to mend.

"First of all I wanted to inform you all that we expended essentially the last of our resources to fix your mechs," Azen said. "We had enough raw materials in this sub-hive to build one more Gold unit, or repair your ten Titans. We chose the latter, as a token of our appreciation. You came to our aid, and it is only right that we should come to yours."

Well that explained that.

"Thanks, I guess," Bender said. "Though I'm guessing you expect us to owe you now."

"Not at all," Azen said. "Any help you render from

this point forward is completely voluntarily. You may leave at any time and return to your space, if you so wish it. Surus has instructed Noctua to allow each and every one of you to pass freely on the other side."

"Well that's somewhat good to know," Lui said. "Though it's too bad we're not that kind of people. We said we would fight, and we will. The Greens needed our help. We're here. Use us."

"Do the rest of you share the same sentiments?" Azen asked.

He was greeted by a chorus of ayes or yeses. Except for one person.

"No?" Bender said. "Am I the only sane one here? Actually, just messing with y'all."

"Thank you," Azen said. "I was hoping you would all stay. Surus already told me none of you would be deterred after that battle. And I admit I expected as much, having fought at the side of some of you during the First Alien War. You are the greatest examples of your species I have ever met, showcasing all that is right, honorable, and good about humanity. You have your flaws, like most humans do, but I would prefer to fight with no others of your kind. You are indefatigable."

"Wait a second, did he just say we have flaws?" Bender transmitted.

"He's talking about you Bender," Manic said.

"Oh yeah, of course," Bender said. "And not the moron whose name rhymes with panic."

"What are you trying to imply?" Manic said. "That I panicked during the fighting?"

"Uh, yeah?" Bender said. "You were flying around like a chicken without its head on out there."

"*Whatever* man," Manic said. "I was doing the best I could. If you weren't so busy trying to show off to your girlfriend Surus there, you would have realized I had seven kills."

"Ooh, a whole seven," Bender taunted.

Rade cleared his throat. "Uh, guys? If you wouldn't mind?"

"Sorry boss," Manic said.

Rade looked toward Azen's imposing golden mech.

"Thank you," Azen continued. "As I was saying, I am happy you have chosen to assist us. There is a special mission I have in mind for you all. Something that will suit your unique skill sets, I think. A covert operation of sorts. Let me digress to explain the socio-hierarchy of the Hydra, for a moment."

Let me digress, Bender texted on the common band. *This guy sounds like one of the pedantic instructors we used to have in bootcamp or something.*

Shh! Tahoe texted back.

"The Hydra follow a supreme leader," Azen said. "An all powerful figure, similar in rank and position to the ancient Roman emperors of Earth. This leader is currently a female member of the species. I will call her Medea, though her name has no translation in your language. She assumed command after assassinating her husband, the emperor. As empress, Medea presides over the vast Hydra Empire. Or what remains of it after the war against the Phants. When the Phants departed, the Hydra nation was left in tatters, a fragmented collection of warring sub-states. But Empress Medea rose to power among the factions, uniting them with hatred for the Phants that did this to them, and planning the ultimate revenge.

"Not all of the factions joined Medea, knowing that the extermination of every Phant homeworld would be a long and likely impossible task, and they ignored her message of hate, knowing it for the ruse to gain power that it was. But the brutal methods employed by the empress allowed her to swallow several of those disparate factions that defied her—she dispatched a network of assassins to eliminate many opposing warlords. She couldn't bring every faction under her fold, though she tried, I'm sure. Many warlords grew wise to her techniques, and found ways to protect themselves, while others ruled territories or populations too small to attract Medea's notice.

"One of the more powerful surviving factions is led by a relative of the empress. Our spies tell us she has been secretly gathering an army, and uniting with other opposing factions. To what end, we are not certain. Perhaps she merely intends to defend her planet against the day when Medea finally turns her conquering eye toward them. Or perhaps the relative plans to someday move upon the empress. It is my intention to spur her into taking the latter action as soon as possible. Empress Medea is at her weakest while attacking our hive. She has stretched her forces too thin, scattering them across the upper atmosphere of this planet. An attack on two fronts will break her army."

Lui shifted in his mech. "So let me guess, your plan is to visit this relative, and just like that you're going to convince her to attack the empress? What makes you think she's going to listen to you? Do you have some psi powers like the Black Phants that we don't know about, or something? You already said these Hydras hate all Phants."

"I knew the relative I speak of," Azen said. "Once, long ago. I will call her Bethesda. I helped liberate her from the Phants when the Hydra homeworld fell. I should have intervened further, and used what leverage I had then to ensure she became empress, but I chose not to. I have never regretted anything so greatly. If I had moved then, none of this might have ever happened. Bethesda knows the Greens are good; she would not have stirred the other factions into attacking us. In any case, yes, we must go to this planet and plead with Bethesda, and convince her that it is in her best interest to attack now. Together, we can dethrone Medea."

"How is this a covert operation?" Lui said. "You said you might need our specific skill sets. Well I don't see it."

"Your skills will be needed to get us out alive, if she refuses," Azen said.

"Oh."

"You said you have spies," Shaw interjected. "I'm guessing some of them would have a means of contacting Bethesda. Why not arrange everything remotely?"

"I lost all contact with my spies in Bethesda's court shortly before Medea's army arrived above our world," Azen said. "I believe there was a culling of some kind."

"So wait, you're not even sure if Bethesda is still in command of her faction?" Tahoe asked.

"I didn't say that," Azen replied. "I believe that Bethesda herself instituted the culling. I have evidence pointing to this: she had begun killing those in her court who she suspected spied for Medea. Mine were just lost as collateral damage."

"Convenient," Rade said. "So, how do we get there?"

"By ship," Azen replied.

Fret gestured toward the black monolith hovering in the sky above the energy shield. "It's going to be a little hard to escape with that thing guarding the upper atmosphere. Especially considering your hints that there are more ships like it up there."

"We will take an Acceptor to a backup base we have in another system," Azen replied. "The same planet where we have slowly been evacuating our citizens. Once there, we will board a ship to the Hydra colony world."

"Why don't you just evacuate everyone to your backup base?" Lui asked. "Why bother fighting for this hive, when it basically seems like it's lost already?"

"What you see here," Azen said. "Is only part of the hive. There are hundreds of similar energy spheres dispersed across this gas giant, sub-hives housing over a billion Greens in total. Together, we form one giant, distributed hive. As I mentioned, Medea has scattered her forces across the upper atmosphere of this planet: similar ships to the one you see above have gathered above each of our energy spheres, and attack in waves. We can't evacuate all of our hive components in time—it would take many years to do so. And even if we could, allowing the Hydra to destroy all Acceptors leading to this place, then we would have to spend the next four thousand years traveling through ordinary space to return, as this is one of the last sources of natural geronium in this region of the galaxy. Many Greens would succumb to starvation. The atmosphere of this giant is particularly rich in geronium. We have not discovered any other such planets in our probings of this region of space, and we cannot simply abandon such a massive food source, not when it will feed us for at least a hundred thousand years. It will take us at least that long to find another source such as that in this galaxy."

"Kind of makes me wonder why the other Phants

didn't try to take this world from you," TJ said.

"They don't know about it," Azen replied. "Or rather, they don't know how abundant the geronium is. They detected this planet long before we did, but left it alone because they believed it contained only a minuscule amount of geronium, similar to other gas giants, and thus hardly worth their interest. And as you know, they create their own geronium fuel sources by conquering populated worlds, so it's not as if they go out of their way to search for planets such as these."

"So wait," Shaw said. "Could the Green Mothership stand up against all those Hydra ships up there?"

"It has a fighting chance," Azen replied.

"Then why not call *it* for help?"

"They're busy fighting the other Phants who are on the long voyage toward Earth, remember?" Azen said.

"Ah, that's right," Shaw said. "Surus told us they were six years away, didn't she?"

"Yes," Azen said. "I'm afraid we have no choice but to reach out to Bethesda."

"So I'm flattered that you want to bring us along and all that," Rade said. "But what's the value proposition? You say our skills might be needed to get us out alive if she refuses to provide aid, but how is bringing us along in our technologically inferior Titans more helpful than simply dispatching your golden mechs?"

"It has been a long time since I met with the cousin of the empress," Azen said. "Bethesda may believe we Greens have become ruthless conquerors like the rest of my species. And there will be members in her court who hail directly from the empress. Some of them may be her advisers. It is my hope that by bringing you along I will demonstrate to her and all of them that we have actual aliens allied with us whom we have not conquered."

"How do we know they won't assume we've been possessed by Phants?" Harlequin asked.

"They can detect the presence of Phant possession in organics and robots," Azen said. "They will know that you are helping of your own free will. And it will puzzle those belonging to the camp of the empress. They will have to face the painful truth that we aren't like the rest of our kin. And hopefully, they won't vote to block any motions to assist us that Bethesda might decree. She doesn't operate in quite the same autocratic manner as the empress, you see."

"Yeah, well, either way, you already said there's a chance this Bethesda won't be receptive to our arrival," Tahoe said. "I'd hate for us to go all that way just to get 'no' for an answer."

"I have no guarantee she will help us, this is true," Azen said. "But it is a risk we have to take. There are no other Green hives close enough to help us at the moment."

"Let me get something straight," Lui said. "Basically the plan is to convince Bethesda to attack the existing empress, with the goal of deposing her, in order to give this Bethesda the crown. Right?"

"That is one potential outcome, yes," Azen said. "Though in truth I only wish to drive the existing empress off. But Bethesda may potentially ask for our aid in deposing of Medea, this is true."

"And you'll help her?" Lui pressed.

"Of course," Azen said. "If it means securing her aid."

"So essentially, you're asking us to be the instruments of regime change."

"If it comes to it, I suppose so," Azen said.

"It's not like you've never done anything of the sort before," Surus said. "I've been following the exploits of your team for a long time..."

"Don't get me wrong," Lui said. "I'm all for ousting the existing empress. I just hope you're really sure this Bethesda will have your best interests at heart. Assuming she doesn't kill us the moment we set foot into her space, of course."

"As I said, Bethesda becoming empress is only one potential outcome," Azen reiterated.

"Question," Bender said. "Can we pilot the giant golden mechs for this mission?"

"We need them for the defense of the colony," Azen said. "I'm sorry. I should mention, we will have to operate in liquid methane environments at different points. The golden mechs are ill-suited to these environments."

"Well our mechs aren't designed for underwater usage, either," TJ said. "In the simulator, we practiced on Titans specifically modified for deep sea operations. They had fins, turbines, etc. That's what we need."

"I believe Surus has already made the necessary modifications to allow your Titans to function more suitably underwater," Azen said. "Namely, hydrodynamic additions to improve drag when operating in high viscosity, incompressible fluids. Isn't that true, Surus?"

"Yes, I have," Surus said. "AIs, go ahead and show them these additions."

Electron spread its arms and legs wide, as did the other Titans. Wings, or fins, erupted from the flanks, filling the space between the arms and the hips, locking the limbs into place. There were four turbines in those fins, two per side. The propellers were obviously designed for movement through fluids, with five broad, angled blades slightly overlapping at the base.

Another wing shape lifted directly outward from the jumpjet tanks, forming a dorsal fin. Shells systematically unfolded at various locations along the hull, smoothing out hard angles to give the Titans a more hydrodynamic profile.

"Ah hell," Bender said. "You bitches have gone and messed up our Titans."

"Not at all," Surus said. "These editions were completed back in human space, before I gave you the Titans. And you all practiced in these variants in the simulator."

"Yeah but we always assumed those were completely different models of Titans," TJ said. "You never told us that you made 'transforming' versions."

"Well, I'm sorry," Surus said. "I guess I didn't make that clear."

"These changes could affect the operation of the mechs in unknown ways," TJ said. "We don't need key systems failing in the middle of a battle."

"They're my mechs," Surus said. "I own them, remember that."

"Yeah, but we have to fly them," Manic said.

"I assure you," Surus said. "The modifications were made in the most delicate manner possible, and my team triple-checked the effects the changes would have on other systems. The power draw of the turbines on the Titan reactor cores is well within operational parameters. They will function precisely the same in real-life liquid methane environments as in the simulator. And you've already seen that the land-based behavior is the same."

"I dunno..." TJ said.

"We Greens are well-acquainted with human technology," Azen said, apparently trying to reassure them. "If you'll recall, the mech I am piloting now is partially based on your own designs."

"Yeah we recall," Bender said. "You stole the tech from us. Typical of you Phants, who have no creative ideas of their own."

"You forget all the patents Surus has issued," Harlequin said. "That has to count for some creativity."

"You would jump to her defense," Bender said. "But honestly, who knows what other races she pillaged from to get those patents? Remember, her little bitch Noctua is a wellspring of alien tech, containing the knowledge of a thousand races."

"We're glad to help, Azen," Rade said emphatically, wanting to end the discussion right there. "Some of my crew will grumble, sure, but we're here to fulfill our promise of help. We owe the Greens, and we'll do whatever you need us to do. If that means piloting transforming mechs, then so be it."

"Thank you," Azen told him. "If you are ready to begin the mission, I can take you to the appropriate Acceptor?"

"We're ready," Rade said.

eight

Rade and the others took the Acceptor and emerged on the dark side of a small planet that lacked an atmosphere of any kind. Overhead Rade could see the outlines of a vast, enclosing energy sphere: different concave areas along the surface occasionally flared a dim yellow in the dark. He saw green dots floating in the sky far above. He zoomed in, and saw those green dots were the illumination coming from different ships. They were small, cranial-shaped starships; the green glow came from hollow areas on the front, which marked the areas where eye sockets and nose holes would be on an animal skull. In the area where the mouth would be, he saw pyramidal projections illuminated by the dim glow.

"Well there's a sight I never thought I'd see again," Lui said. "Skull ships."

"Yeah, but these ones are tiny," Fret said. "And colored a friendly green."

The group activated their headlamps, illuminating the red dust of the surface below them. The gravity was about half of what they were used to, allowing Azen to lead the Titans bounding across the terrain. They passed various resinous structures containing decagonal cells tended to by Green mists and the requisite jellyfish. Those structures were organized into plates, smaller version of those Rade had seen on the gas giant hive.

"What are all these plates anyway?" Lui asked. "I mean, what purpose do they serve?"

"They're essentially Phant habitation units," Azen said. "Or houses, I suppose you would call them."

"And the jellyfish?" Tahoe said.

"Jellyfish?" Azen sounded confused. "Oh. They are the shared organic interfaces we use when in our natural state to access this reality. The Servants have no minds of their own: their ganglia are essentially blank slates for us to control as we see fit, via special cybernetic receptors that allow us to link without destroying them. We designed them from the ground up to fulfill this role."

"And I wondered why it was so easy for you to control our robots," Lui said. "It sounds like you've practiced interfacing with cybernetics—and hence machines—for thousands of years."

"Millions of years would be more accurate," Azen said. "If it relies on some form of electrical- or quantum-based neural network, we can control it. Of course when encountering a new design, it will take us some time to figure out how to access the various features and components, but since we share knowledge in a telepathic cloud, our learning of new designs is exponential."

"Servants, you call these jellyfish?" TJ asked. "A species genetically engineered specifically for the servitude of another. Sounds kind of cruel. Remind me why you're the good guys again?"

"Because we haven't conquered you?" Azen said. "I don't see anything wrong, morality-wise. Is it anything different from the robots and AIs that humanity creates to serve its species? "

"Yeah but, we don't reach into their minds and take control of them," Fret said. "I agree with TJ on the cruelty comment."

"Considering that the Servants are not self-aware on their own, it can hardly be considered cruelty," Azen argued. "It's like humans growing biolimbs or meat from harvested cells."

"All right," Fret said. "Then what about what you're doing to our Artificials at the moment? Emilia Bounty for Surus, and whatever Artificial you possess. They are self aware. But you've taken control, and I'm not sure that's ethical."

"Emilia acts as my host at her consent," Surus said. "The same is true of Azen, I'm sure."

Azen hesitated. Then: "Yes, I would not force my will upon anyone."

"Hmm," Manic said. "Did anyone else hear that suspicious pause before he answered?"

Azen didn't comment. The group continued in silence for a few moments.

"Ah, the Phant mythos," TJ said. "We cannot escape them. Though we travel far and wide, our path always finds its way back here. It is our destiny to either hunt Phants, or aid them."

"You don't sound too happy," Harlequin said.

"You weren't there during the First Alien War," TJ said. "If you were, you'd understand."

"I have watched footage from the war," Harlequin said.

"Actually being there is a different story altogether," Lui said.

"I've fought against Phants with you," Harlequin insisted. "And I've been possessed by them. So don't try to give me that I'm-more-battle-hardened-than-you bull."

"Ooo," Bender said. "The AI is touchy today. What's got your balls in a snitch, Harley boy?"

"I've decided I'm going to stand up for myself," Harlequin said.

"An honorable choice," Fret said.

"Ha, good luck with that," Bender said.

"Yeah, we're all assholes, remember?" Manic said, referring to a post a troll had made on their security consulting InterGalNet site.

"Harlequin is a gentleman among assholes," Surus said.

"I think the alien has the hots for you, Harleykins," Lui said.

"She has good taste," Harlequin retorted.

"I've always thought of you all as assholes with heart," Shaw said, sounding earnest.

"That sounds about right," Tahoe said.

"Except Rade of course," Shaw said. "He's not an asshole. Most of the time. But he has the biggest heart of you all."

"Hey, don't do that to me," Rade said. "Make me the odd one out. As far as I'm concerned, I'm the biggest asshole of them all."

"Yeah boss, we agree," Bender said. "Especially for all the times you've docked our pay for nothing."

"Maybe if you stopped having physical altercations with Manic your salary might be a bit higher," Rade said.

After passing between several of those cell-covered plates, eventually the bounding Titans reached a clearing of sorts on the red surface, the resinous structures parting to reveal a broad disk carved with Fibonacci spirals. It was an Acceptor large enough to transport three Titans at a time.

"This is going to take us to one of those ships in orbit?" Rade asked.

"Yes," Azen replied.

"How many of the other ships are coming with us?" Tahoe said.

"Our ship will be the only one, I'm afraid," Azen said.

"We're on a mission that could potentially save the homeworld of you Greens," TJ said. "And yet we're only bringing one ship, when we obviously have at least a small armada up there? Seems like a bad decision if you ask me."

"Yes, but we have to be very careful, diplomatically," Azen said. "Relations between the Hydra and our species are obviously not at their best. Even if the relative of the empress is sympathetic to our cause, many who work for her will not be. Too many of our ships arriving at their borders will be perceived as a threat. One, not so much. I'm almost certain Bethesda's border guards will allow us passage to the colony world if we come alone."

"Almost certain," Lui said. "Is not the same as certain."

Azen disembarked from his golden mech.

"You're not taking it with us?" Shaw asked.

"No." Azen stepped onto the Acceptor, leaving the tall mech standing alone on the red sand like a sentry. "Unfortunately, it's far too large to navigate the passageways of our destination ship. It will stay behind and guard this colony instead. Your Titans will fit, of course."

The remaining mechs moved onto the Acceptor and vanished in threes. Azen went with the first party. Surus remained behind to transport the remainder.

Rade, Shaw and Fret stepped onto the disk. The

landscape vanished a moment later, replaced by a vaulted chamber. Rade's headlamp illuminated an Acceptor of similar size beneath his feet. Several thick ribs spanned outward across the floor from the edges of the teleportation device. Those ribs, and the deck, bulkheads and overhead around them, were formed of small, dark metal pipes that crisscrossed one another, and slowly undulated as if alive.

Rade felt heavier after the lighter weight of the planet below.

"Man, is this gravity twice that of Earth or something?" Fret said.

"I've had the artificial gravity set to Earth levels to accommodate you," Azen said. "Though compared to the lower gravity of the previous planet, it will take you a few moments to accustom yourselves."

"Geez, now I know what it feels like to weigh as much as Bender," Fret said.

"Yeah bitch, and that's all pure muscle I'm packing on my frame, remember that," Bender retorted.

Rade stepped off the disk and waited for the others to arrive.

"Electron, is there an atmosphere out there?" he asked his AI.

"Negative," Electron replied. "I am detecting void conditions."

That was different to the other Phant ship Rade had once been inside. Then again, that ship had belonged to a rival Phant faction, and was far more massive.

When everyone materialized, Azen led them from the chamber and into the dark passageway beyond.

The party proceeded onto a raised walkway formed by that moving lattice of tubes on the deck. Sometimes the undulating pipes formed gaps in the floor that would have been wide enough to trip a human in a jumpsuit, but given that the Argonauts were all inside Titans, the broad feet of their mechs easily spanned any breaks that arose.

"Damn things give me the creeps," Bender commented as they made their way through the passageway.

"Why do those pipes move like that anyway?" Lui asked. "Are they alive?"

"They are, in fact," Surus said. "The ships flown by the Phants are living entities capable of self-healing. Though a better description would be cybernetic, since they are half machine. All of our ships are based on this same design, scaling from the smallest to the moon-sized Motherships. It has a mind, essentially the equivalent of your AI cores. This mind can be placed some distance outside of the ship for protective purposes, though that is not the case for these. I believe you called them Observer Minds at one point. These minds are composed of specialized Phants— neutral Oranges—linked together to form a massive neural network spanning the supra-dimension, allowing for unified operation of the ship."

"All right, that kind of went over my head, but hey," Manic said.

"You know how in some villages there's always someone who's the idiot?" Bender said. "That someone is you."

"And what's that make you?" Manic asked.

"Man, compared to you, I got an IQ of ten thousand," Bender said.

"An IQ of ten thousand," Manic said. "And you don't know how to conjugate verbs? Riiiight."

"I said *compared* to you," Bender replied. "Damn. Get a hearing aid."

In those dark passageways the Titans occasionally passed Greens in mist form. The living vapors moved with purpose, and Rade was left with the impression the gaseous aliens had some important errand to run; nonetheless, they always deferred to the mechs and swerved to avoid the individual party members. While there might have been an element of courtesy to their behavior, Rade thought they deferred mostly because of the Phant-repelling emitters the pilots had: after the possession fiasco of the last mission, Surus had those emitters installed in all of their jumpsuits.

"How big is this ship?" Tahoe asked.

"It's about as big as the *Argonaut*," Surus replied.

"Does it have a name?" TJ asked.

"The name is unpronounceable to the human tongue," Azen said. "But you may call it the *Yarak*, based on the Persian word for strength."

"It can also be applied to a trained hawk," Harlequin elucidated. "When a hawk is said to be 'in yarak,' it means the hawk is fit and in proper condition for hunting."

"Well, I suppose that applies to us readily enough," Lui said.

"*Yarak*," TJ said, sounding unimpressed.

"Sounds like a word you'd use when complimenting a chick," Bender said. "Yer rack is hot, bitch."

"If you think that's a compliment, I can see why you don't have a girlfriend," Manic said.

"Ha! You should talk."

Azen brought them to a wide compartment. "This will be the storage bay for your mechs. Please find a suitable spot and debark."

Rade brought Electron to one corner, then opened the cockpit and climbed down the rungs to the deck.

Everyone else did the same, leaving their mechs inside the compartment.

"Your shared berthing area is just this way." Azen led them out into the shifting hallways. "Watch your step."

Rade took care not to step between the gaps in the pipes that formed the walkway. He definitely didn't want to get caught by those moving things.

"Strangely, I feel really vulnerable at the moment," Fret said.

"There's certainly something about wandering around a Phant ship while wearing only a jumpsuit that's disquieting," Lui said.

"Why does it feel like he's taking us to a room full of robot arms waiting to attach cybernetic components to our backs?" Fret asked.

The team approached another Green along the way. The mist moved aside, though giving them less of a berth than other Greens had when the Argonauts had still resided within the Titans. The proximity of the things made Rade a little nervous, and he wondered if they should boost the power levels of the EM emitters; like Fret, he definitely felt exposed without his Titan.

Azen reached what appeared to be a dead end. A moment later the undulating pipes that composed the bulkhead parted, revealing a smaller chamber inside.

"Everyone, please," Azen beckoned toward the compartment.

Rade regarded the cramped area uncertainly, then sighed.

We've gone this far...

"Come on, guys." He entered.

nine

The others squeezed inside after Rade. It had just enough room to fit them all.

When they were all packed within, the bulkhead sealed once more behind them, and air misted into the chamber from vents hidden in the overhead.

"Well lookee here," Bender said. "The Phants have gone and made an airlock."

"Correct," Azen said. "This membrane is human style. We also have the technology to create energetic membranes that allow for the passage of organics, but not atmospheres, eliminating the need for inner and outer hatches."

"Quit your bragging," Bender said.

"So if you have the tech, why didn't you use it?" Fret said. "It'd be interesting to see one of these energetic membranes as you call it in action."

"Such membranes constantly draw power," Azen said. "Whereas the airlock before you is far more energy efficient. And safer, in the long run. For example, if the power were to fail in any way, you would still survive. With an energetic membrane, the power fails, and instantly the chamber experiences explosive decompression."

"We've actually seen the tech already, Fret," Lui said. "Well not you, maybe, since you never boarded the Phant mothership all those years ago, but *I* remember. There was a layer of void in the outer regions of the ship, which soon gave way to trace gaseous elements. The air pressure slowly rose until we had completely transitioned into the inner atmosphere. You couldn't even tell that there was any sort of energy membrane present at all."

"Exactly so," Azen said. "That is an example of a location-dependent membrane, with the atmosphere becoming denser the deeper inside one travels."

A moment later the bulkhead on the opposite side opened and Azen led them into the wider compartment beyond. While the bulkheads and overhead here were still fashioned from those undulating pipes, the deck had been covered over in what appeared to be some sort of vinyl laminate meant to imitate tiles. Distributed among those false tiles were a few horizontal light planes, strategically placed to illuminate the entire chamber; the color temperature matched that of natural sunlight, so that the planes gave the impression that they were skylights, except situated on the floor. It was relaxing, somehow. Almost homey.

Small pieces of furniture had been provided: mostly hard-backed chairs and coffee tables. It looked like the items had been quickly 3D-printed out of polycarbonate. There were also several pillows, spaced evenly across the deck on one side.

In one corner resided a United Systems surgical Weaver unit.

"You even have a Weaver aboard," Fret said. "You Phants have thought of everything haven't you?"

As they entered, they turned off their headlamps,

as there was no need to waste power while those light planes were active. When everyone was inside, the bulkhead sealed behind them.

Manic paused beside one of the floor lights. "You know, normally we put these on the ceiling."

Bender stared down into the illumination beside him; his faceplate reflected the blue color. "So goddamn featureless. Feels like I'm staring down from an observation deck above Neptune."

"I bet you think the same thing when you look in your pants," Manic said.

"Lui, how's the air?" Rade asked

"Definitely breathable," Lui said. "The gas ratios are similar to what we have on our own ships. Seventy-eight percent nitrogen. Twenty-one percent oxygen. One percent argon. Trace amounts carbon dioxide, neon, and helium."

"What about contagions?"

"I'm not detecting any," Lui said.

"Yeah, but that doesn't mean there aren't any," TJ said. "There's a reason why we have a rule about not taking off our helmets when aboard alien ships or on alien worlds, even when the air is breathable."

"There are no contagions, I assure you," Azen said.

"Do we really want to believe this guy?" Bender said. "We take off our helmets, blink, and a moment later we got some retrovirus crawling through our bodies, messing with our DNA to create bugs inside us just waiting to burst from our backs. Either that or we change into bugs ourselves."

"Keep your helmets on, then," Azen said. "And wear them until your oxygen supplies exhaust. Or your liquid food supplies are empty. Whichever comes first. It's your choice."

"When we get back, I can reserve a building on the Green Systems base specifically for you all," Surus said. "To serve as a decon ward. If that will make you feel any better."

"Works for me." Rade opened up the latch on his neck assembly and removed his helmet. His face felt cold, exposed as it was to the air of that compartment.

Shaw and Tahoe joined him, also leading by example.

"The air smells strangely good," Tahoe said. "Certainly better than the stale air of the jumpsuits we've been breathing."

Shaw nodded. "There's a hint of mint to it."

The other members of the crew followed their lead and removed the helmets they wore.

"Shaw, what the hell?" Bender said. "There ain't no mint scent to the air."

"I know," Shaw said. "But it got you to take off your helmet, didn't it?"

Tahoe took a seat at one of the tables. "So when do we get to eat?"

"Ah, I love you ex-military types," Shaw said. "Always putting your stomachs first."

"Food will be provided shortly," Azen said. "I've assigned our bioengineering group the task of growing chicken breasts and potatoes."

"Ooh, chicken breasts," Bender said. "You've outdone yourself."

"Where do we relieve ourselves?" Fret asked.

"Keep your suits on," Azen said. "And utilize the waste collection facilities therein. When you need to expel the waste matter from the suits, open this slot and deposit the material inside. It leads to an incinerator." He walked to a small handle on the deck and opened it, revealing a chute. When he closed it,

Rade heard a brief suction sound that reminded him of the noise a toilet made on an aircraft.

"Well, it's better than an open latrine, I suppose," Fret replied.

"Like the kind you keep in your house?" Bender quipped.

"Surus will remain here with you," Azen said. "She will keep you updated on the status of the ship."

"Are there any external cameras we can get access to?" Rade asked. "Or a tactical display?"

"No," Azen said. "Our technology is quite different than your own, I'm afraid. In any case, if there are no further questions, I must take my leave."

"You're going to the bridge?" Tahoe asked.

"Phant starships don't utilize the human concept of a bridge," Azen said. "I interface with the ship from my quarters as necessary."

"How long is it going to take to reach the colony?" Lui asked.

"Three weeks," Azen said.

"Are we actually using propulsion to fly there?" Lui pressed.

"We are," Azen replied.

"I thought Phant ships used mini-Slipstreams to move forward? You know, hopping from place to place to cross a system, creating temporary Slipstreams to facilitate the motion."

"We can," Azen said. "Though it is dangerous. When there are no wormholes available to facilitate interstellar travel, we prefer to pass the heliopause into the lifeless void between star systems before utilizing the technology. Other Phant hives will sometimes create mini-Slipstreams inside systems to surprise enemies, however. They did it to humanity a few times, I believe."

"Are there wormholes leading to our destination?" Tahoe asked.

"There are," Azen said. "And we intend to use them. If we did not, the journey would take ten times as long."

"If it takes three weeks to get there, it will take at least as long to return," Tahoe said. "Are you sure the Green homeworld will be able to hold out that long?"

"They will hold," Azen said. "They have no choice. Some individual sub-hives may be lost, along with the constituent populations, but the rest will keep fighting. Now please, I must prepare for departure."

"Azen, we're going to need some curtains, and frames to hold them," Rade told him. "For privacy reasons."

"It will be done." Azen approached the far bulkhead, which opened for him. He glanced askance. "If you wish to depart this chamber, Surus can open the airlock. Though I don't foresee you will have the need."

"Azen is right," Surus said. "The only time we'll need to leave is when we're ready to deploy. If we vacate this chamber before then, it means the *Yarak* is in big trouble."

Azen entered the airlock. "Water has arrived. Food will come later."

"Could use a drink." Bender started walking toward the airlock.

The bulkhead abruptly resealed in front of him.

"Well that was rude," Bender said.

When the bulkhead opened again, Azen was gone. Bender and a few others went inside.

"There's a barrel in here," Fret said. "It's like a keg or something."

Bender grabbed one of the provided polycarbonate

mugs.

"This is my glass," Bender said. "No one touch it. Now get back, I'm first."

Bender held the mug under the spigot and filled it. He stepped back, giving the others room. He was staring into his mug with a sour expression. "Looks cloudy."

Fret filled another mug and gazed at it. "Yeah."

"Lui, scan this crap," Bender said, holding out the mug.

"Seems fine," Lui replied a moment later.

Fret took a sip.

"Tastes like bilgewater," Fret said.

Bender sipped from his own mug, then spat it out.

"Bilgewater?" Bender said. "No, Bilgewater is a luxury compared to this! Tastes like *piss*."

"How would you know what piss tastes like?" Manic asked.

"All right, let me rephrase that," Bender said. "It tastes like piss smells like."

Rade took a sip. It was a bit sour, but he wasn't going to show it. "Tastes fine to me." He offered his mug to Shaw.

She took a sip and shrugged. "Good enough for me."

That basically silenced the complaints going forward.

The curtains and their frames arrived later that day, and Rade and the others partitioned the chamber into different "rooms," giving them privacy.

The days passed. The Argonauts became restless from being cooped up in that chamber. Rade led them in PT three times a day, doing calisthenics right there on the vinyl laminate deck. They engaged in VR war games via their Implants. They had Azen print up a few mats and used them for sleeping, and sparring.

Manic and Bender went too far during one of those sparring matches; the latter emerged with a black eye, the former a broken arm, despite Rade's warnings to cool it. They continued fighting even after their injuries, until Rade and Tahoe pulled them apart.

As the Weaver worked on them, Rade imposed his usual punishment of docked pay.

"You've got to be what, at negative two hundred a month now?" Fret mocked Bender.

"Nope," Bender said. "You do know I get paid three times your measly salary, don't you? So even though I'm down two hundred, I still make twice what you do."

"Ha," Fret said. Then his expression became worried, and he glanced at Rade. "Is that true?"

At the designated night times, the floor "skylights" dimmed, allowing the crew to sleep. During those late hours, Rade and Shaw occasionally stripped down and made love quietly in their curtained off area. They placed their helmets outward and activated the noise cancelers with the hope that it would mute whatever sounds they couldn't contain.

No one ever said anything the next morning, though Rade was sure they all knew what he and Shaw were up to. That fact made his lovemaking restrained. Well, that and the fact Rade was embarrassed of his growing smell—he had washed himself as well as he could with the water from the barrel, letting himself air dry afterward, but without soap he had trouble getting rid of the odor produced by problem areas. Shaw didn't seem to mind. She had her own smells, of course, but seemed to do a better job of curtailing them than he did.

Surus kept them up to date on their progress.

Apparently the Hydra colony was three jumps away via the network of wormholes the inhabitants of that region of space relied upon. When the *Yarak* took the first wormhole, the system beyond proved empty. The second system was populated by automated Hydra probes that moved to and fro between the planets and wormholes, but otherwise left the party alone.

It was shortly after breakfast at the start of the third week when Surus announce that they had just emerged into the final system.

"A contingent of three Hydra ships was waiting on the other side for us," Surus said. "They haven't fired yet. Azen is currently engaged in negotiations for our safe passage to the colony."

A few hours later Surus told them that the *Yarak* had been allowed through. "One of the Hydra vessels is escorting us to the planet. Two more are expected to rendezvous with us along the way."

It took another three days to reach the planet in question. They spent two days in orbit waiting for an audience with Bethesda. Finally, on the morning of the third day Azen came to berthing area to update them.

"So, I just finished conversing with Bethesda's high council," Azen said. "Apparently, she has been kidnapped."

"Kidnapped?" Rade said.

"Yes," Azen said. "By agents of Empress Medea. This is a change from the usual assassination methods of the empress. The high council believes Medea wishes to brainwash Bethesda and use her as a puppet to assume control of the army her cousin has been gathering in secret. If Medea were to assassinate Bethesda outright, perhaps a few of the warlords formerly under Bethesda's command might fight among themselves for rights to her territories, but the remainder would simply disband. Those warlords are far more useful to Medea as a unified whole. Hence, the kidnapping."

"So we came all this way for nothing," Fret said.

"Not entirely," Azen replied. "The council has listened to our request for help, and they have allowed us to render aid as a show of good faith. They have not guaranteed they will help us, but if we can rescue Bethesda, that will go a long way into securing their assistance."

"So what's the plan, then?" Bender said. "We're going to intercept an alien ship and rescue some bug?"

"Almost," Azen said. "We're going to join an armada destined for a system two jumps away. By the time we get there, Bethesda will have already been brought to another colony, and detained deep beneath the liquid methane ocean by the agents of Medea. While the armada engages the enemy from orbit, we're going to drop to the surface with their skirmisher units and attempt a daring rescue."

"Fighting side by side with aliens you consider your enemies," Shaw said. "That's an interesting concept. And something we've never really done before. Well, discounting when we fought beside you and Surus."

"Whether they prove to be friend or foe remains yet to be seen," Azen said. "I don't need to tell you that we must be cautious at all times. Once we rescue Bethesda, for all I know she may order the armada to shoot us down."

"You mean if Medea's agents have already brainwashed her?" Fret said.

"She might give the order to fire at us even if she's herself," Azen said. "Because let me just say, the initial reception I had with the high council was frosty, to say the least. I could almost feel the methane turning to ice around their bodies."

ten

The *Yarak* joined the Hydra armada. There were twenty-two ships in total. When Rade asked for a description of those ships, Surus told him to imagine slightly smaller versions of the monolithic vessel he had seen in orbit above the Green homeworld, replete with three talon-like prongs protruding from the nose.

The next two weeks passed in a blur of system jumps and interplanetary travel, and in no time at all it seemed the *Yarak* was closing with the destination planet.

"The Hydra armada is engaging with the defending forces the agents of the empress have placed in orbit," Surus announced.

The deck rumbled twice in a row shortly thereafter.

"Bender, did you eat yet?" Fret said. "I can hear your stomach growling."

"When my stomach growls, it shakes the ship," Bender agreed.

"Are we absolutely certain that came from Bender's stomach?" Manic said. "And not a more nether region of his anatomy?"

A few minutes later the deck shook a third time,

worse than ever. Rade and the others exchanged worried looks and then donned their helmets to pressurize their jumpsuits.

"Bethesda's fleet just lost four ships," Surus said.

"I'm surprised the enemy hasn't concentrated their forces on us," Tahoe said. "We stick out like a sore thumb."

"Apparently the enemy is afraid," Surus said. "Bethesda's armada is using our presence to instill fear in the defenders. It has been a long time since a Phant skull ship, even if a small one, has appeared in these parts. And the memories the Hydra have of that last time are not pleasant."

Half an hour of intermittent shaking passed. Then the inner bulkhead of the airlock peeled aside, revealing Azen. "It's time."

The Argonauts followed Azen through the undulating passageways to the compartment where they had stored the Titans. Rade loaded inside his designated mech.

"Welcome back, boss," Electron said.

"Did you miss me in the long time we were parted?" Rade asked.

"Like a face misses its beard," Electron said.

"Hmm," Rade said. "I'm not sure if you meant that as a complement or an insult."

"Probably a little of both," Electron replied.

Azen, wearing a jumpsuit, loaded into the passenger seat of Swift, Surus' mech. During the intervening weeks since their arrival, Surus had made frequent trips to the mech bay with TJ and Bender to upgrade her passenger seat, giving it a complete glass enclosure in the form of a globular tank; once Azen was in place, the glass sphere sealed over him, giving the Artificial essentially his own pressurized observation deck.

Surus had also apparently increased the power output of all the zodiacs and cobras the Titans possessed, improving the effective range of the weapons against the Tech Class IV armor of the skirmishers. When Rade asked why she hadn't done that in the first place, she told him it was because she lacked certain parts that were unavailable in human space.

"This way." Surus led the party in her mech.

"Now I'm feeling a bit better," Fret said.

"Give a man a mech, make him feel secure," Tahoe said. "Give a man ten mechs, make him feel invulnerable."

"What if, instead of a man, you're an Artificial?" Harlequin said.

"And what if you're a woman?" Shaw added.

"Hey, it was just a spur of the moment saying meant to inspire confidence, cut me some slack," Tahoe said.

"I'm so looking forward to this shit," Bender said. "Last time we had to deal with an alien queen, this time we gots ourselves an alien *empress*." He broke into spontaneous song. "Giant bugs roasting on an open fire... Jack Frost nipping—"

"Stop ruining Christmas songs!" Manic said.

"So uh, one question," Fret said. "How do we intend to return to orbit without booster rockets?"

The bulkhead folded aside up ahead, revealing a wide bay. Several 3D-printed booster rockets were arrayed within. "Never mind. Our hosts have thought of everything, it seems."

When the last of the Titans entered, the bulkhead sealed behind them.

"Line up against the far wall in front of the booster

rockets," Azen said. "And face the bulkhead."

The group complied.

When they were in place, the bulkhead in front of them rapidly peeled aside. There was no decompression of any kind, as there was no atmosphere in the bay in the first place.

Past the opening, the horizon-to-horizon hemisphere of the planet was revealed before them. Between clouds that looked like runny egg yolks, brown land masses dotted with gray mountain ranges vied for dominance of the surface with featureless yellow oceans.

Several dark shapes interrupted their view of the planet, placed as they were between the *Yarak* and the surface. These were the long, stretched ovules of the black Hydra vessels; some of these ships faced the *Yarak*, others pointed away, as determined by the positioning of the three prongs protruding from the noses.

Streaks of darkness erupted from the Hydra ships that faced the planet; their allies were launching the skirmishers that would join Rade and his team in the rescue operation beneath the oceans below. Other streaks, these ones colored a bright white, occasionally emerged from both sides; those were aimed at the different ships, and where they struck, large portions of the hulls dissolved.

"Um, why does this feel like we're back in the alien wars?" Fret asked.

"That's because, essentially, we are!" Bender replied.

"Except this time we're fighting on the side of the aliens, against the aliens!" Manic said.

"So?" Bender transmitted. "I'll take whatever excuse I can to kill bugs any day."

"Deploy the booster rockets," Azen said.

There were apparently no launch platforms for the boosters, so that meant it was up to the Titans to pick up the rockets and hurl them outside. Rade wrapped his arms around the bulky rocket payload in front of him and, twisting his torso, he threw the heavy object outside.

The others seamlessly tossed the remaining boosters outside; thrusters activated on the units, decelerating them so that they instantly vanished from view.

"On my mark..." Azen said.

Several moments passed.

"Drop!" Azen said.

Rade leaped his mech outside. He felt the stomach-turning weightlessness of space instantly.

"Match my deceleration vector," Surus said. "We'll be landing in the ocean here." A highlight appeared on the overhead map.

"Electron, match it," Rade said.

"Matching," the AI replied.

Around him Rade saw more of the dark streaks launched from the armada, and destined for the planet. He zoomed in. The objects looked the same as the skirmishers that had attacked the Green hive: miniature versions of the Hydra warships with weapon turrets protruding from the nose sections, and four or five segmented tentacles extending from the aft quarter behind them. The number of those rear tentacles dictated their respective ranks, he guessed.

Rade was a little glad those units were on his side, as he remembered how much trouble he had with them in the previous attack. Azen had warned them they could expect more of those skirmisher-style robots waiting in opposition below, along with worse opponents. Rade was just glad Surus had updated their weapon effectiveness.

White streaks continued to erupt from the starships on both sides. Some of those streaks, launched from the opposing fleet, occasionally struck the approaching skirmishers and disintegrated them. He was nearly hit by one himself.

"Close one," Shaw commented.

He glanced at his overhead map, and saw that she was following him not far away. Tahoe was beside her.

The incoming energy streaks intensified as the mechs and skirmishers came closer to the Hydra warships guarding the planet. Rade held his breath as he passed between several of those starships, and then, just like that, he and the others were through the defensive line. There was no longer anything between them and the planet.

Rade searched the immediate area for signs of orbital defense platforms, but couldn't see any. He braced himself for the expected surface-to-space attacks, but they did not come.

"The first wave managed to take down most of the planetary defenses before the drop, in case you were wondering," Azen commented. "It should be clear sailing here on in. At least until we get closer to the submerged base."

The planet quickly grew larger below them until it ate up Rade's entire vision. Gyroscopic thrusters fired, stabilizing his descent. The aeroshell heat shield deployed underneath him just in time for flames to lick the edges. The fire soon expanded until all he saw was orange.

And then the flames were gone, their brightness leaving only a momentary afterimage in his retina. The spent aeroshell shield fell away, disintegrating, and

Rade descended into the yellow cloud coverage. When he emerged, he was headed directly toward the featureless methane ocean.

He glanced at his HUD. On the overhead map, the blue dots representing the Argonauts were strung out in a wide, zig-zagging line that closely followed the descent of Surus and her mech. Everyone had survived the reentry.

There were other dots in a darker shade of blue, indicating the allied skirmishers; those units transmitted a special signal that Azen parsed for the humans, marking the aliens as friendlies on the overhead map. Enemy skirmishers would automatically be indicated in red, as they did not transmit the signal.

Apparently, Azen had likewise installed markers in the Titans to prevent their temporary allies from accidentally targeting them during the battle.

In a few minutes, the ocean grew until it filled Rade's vision. Electron engaged the air brakes and fired the aerospike thrusters in the feet, slowing Rade enough to impact the ocean without destroying his mech.

He plunged into the liquid and continued descending rapidly.

"Do not transform until we are closer to the ocean floor," Azen said.

Apparently, the Hydra utilized sonar and echolocation to "see" in the liquid methane environment. In the last mission, Surus had developed special emitters that could shield jumpsuit-sized units from detection via sonar and echolocation, however those emitters didn't function for something the size of a mech. Unfortunately, because of the expected liquid pressure involved in this mission, mechs were required—they couldn't simply approach the target in their jumpsuits.

The plan was to stay close to the ocean floor to reduce their sonic profile—with luck, they would blend right in with their surroundings.

Rade's mech continued rapidly descending through the cloudy yellow liquid. Soon he reached a level where light did not penetrate, and he was surrounded by darkness.

The moments passed, and as the depth became ever greater, Rade could almost feel the weight of the liquid methane pressing down on top of him. He knew if he ejected now—assuming he could even open his cockpit—he'd be crushed to death.

"Argonauts, activate LIDAR for mapping purposes," Rade transmitted. "Three bursts, two seconds apart."

Electron sent out the requested bursts of LIDAR and in moments a white, three-dimensional grid of the distant ocean floor appeared below. He could see the small protuberance of their target far ahead, set upon the sea floor. The entire area appeared to be part of a continental shelf. Far to the left, away from the colony, the LIDAR mapped empty space—that would be the open ocean.

Some distance away, Rade could see the three-dimensional representations of the allied skirmishers that had arrived ahead of the Argonauts. Closer were small white dots representing schools of alien fish. There was a larger whale-type creature that prowled not far from those schools. Rade hoped it left them alone.

All of those representations were frozen in time, of course, due to only the three bursts Rade had authorized. The enemy could detect LIDAR because of their high Tech Class, so by using it in bursts, Rade only gave away his position for a fraction of a second. Even so, because the enemy would be relying upon echolocation as their main mode of target detection, it meant he couldn't release another burst until the team had descended closer to the seabed. They'd just have to run on outdated information until then.

The accelerometer and gyroscope in the Titan would account for his speed and heading to update his position in relation to the recorded topographic map of the seabed anyway, with only a small margin of error.

When they were fifty meters from the ocean floor, Azen transmitted: "Stabilize depth and transform into Titan submarines."

Rade fired a quick burst of stabilizing thrust and instructed Electron to change. The Titan's arms and legs spread out, and fins extended from the rib area to fill the space between the arms and the torso. He knew a dorsal fin had also appeared from his jumpjet tank. Shells unfolded along the hull, smoothing out the sharp points of the Titan. The metallic skin of the transforming mech moaned in complaint during the process, not liking the immense pressure down there at all.

"How is the submarine frame holding up?" Rade asked.

"Surprisingly well, given the pressure," Electron replied. "Surus wasn't kidding when she said she had given the design much thought."

"But we're not even close to the open ocean," Rade said. "The target colony appears to be on a continental shelf. The pressure can't be all that bad."

"Unfortunately it is," Electron said. "You can't discount the different hydrodynamic properties of liquid methane versus water, plus the higher gravity of this world as compared to Earth. The liquid simply weighs more here, I'm afraid, and for comparable depths on Earth the pressure is greater."

He felt his torso vibrate as the turbines activated in the flanking fins. He had continued to descend during the transformation, but the forward motion had countered the plunge, and he was now climbing slightly.

"Proceed toward target," Azen said. "And descend once more. Depth objective: ten meters from the seabed."

eleven

Rade compensated his heading to proceed toward the target at the requested depth.

On the overhead map, the booster rockets showed up about a kilometer to the east, where they had sunk to the ocean floor on the continental shelf.

"Set your AIs to emit LIDAR bursts every twenty seconds," Rade said. "Tahoe, give me two fire teams, traveling overwatch."

While Azen was in command of the overall operation, Rade was in charge of combat procedures. Thus, Tahoe broke the team into two units as per his instructions, and sent the first team forward. Rade, part of the second team, followed.

Rade instructed Electron to interpret the positional information returned by the friendlies in realtime, and to overlay them on his vision. That way he would know where the Argonauts and their Hydra allies were at all times, regardless of the twenty second burst intervals.

In moments he saw the skirmishers on his HUD; they led the way toward the distant valley up ahead. Surus followed close behind in her Titan, as part of Fire Team One. The remaining four Titans of that fire team were dispersed in a zig-zag pattern behind her.

Rade and the others followed fifty meters behind, cruising along ten meters above the ocean floor.

"I've been in touch with the Hydra commander," Azen said. "He's agreed to transmit positional information of any enemies detected by his skirmishers in realtime. What that means is, in between LIDAR bursts, you'll still be able to see the enemy positions, but you just won't know what they're doing."

"What do you mean we won't know what they're doing?" Lui said. "What kind of positional information is this? Can you clarify whether we'll see them at all times? As in, their full bodies?"

"No, the enemy will appear as a red sphere between updates," Azen said.

"Nice."

The LIDAR updated the topography of the seabed below. The background remained absolutely black of course, with the white wireframes representing three-dimensional objects overlaying the darkness. Some of those wireframes looked like small streamers that might have been seabed flora—maybe the alien equivalent of seaweed or kelp. There was more fauna, too—strange crablike and tentacled creatures. All frozen in their last recorded positions, thanks to the LIDAR burst. Rade guessed the Hydra didn't count the numerous sea creatures as part of the enemy, since he never discerned any red spheres between updates.

Rade's weapon mounts were still free to swivel while he was in "submarine" mode, and he aimed his scope at the white wire frame representation of their target. He zoomed in. The LIDAR data obtained at that distance was somewhat coarse-grained, and he couldn't make out much detail. It appeared to be a gargantuan reef-life structure set amid a rocky basin. He spotted several treelike structures of varying sizes and shapes, similar to coralline; tall arches covered in platelets; and spirals that reminded him of minarets. It was definitely a colony of some kind, about the size of a small town.

Floating in the sea above it were hundreds of skirmishers tagged in red, along with other objects that Rade guessed were sea creatures—they had the tentacles of octopuses protruding from the heads of lions, replete with manes, at least on the LIDAR. While their positions were frozen, small red spheres overlaid them all, drifting subtly to the left or right; every twenty seconds the wireframes updated to match the latest location of those spheres.

Rade tried thermal vision. It didn't help. Apparently the creatures, as well as the enemy skirmishers, were the same temperature as the outlying liquid. The team's Hydra allies didn't show up on that band either, Rade noted.

"Anyone want to come up with creative names for those new baddies?" Lui asked. "The ones that look like a lion and an octopus got together and had a baby?"

"Octolion?" Fret said.

"Sounds like some kind of drone," Lui replied.

"How about Lion Pussies?" Bender said.

"Doesn't do it for me," Lui commented.

"Lionsquids," Tahoe tried.

"And the winner of the naming contest goes to Tahoe," Lui said.

Rade maintained the traveling overwatch formation for the moment, because while he could see where most of the enemy was waiting, he wasn't sure if more might attempt an ambush attack from the seabed along the way.

"I'm detecting laser fire," Electron said. "Coming

from our allies. And now the targets are returning fire."

The red spheres of the lionsquids abruptly shot forward, while the spheres representing the skirmishers quickly descended instead. A moment later, when the LIDAR updated, the wireframes of the lionsquids were that much closer to the incoming units, while the defending skirmishers had taken cover behind the different coral structures of the colony.

Rade glanced at the distance gauge. During the briefing, Azen had requested that the party attempt to close to within five hundred meters of the submerged city before digging in, explaining that the updates to their weapons would enable them to readily inflict damage at that range. Rade told him his Argonauts would do their best to attain that distance, but he refused to guarantee it, telling Azen the safety of his brothers and sisters was the highest priority.

"Evasive maneuvers, people!" Rade sent. "Don't let those enemy lasers target the same spot on your mechs too long! And fire at will!"

In submarine mode, while it was possible to rotate their shields into place, doing so wasn't feasible as the drag slowed down their mechs too much. So evasive action was really all they could do at that point. That and fire back. Surus had reinforced the head and shoulder armor to give about half as much protection as the shields during sub mode, but unfortunately that wouldn't last long against the starship-equivalent heavy lasers they faced.

"Argh!" Lui said. "This isn't working. Both my right turbines got shot out. I'm going to have to dig in here. Sorry."

A moment later:

"Just took a shot to my Titan's head," Bender

transmitted. "It nearly drilled through to my cockpit. I gotta drop out and deploy my shield."

Bender and Lui descended to the seabed, transforming into mech mode, and fire team two passed them.

"Electron, target as many of those skirmishers as you can," Rade said. "Record the positions where they dropped behind the coral to take cover, and fire rockets to intercept! Two per tango!"

Electron unleashed several rockets a moment later, dispatching two per skirmisher target as requested. Meanwhile, Rade concentrated his cobra fire on the spheres of the rapidly approaching lionsquids. He held the zodiac in reserve, as it didn't work as intended in liquid environments, dispersing its electrical energy in all directions and dissipating in six meters. However, it produced an even louder noise than when deployed on the surface, and could potentially be used as a stun weapon when the opponents were closer. In retrospect, Surus probably should have exchanged those zodiac mounts for second cobra lasers instead. Another reason why she needed to consult with him earlier and more often.

Every one of those lionsquid spheres he targeted ceased advancing when he pointed the targeting reticle of his laser over them and squeezed the trigger. Meanwhile flashes in the distance told him that his rockets had struck their intended targets.

The incoming force had similar success, not just the Argonauts, but the allied skirmishers. Rade saw lionsquid spheres and their respective updating wireframes descending toward the seabed in droves. But there were too many of them, and they kept on coming while the enemy Hydra fired from behind their cover within the colony.

The first fire team was going to be overwhelmed by the lionsquids.

"Fire team one, reverse course!" Rade said. "Get back here! Fire team two, time to dig in. Walker mode, people. Cover them!"

The first fire team had closed to within six hundred meters of the outskirts of the colony. When they reached fire team two, the distance for the overall squad would be six hundred fifty meters from the target. That would have to be near enough for Azen. Other skirmishers were digging in not far beyond them. To continue approaching in the open like that would have been a death sentence with all the lasers tracking them. At least in the unshielded "submarine" mode.

Rade transformed back into "walker" mode and descended to the seabed. He folded his shield into place in his right arm, and kept his laser aimed at the incoming lionsquid spheres; he took down another every few seconds. He also began to fire rockets at the lionsquids to keep them at bay. He heard a thundering sound, and realized someone had used their zodiac.

He saw several of the lionsquids converge toward Tahoe's mech, which was still in submarine mode for the retrograde.

"So much for the theory that the electrolasers can actually stun them," Tahoe said. "Looks more like they *attract* them!"

Rade aimed at the lionsquid spheres and eliminated two of them before they could reach Tahoe. Harlequin, near Tahoe, swerved his mech toward two of the incoming lionsquids, firing his rockets at them before continuing the retreat.

In moments the Titans of fire team one rejoined Rade and the others and dropped to the seabed, switching to walker mode.

One of those red spheres was coming right at him. Rade swung his cobra toward it, but before he realized what was happening he was being lifted off the seabed. He couldn't move his arms—they were pinned to his side.

"Warning, cockpit pressure rising," Electron said.

Rade activated his Lighter, electrifying his hull. Nothing. His captor refused to release him.

Rade switched on his headlamps, not caring if he exposed his position. He needed to see his opponent right now.

A cone of light cut through the darkness, filled with small particles. The tentacles of a lionsquid had wrapped around him, pinning his arms to his side. They were drawing him toward a saber-toothed maw.

The rockets on Rade's shoulder were still free to rotate, but he knew they wouldn't detonate at that range, not while the proximity fuse safeties were engaged. Unless Rade disabled those safeties. Did he dare, given the current pressure his mech endured...?

"I got you, Rade," Tahoe said.

A moment later the lionsquid hurtled toward the seabed, but it didn't release him. Tahoe had struck the creature with his cobra no doubt, but it wasn't enough to kill it. The thing smashed into the seabed and dragged Electron along the surface for several meters before coming to a halt.

Then the creature stirred, apparently tightening its tentacles, because Electron said: "Warning, cockpit pressure approaching critical levels."

It drew Rade toward its maw once more. Those jaws parted in anticipation.

Rade's arms were still pinned. He couldn't swivel any of his weapons into a usable position. He tried firing his electrolaser, but all he got was a shuddering across his hull and a ringing in his ears as a reward. The lionsquid did tilt to one side, however, obviously not completely thrilled by the weapon.

Rade tried activating his jumpjets. The thrust unit was completely watertight, and was supposed to be fully functional even at depths such as these, however it had no effect on those gripping tentacles.

"Tahoe..." Rade said.

He thought once more of the rockets.

Those teeth closed around his head. Rade fingered the rocket switch...

Before the darkness swallowed his video feed, Bender and Lui leaped onto the lionsquid, firing at point blank range. They had apparently been slowly making their way forward along the ocean floor from where they had dropped out farther back. In moments they had killed the creature and torn Rade free.

"Thanks," Rade said. "Owe you both."

"We're just paying you back for all the times you've saved our asses," Lui said.

"Sorry about that," Tahoe said, arriving a moment later. "I was occupied."

A lionsquid swooped down at Tahoe's mech from behind, and Rade fired off his cobra and took it down.

"Well, I can see why you have been a target with that light of yours shining so bright." Bender walked up to a large rock that jutted from the ocean floor. It shielded Rade from view of the colony beyond. "Might want to turn it off before stepping past."

Sufficiently scolded, Rade deactivated his headlamp, plunging the scene into darkness. The white wireframe of the topography filled his view once more. He rotated his shield into place and proceeded past the rock with Tahoe, Lui and Bender to rejoin the others.

Red spheres appeared from nowhere right beside them. Rade activated his headlamp in time to witness the seabed erupting with tentacles.

All four Titans were caught by lionsquids that had lurked in ambush upon the ocean floor, hidden within the detritus. The arms of the mechs were pinned.

"Argonauts!" Rade said. "We could use some help!"

He tried his Lighter. Useless once again.

He was being dragged down into the seabed, pulled into the silt. The LIDAR faded as he was swallowed by the loose soil.

He was reminded of another time, when aliens had lain in wait within the dunes of a desert world, and then pulled his team under one by one. Killing them.

And he was filled with an abject terror.

Not for himself.

But Bender, Tahoe and Lui.

Rade remembered his rockets.

"Electron, disable the proximity fuse protections on one of my rockets," he said. He was surprised at how calm his voice sounded.

"By doing so, you risk both our lives," Electron said.

"The explosive gases will seek the path of least resistance," Rade said. "Much of the detonation will be directed upward, because of the seabed, toward the lionsquid. There is a chance we may die, yes, but a greater chance the lionsquid will suffer the majority of the damage."

"I have disabled the proximity fuse," Electron replied. "Launch when ready."

Rade fired.

twelve

His cockpit reverberated with an incredible bang. G-forces assailed him. He realized he was spinning.

And then he hit something. Hard.

An alarm sounded repeatedly.

"We have suffered multiple hull breaches," Electron said. "Liquid methane is seeping into the cockpit. Hull pressure has surpassed critical levels, and is steadily increasing as the weakened structural frame yields. The cockpit could implode at any time."

The Titan was surrounded by cloudy liquid... it slowly cleared, allowing the headlamp to penetrate the darkness. He had drifted to the ocean floor, having struck a boulder that protruded from the seabed. A lionsquid lay beside him, its insides open, dark blood expanding outward. Small, opportunistic sharklike creatures were tearing away at its flesh.

The alarm continued to sound.

He glanced at the hull pressure indicator. It was rising into the red. He was screwed.

"Liquid methane has nearly suffused the cockpit," Electron said. "The electroactuators are still insulated, however, and will continue to function. At least until the cockpit collapses entirely."

Rade turned toward the other three lionsquids, whose heads he could see protruding from the seabed nearby. If he was going to die, he planned to save his men first.

He fired his cobra three times in turn, taking out the lionsquids that were attempting to grind Tahoe, Bender and Lui into the seabed. The three Titans tore free.

Two new mechs appeared from behind a nearby coralline structure. His HUD labeled them Harlequin and Shaw.

"Rade, what the hell are you doing?" Shaw said.

"I took a bit of damage," he told her.

"We have to get you to the surface!" Shaw said.

"All right," he responded.

"And turn off your headlamp!" Shaw said.

He did so.

Shaw and Harlequin grabbed his mech by either arm and transformed into submarines to carry him away from the battle. They were staying close to the ocean floor, at least at first. Rade didn't dare transform his own mech, not while the structural integrity was so low.

"Are you hurt?" Shaw asked.

Rade realized he wasn't actually sure, so he checked his own vitals as displayed on the HUD. They were green.

"Don't think so," he told her.

On the overhead map, he watched the blue dots of Tahoe, Bender and the others recede behind him. Rade regretted leaving, but there wasn't much more he could do at the moment. Not when his cockpit was close to collapse.

"Tahoe, you're in charge until I get back," Rade instructed.

"Where are you going?" Tahoe asked.

"I'm making a quick surface run to repair a hull breach," Rade replied.

When they were a kilometer and a half away from the battle, Harlequin and Shaw changed course and began climbing. They all activated the inflatable balloon attachments Surus had installed, allowing them to make their return to the surface with far less power.

The pressure warning indicator changed from red to orange to yellow as Rade ascended, indicating his reduced chances of suffering a sudden cockpit implosion.

"What were you thinking back there?" Shaw transmitted on a private line. "We had almost reached you. We could have saved Tahoe and the others without you having to compromise the hull integrity of your mech. Didn't you look at your map?"

Rade shook his head. "I messed up."

"You did," Shaw said. "Big time. And I can't tell you how pissed I am right now. That you'd risk your life so unnecessarily like that..."

Rade felt a well of indignation inside him. How dare she chew him out like that. *She*, of all people. After everything he had done for her.

But he realized she was right.

They continued the ascent in silence.

He remembered what Shaw had told him near the beginning of the mission. *You've built up a house of cards, and if you don't watch yourself, it's all going to come tumbling down.*

"It's almost hard to believe I was once a member of an elite military force," Rade said over the private line. "All that training. All that discipline. And I can't even fight a battle anymore. You can see why I left the military. I'm not cut out for this business anymore."

Shaw didn't answer right away.

"Maybe I was a bit too hard on you," she said finally. "Listen to me, you *are* cut out for this. We all make mistakes sometimes, elite or not. But next time wait for us to come to you instead of taking matters into your own hands at all costs, okay?"

Rade was about to agree, but something deep inside of him refused to. When he finally realized what that something was, he spoke. "If I see a situation where my men are in trouble, and there's a chance I can save them, even at great risk to myself, I'm going to take it. I'm sorry. That's all there is too it."

Shaw gave no rebuttal.

But as they neared the surface, she said: "Now you know why I want to have kids so badly. So that you think twice before risking everything for your men. So you have something else to live for. I had hoped having me would be enough, but it's not. I realize that now."

"I'm not sure kids would make a difference," Rade said. "These men are my brothers. If you knew everything we've been through, and I mean *everything*, since bootcamp, through MOTH training and all the missions afterwards... if you knew, you would understand."

"Ah, my warrior," Shaw said. "My dearest warrior, what am I going to do with you?"

When they surfaced, they left the balloon attachments inflated to keep the mechs afloat; the Titans lay prostrate, side-by-side, bobbing on the surface, their metal hands interlinked. Rade opened the battered cockpit hatch with some difficulty and emerged into the orange hued atmosphere in his jumpsuit. The sun was a red giant the size of his fist in the sky. Meteorites composed of falling ships and debris streaked across the sky. Rade had no way of knowing which side those ships belonged to, Bethesda or the empress.

Underneath him, his cockpit was completely full of liquid methane.

"Well, that's no good," Rade said.

As damaged ships continued to streak past overhead, sometimes issuing sonic booms, Shaw and Harlequin helped Rade patch his hull. They used the laser welding kits and extra armor plates they had in their storage compartments.

Rade remained in communication with the Argonauts far below, though the connection was sketchy. He glanced at the team's vital indicators now and again to confirm everyone was all right. After the first hour, apparently all of the lionsquids had been eliminated. That left only the enemy skirmishers dug in within the colony itself.

It took Rade, Shaw and Harlequin five hours to return his mech to an adequate level of hull integrity. By then the number of ships streaking through the sky had diminished to only one or two per hour.

After Electron's armor was repaired, Rade and the others packed away their equipment into the storage compartments. Shaw hadn't loaded into her Titan, like Harlequin had; instead she lingered at the edge of his mech, staring into the yellow ocean beside him.

"What's wrong?"

"Nothing," Shaw said. "It just looks so deceptively calm from up here."

Rade gazed at the gentle waves. "You could almost forget why we're here."

"I'm certainly not looking forward to going back down there." Shaw sighed, then leaped onto her prostrate mech and slid into the cockpit. "Might as well get it over with."

They began the descent into the dark depths once more. They spent forty minutes returning to the Argonauts below, first landing a kilometer and a half out, then making their way forward stealthily, using the LIDAR bursts for vision.

The battle hadn't changed much by then. The main colony was still under siege. The floating bodies of dead lionsquids littered the seabed; small alien sharks feasted on their flesh, tearing away large chunks that dispatched fresh clouds of blood.

The Argonauts had closed to three hundred meters of the colony outskirts. They were divided into two teams, spread out in a line behind a pair of small reefs separated by twenty meters.

"Boss, make sure you completely deactivate your forward LIDAR," Tahoe sent as Rade grew near. "No bursts. The enemy doesn't know where we are, and we'd like to keep it that way."

"Got it," Rade said. "Harlequin, Shaw?"

"Done," the two replied in unison.

"So we're relying exclusively on our Hydra allies for targeting information?" Rade asked over the general comm.

"We are," Azen replied.

He could still see the outlines of the Titans—and other nearby allied skirmishers—thanks to the "friendlies" overlay mode Rade had kept active on his HUD. Rade noted that save for himself, Harlequin and Shaw, no one had any rockets left. He glanced at the team vitals once more to confirm everyone was okay.

As he neared, Rade transformed into walker mode and low-crawled along the seabed to the first team; he joined Swift near the edge of the reef Surus' Titan used for cover. He peered past into the darkness, at the wireframe outlines overlaid onto the murk from previous LIDAR scans. He saw a few red spheres denoting where enemy targets were hidden behind the different coralline structures.

He pulled back and glanced at the glass enclosure on Swift's back. He saw Azen within once again thanks to the "friendlies" overlay feature.

"The enemy skirmishers are dug in extremely well," Azen said. "Even so, in any battle, there's only so much one can do to defend from a siege position. The allied Hydras have moved to flanking positions. We're slowly closing the noose. Meanwhile in orbit, Bethesda's armada has achieved dominance, routing the agents of the empress to the far side of the planet. We may be receiving more skirmishers shortly. The commander tells me the warships can safely launch their troop shuttles now."

"Didn't know we were waiting for them to do that." Rade edged his cobra past his cover and scanned the enemy positions through the scope, waiting for a target to expose itself. None were obliging. He could use up the last of his rockets and target some of those spheres hidden behind the different coralline trees and minarets, but he decided it was better to save the Hellfires until he really needed them. Besides, many of those indicators were likely inaccurate, especially if the tangos had repositioned since taking cover.

The occasional moan or clacking drifted through the liquid methane. Because of the paucity of sounds, Rade assumed that most of the enemy communications were done over a private communication band, like those of the allies.

"This is like our very first deployment in Mongolia, huh boss?" Tahoe said. "You spend hours staring through your scope into the city, waiting for a tango to do something stupid and expose himself, while I watch your back."

Tahoe was indeed guarding Rade's back; he had taken up a position on drag in the first fire team to cover the rear. Lui meanwhile watched the left flank. Manic, in the second fire team, guarded the right. Though all forward LIDAR was currently inactive, the three of them would continue sending out LIDAR bursts away from the colony, Rade knew.

"You know, if this were a sci-fi movie or VR experience," TJ said. "The bugs would be popping up their heads for us to shoot, or they'd rush us, placing themselves in our line of fire so we could mow them down. Either that, or we'd be the impatient ones, and we'd be rushing the enemy positions and killing the bugs one by one, execution style, and saving the day."

"Yeah, but this isn't a movie," Manic said. "We rush out there, we're dead men."

"Oh I know," TJ said. "I'm just saying, never trust anything you see in movies."

"Ha!" Tahoe said. "If I trusted everything I saw in movies, I'd be dead a long time ago. My favorite is those action movies, you know, where they punch someone in the head and then the recipient is out cold. Permanently! Uh, last I checked, you get hit in the head, unless you've suffered a major concussion, you're waking up a maximum of ten seconds later."

"I can agree with that," Bender said. "I've got a bit of practice in that department, after all. From all the times I've knocked Manic unconscious."

"You've never knocked me unconscious," Manic said.

"Need I remind you of that sparring match we had a few weeks ago?" Bender said. "The one where I broke your arm? When I smashed your noggin I sent you to la-la land."

"Yeah, for like three seconds," Manic said.

"See?" Tahoe said. "My point exactly. Movies like to do the knock-out thing to the extreme. Want to show how nice the hero is by not killing anyone? Let's have him conveniently knock everyone out with a few well-placed punches. Time to cut to a new scene? Let's have the hero get hit in the head. Oh, and now he wakes up half an hour later in a completely new scene. But if he was out that long, how come he's not suffering head trauma? I can only laugh when I see that done. They think we viewers are so clueless."

"Hey, it's all about the enjoyment of the experience," Fret said. "If you're noticing stuff like that, then there's something wrong."

"I sometimes notice hairstyles changing between cuts in the same scene," Harlequin said.

"See, then there's something wrong," Fret said. "If you were engaged in the story, you wouldn't notice, or even care."

"I think in this case there's something wrong with the viewer," Bender said. "As in, Harlequin's a freakin' AI!"

"It is one of my curses," Harlequin said. "To be distracted by the strange grooming habits of humans. So much time, effort, and money expended in the pursuit of the perfect coiffure, something that is quite impossible to achieve, given the chaotic nature of hair."

"And here I thought I was the only one distracted by their grooming habits," Surus said. "You and I simply have to think a command, and instantly our tresses assume one of many preset styles, thanks to the tensile structures attached to the microfibers. Whereas humans, they have to spend hours and hours."

"Longest I've ever spent on my hair was two seconds to throw in some gel," Tahoe said.

"I never comb my hair," Fret said.

"Don't have any," Bender replied.

"Man, the things we talk about on mission..." Lui said.

Rade had kept the video feed from his cobra scope piped to his vision; he continually scanned the white wireframes representing the structures. Occasionally one of the tangos moved into his sights, as indicated by the appearance of a red sphere; sometimes he was able to position the crosshairs over the target in time, other times it descended into cover before he could take the shot.

"Boss, I'm detecting incoming on our six," Tahoe said.

thirteen

Rade glanced at the overhead map and saw the red dots appearing behind them. A whole lot of red dots.

"Those would be the reinforcements," Azen said.

The objects turned from red to blue on the overhead map.

Rade exhaled in relief.

The skirmishers passed them, staying close to the seabed, and took up defensive positions nearby. Some went on to skirt the colony, heading toward the far side to continue outflanking the enemy.

"I don't suppose our Hydra allies can drop the equivalent of a bunker buster from orbit, can they?" Fret asked.

"They won't risk killing Bethesda," Azen said.

"Oh yeah," Fret said. "Forgot about her."

"You *forgot* the whole reason we're out here?" Bender said.

"Yeah," Fret said, sounding sheepish.

"Me too," Bender said. Rade could almost imagine him flashing that gold grille of his.

Another two hours passed without much action, at least on the part of the Argonauts. Rade terminated three more tangos, but the remainder refused to reveal themselves.

Their Hydra allies made a few tentative incursions, but always the firmly dug-in defenders repelled them, usually at a high casualty cost to the allies.

"Boss," Tahoe said. "I got something on the rear LIDAR again."

"More incoming?" Rade glanced at his overhead map. Three red dots had appeared about a kilometer behind the party.

"No, these are outgoing," Tahoe said.

"There must be a secret channel here," Shaw said. "Maybe hidden by holographic emitters. Or maybe an underground tunnel. Either way, they snuck right past us."

"I've alerted our allies," Azen said.

Just then Rade felt a rumbling.

"What the hell is that?" Lui asked.

"An earthquake?" TJ said.

"I don't think so," Rade said. "Electron, link up with the other Titan AIs and see if you can triangulate a source for the seismic activity."

The reverberations continued. A moment later: "It appears to be coming from the city."

"I figured as much," Rade said. "Azen, what do our allies have to say?"

"They're telling me to wait a moment," Azen said. "I'm hearing a lot of confused chatter on the line."

"We need to a get a live feed on what's happening out there," Rade said. "I'm going to reposition so I can activate forward LIDAR without drawing attention to the rest of you. Cover me."

Rade jetted from his hiding place, momentarily transforming into a submarine as he made his way toward a nearby arch covered in coral platelets. He sent out a burst of forward LIDAR before switching back to walker mode and assuming a position behind the arch.

The resultant wireframe image showed him that a large, iceberg-shaped structure had broken free of the colony and had drifted twenty meters above the seabed.

"Nice," TJ said. The image would have been transmitted to all of the Titans courtesy of the comm nodes in the mechs.

Rade leaned past the arch and launched another burst. The large structure had moved another twenty meters higher. It was obviously surfacing.

The Hydra allies with them were leaving cover in droves to converge on that structure. Meanwhile the tangos still residing in the colony below were shooting them down.

"Uh," Lui said.

"Who wants to bet that's a diversion?" Tahoe said. "To draw our attention away from the group making a tactical retrograde behind us?"

Rade glanced at his overhead map. The three tangos in the distance behind them continued to move away. Only five of the allied skirmishers had broken away to pursue.

"Azen, tell them to send more skirmishers after them," Rade said.

"They're not listening to me," Azen said.

"Damn it," Rade said. "If we want something done right, we always have to do it ourselves. Argonauts, turn around and transform. We pursue. Stay close to the seabed. Make random left and right movements between LIDAR bursts... don't let them target you."

Rade switched back to submarine mode and piloted Electron into the repressive murk.

The Argonauts followed his lead and proceeded

after the retreating targets, trailing the five skirmishers that led the pursuit.

One of those skirmishers simply halted in place and slowly drifted downward.

"Looks like they're taking fire," Lui said.

Rade continued to send out LIDAR bursts. Electron was automatically adjusting the turbine power levels to swerve left and right between bursts, preventing the enemy from hitting him—assuming they targeted his last known position as revealed by the LIDAR. And if the enemy also used echolocation for tracking, the positional information of the Titans would be well out of date before arriving back to the pursuers. Still, that didn't mean a lucky shot wouldn't take one of them out.

Rade zoomed in on the target. The Hydra allies provided three red spheres to aid in tracking, but Rade ignored those, and focused on the last LIDAR impressions the targets had made. Two of the tangos were about the same size as skirmishers, but the center object was about twice the size, like a small transport shuttle or something. It was the same ovule shape as the others, but in front, instead of three prongs, it had a more hydrodynamic nose, which tapered into a point. At least that was the impression Rade had from the current viewing angle, which was slightly to the left and underneath the tangos.

"Azen, tell our four remaining friends to target the two skirmishers on either side of the larger tango," Rade said. "The rest of you, if you get a shot on those flanking skirmishers, take it."

"You think Bethesda is in the center craft?" Shaw asked.

"That's my hunch," Rade said. "And even if she's not, it has to be someone important they're smuggling out."

Rade glanced at the rear LIDAR view. Far behind them, the breakaway piece of the colony continued ascending toward the surface, drawing the attention of most of the skirmishers.

They really should have sent more this way.

Rade focused on the forward section once more. Another Hydra pursuer dropped out.

A moment later both of the fleeing escorts halted, letting the center craft travel forward on its own.

"Looks like we got the escorts," Tahoe said.

"That was me," Bender said. "I got the one on the left."

"And the Hydra got the one on the right, apparently," Azen said. "They've asked us not to fire on the remaining craft."

"I'm undecided on that for the moment," Rade said. "Lui, is the remaining craft firing at us?"

"It seems to be firing intermittently, yes," Lui said. "So far, it's been targeting the pursuing Hydra craft."

Another of those craft dropped out. That left two, plus the Titans.

"The target is increasing speed," Lui said.

"Electron, can we match?" Rade asked.

"We can match, and surpass," Electron replied.

"I want maximum speed, Argonauts," Rade said. "And let's see if we can target the source of those lasers. I've been studying the wireframe representation of that craft. It appears there are a few cylindrical shapes protruding from the rear quarter. I'm willing to bet those are the turrets."

"Yes," Tahoe said. "But we'll never hit them if we stick to LIDAR burst mode. Not with the way the craft is zig-zagging back and forth like us."

"One of us is going to have to engage active

LIDAR, and risk giving away his or her position to track those turrets," Rade said. "Who wants to do the honors?"

"I'll do it," Bender said.

The positional wireframe of the zig-zagging craft began updating constantly; Rade knew Bender was tracking it with active LIDAR in that moment, his comm nodes transmitting the positional information to the rest of them.

"I got direct hits on the turrets," Bender said.

The wireframe froze as Bender went back into burst mode.

"It's stopped firing," Lui said.

"The two Hydra with us have given me a warning," Azen said. "If we fire on the craft again, they will take us down."

"Warning noted," Rade said.

"Yeah," Bender said, his voice becoming ironic. "Like we're *real* scared. Big bad Hydras are going to rough us up. We'll see about that."

The Titans continued their approach, passing the Hydra vessels, which weren't as hydrodynamic, what with the three prongs protruding from their front areas.

"You'd think, given that these aliens operate so much in liquid methane, that they would have fine-tuned their craft to operate better here," Lui said.

"They *do* have dedicated submersibles," Azen said. "But apparently their inventories were running low on such units, forcing them to use the multipurpose, space-capable skirmishers. Most of their battles are fought in the void, you see."

"Whatever," TJ said. "I'll take whatever advantage I can get."

The Argonauts were slowly closing with the fleeing

craft. Despite its more suitable hydrodynamic profile, the craft's larger size prevented it from outdistancing them.

Harlequin was near the front, and he broke ahead of the pack. "I got her!"

He had stopped zig-zagging, Rade noticed.

"Careful," Rade said. "Keep zig-zagging, Harlequin."

"Sorry," Harlequin replied. His Titan began to swerve back and forth, but only by a few meters at a time. He was definitely eager to catch the craft.

Rade tapped in Harlequin directly. "You don't have anything to prove to us."

"But I do," Harlequin replied.

"You've proven yourself ten times over already," Rade said.

"Not like this," Harlequin said. "Now's my chance to really shine. You sought out my files when you left the military. You brought me back to the living. And yet still, essentially, I'm a clone... my neural engrams transferred over from a backup file of my original. I have to prove that I'm as brave as the old Harlequin. If not to you, then to myself. Please, boss. Let me do this."

Rade hesitated. "Fine. But be careful. I want you to zig-zag more than you're doing. We don't know if we've taken out all their weapons yet."

"Okay," Harlequin said. And he began to zig-zag a little more as he continued to pull ahead.

"We better close soon," Lui said. "According to the LIDAR data we took from above, we're nearing the edge of the continental shelf. We plunge over that, the pressure is going to start rising. Big time."

Rade glanced at the overhead map. Lui was right. The shelf ended about fifty meters ahead of the fleeing craft. Below awaited an unmapped, fathomless pit.

Harlequin reached the craft and latched on.

"Got it!" Harlequin said. "It looks like we've taken out all its armaments. At least the forward facing ones. There's some kind of hatch here. I'm going to pry it open."

Because of Harlequin's "friendly" status, Rade watched in realtime as Harlequin's Titan plunged from view.

"The craft just dove over the edge of the continental shelf," Lui said.

"Do we pursue?" Tahoe asked.

"For now," Rade said. "Keep an eye on pressure levels."

He reached the edge of that shelve and steered his Titan downward. There was only darkness below. All he had anchoring him to his whereabouts was the sheer cliff face of the rock underneath him, that and Harlequin up ahead.

Behind them the two skirmishes pursued.

"Pressure is rising extremely fast," Electron said. "We cannot continue."

Rade glanced at his pressure bar. It was in the red.

"Okay everyone, slow down," Rade said. "Harlequin, you're going to have to come back."

"I've almost got it," Harlequin said.

"Pressure levels are approaching critical," Electron said.

"Full stop, people," Rade said. "We turn back. Harlequin, that includes you."

Rade began decelerating. A moment later the two Hydra skirmishers rushed past, apparently better able to withstand the high pressures.

Rade started the slow ascent back up the cliff face. His turbines whirred with effort. He glanced at his overhead map and saw that the other Titans were all doing the same. They knew when it was time to throw in the sack.

Everyone except Harlequin, that is.

"Harlequin," Rade said. "Harlequin. I said get back here."

Harlequin didn't reply.

"Harlequin?" Rade pressed.

"He's not answering," Lui said.

"I see that," Rade responded. "Damn it." He halted his acceleration and maintained his current depth. Pressure levels were still in the red.

"Electron, how long can we hold this position?" Rade asked.

"Not long," Electron replied. "We could start seeing signs of implosion any moment. Especially considering the recent patches you made to the hull, which have made the frame even weaker than usual. I would recommend returning at least to the top of the shelf."

Rade sighed. "I can't abandon him."

"You must," Electron said.

"Harlequin, come in," Rade said. "Harlequin."

Rade zoomed in on the dot Harlequin had become. According to the HUD, his Titan was roughly six hundred meters below them.

"My hull is starting to give," Shaw said. "Sorry boys, I have to retreat."

One by one the Argonauts returned to the shelf. Rade remained as long as he could, but then he too returned. Bender was the last of them.

"Bender, get up here." Rade said.

"Can't do it," Bender said.

Rade glanced at Bender's pressure levels. They were critical.

"Bender, you can't help him if you die down here," Rade said.

Bender exhaled loudly over the comm. "I'm coming, boss."

Bender topped the shelf and rejoined the squad; everyone waited near the edge, peering over worriedly.

Below, the dots representing the friendlies, and the target craft, began to ascend. Apparently the two skirmishers had wrapped their segmented tentacles around the unit and were hoisting it upward.

But as they got closer, Rade realized that the bigger craft had been abandoned. Instead, the two skirmishers were escorting another, smaller object. It had a similar shape as the skirmishers, except the tentacles at its rear were smoother, implying that it was an organic form of life. The skirmishers weren't aiding the motion of the creature in any way: its tentacles whipped, flagella-like, while the central, bell-shaped body pumped, propelling its ascent.

As it came closer, Rade's LIDAR filled out the frontal section. Instead of three prongs, there were several thick, gripping appendages covered in suckers, ending in a maw of sorts at the base. Within those appendages, Harlequin's Titan was cradled.

Rade heard a strange clicking sound, followed by a whiny moan.

A louder series of clicks and sirens answered, these seeming to come from closer at hand. Rade realized the sounds were sourced from Swift's external speakers.

"Bethesda remembers me," Azen said a moment later. "And she thanks us for our help in her rescue. She says she will never forget the brave sacrifice of the metal one, who gave his life for hers."

"Harlequin no," Bender said. He steered his Titan

over the edge to intercept.

fourteen

Rade and the Argonauts retrieved the booster rockets from the eastern side of the continental shelf and used them to bring Harlequin's broken body back into orbit. The *Yarak* had survived the battle intact, and the team was able to dock without issues.

Harlequin's Titan had suffered severe damage. As had Harlequin himself: the cockpit had imploded, crushing him. His jumpsuit had experienced multiple puncture wounds, and hull fragments had penetrated through his normally waterproof skin, causing liquid damage to his internal systems and shorting out much of his circuitry. It was essentially equivalent to shrapnel damage taken underwater.

After boarding the *Yarak*, Azen had Harlequin and his mech delivered to a team of Greens aboard who specialized in human robotic technology. They worked on salvaging what they could of Harlequin's AI core, as well as that of the Titan, using the scant Earth technology they had available on the Phant ship. Bender and TJ volunteered to assist.

Azen checked in with the Argonauts in the berthing area a few hours later.

"What's the prognosis?" Rade asked.

"Bender and TJ are working hard to revive Harlequin with my team of Greens," Azen said. "They're optimistic that most of his core data will be recoverable. There is a chance, however, that the Artificial will emerge from this with a completely different personality, and perhaps a loss of memory. The same applies to the Titan."

"What kind of time frame are we looking at for his recovery?" Rade asked.

"The repairs to his body are relatively easy, and those will take maybe a half day or so," Azen said. "But at this early stage, it looks like it will take at least a week to regenerate the methane-damaged circuits involved in his neural network. We'll have to melt down some of the existing components and feed them to our 3D printer to create fresh parts. Then we'll have to run a check on the engramic data to ensure none of it is corrupt. In all, a very time consuming affair. Bender and TJ are creating custom programs to aid in the error-checking, with the hope of speeding up the process. I'll keep you updated daily. As will Bender and TJ, I'm sure."

"What about his Titan?" Rade pressed. "The time frame?"

"Its AI core is even more severely damaged than Harlequin's," Azen said. "There is a higher chance of personality change and memory loss."

"That's too bad," Lui said.

"But the repair timetable should be similar," Azen continued. "And I hope it will be finished in about a week."

"What about the damage to our own mechs?" Tahoe said.

"Since the AI cores are intact, I should be able to affect repairs within a much shorter period of time,"

Azen said. "A day. Maybe two."

"Why so long?" Manic said. "After our first battle defending your homeworld, you had our mechs fixed up in no time at all. Hours, not days. What's going on? You guys are slacking."

"We don't have all the resources of a complete sub-hive at our disposal, unfortunately," Azen said. "All we have is one small ship."

"Okay, so forget the repairs for a moment," Rade said. "What's the story with Bethesda? Will she help you against the empress? Or was all of this for nothing?"

"Unfortunately," Azen said. "She refused to grant me an audience or answer my communiqués until we have returned to her home colony. 'Deep space is not the place for negotiations.' Her words. I've told her that time is of the essence, but still she refused, telling me instead that she's already set a course back toward the exit wormhole. She's making a speedy return, I concede."

"It'll take two weeks to reach her colony," Rade said.

"It will," Azen replied. "But I admit we would have had to take that route anyway to return to the Green homeworld."

"And once we reach Bethesda's world, how far to the Green homeworld thereafter?" Rade asked. "Three weeks, like the distance to your backup base?"

"No," Azen said. "By choosing different Slipstreams, some within Bethesda's domain, we should get there in two and a half weeks."

"So by the time we return, potentially almost ten weeks will have passed since we left the Green homeworld," Rade said.

"I know," Azen replied grimly.

"Will the Greens be able to hold out until then?" Rade asked.

"I've made frequent trips back to the supra-dimension my race uses for communication," Azen said. "We will last. But the casualties will be great. Already we've lost two sub-hives and the populations they contained. We'll probably continue to lose at least one every few days. That's almost three million Greens per sub-hive, sucked into the immense gravity of the gas giant, irretrievably lost."

When Azen departed, Rade and the others ate the provided food in relative silence; when Rade finished his meal, he moved off to the curtained-off portion of the berthing area he shared with Shaw. He sat down on the imitation tiles, near one of the floor "skylights" or light planes. By then the illumination from the object had dimmed to night levels, and points of light had appeared within it, meant to mimic stars. He removed the helmet from where he had attached it to his harness and set it down beside the false portal. Then he lay on one side and stared at the fake stars.

Tahoe and Shaw joined him. Shaw gave Rade a quick peck on the cheek before she sat cross-legged beside him. Tahoe perched on the opposite side of the light plane.

"Hey," Shaw said. She activated the noise canceler in her helmet to give the three of them some privacy, and then set it down on the vinyl laminate beside her. If they had been aboard the *Argonaut*, they could have used their Implants to create a cone of silence via the cancelers embedded in the overheads and bulkheads of the ship, but out here they had to rely on their helmets.

"So it's done," Tahoe said. "We completed our mission."

"Have we?" Rade said. "I have a feeling Azen has

more work in store for us."

"What more is there for us to do?" Tahoe said. "We've retrieved Bethesda. All we can do now is hope she'll bring the fight to the empress and drive her off."

"Bethesda will want to do more than drive her off, I'm sure," Shaw said. "You remember our earlier talk with Azen, don't you? Where he hinted that Bethesda might attempt to depose the empress? That's what I would do if I attacked the all powerful ruler of my species. Otherwise, what's the point? Just to make her angry so she'd come looking for you someday?"

"I remember," Tahoe asked. "Though I guess I hoped we wouldn't have to be involved in that."

The three of them gazed at the false stars in silence.

"I hope Harlequin is all right," Shaw said.

Rade sighed. "He was my responsibility. And I let him go."

"It's not your fault," Tahoe said.

"He told me he wanted to prove himself," Rade said.

"Really?" Tahoe asked.

"Yeah," Rade replied.

"But he's done so many times since joining the Argonauts," Tahoe said.

"I know," Rade told him. "But he insists it's not enough. That he has to prove to himself he has the same courage as his predecessor." Rade shook his head. "I wonder if it was a mistake to reactivate him. Transferring over his memory core from the backups like that, without his express consent. I probably shouldn't have done it. He just doesn't feel like he's the same Harlequin. And he's not, I suppose. That's why I couldn't change his name to the callsign I gave him fifteen years ago, before he sacrificed himself for me: Heart. And I figured, that moment wasn't in the backups anyway, so Harlequin would be none the wiser." Rade paused. "I never told him how he died for me. He never asked."

"Maybe he will ask, someday," Tahoe said.

"I doubt it," Rade said. "I don't think he wants to know. It would only make him feel even more unworthy in his own eyes. All I can say is, he has existential issues."

"Maybe when he comes back we should give him a new name?" Shaw said. "If you think it will help?"

"No," Rade said. "A new name won't magically solve all his problems. I guess... I guess all we can really do is be there for him. Just as you and Tahoe, and all the Argonauts, have always been there for me."

Shaw reached across the light plane and squeezed his gloved hand.

"I'm not going to hold your hand," Tahoe said guardedly.

Rade laughed. "You don't have to, my brother."

"Good," Tahoe said. "Because I'm going to hug you." He extended his two arms and leaned forward, forcing Rade to rise to his knees; Tahoe hugged him in his big arms.

Rade patted him on the back of his jumpsuit, then released him to recline once more.

Tahoe and Shaw continued to talk, but Rade had stopped listening. He felt a sudden urge to cave out. He couldn't explain it. Thinking about how Harlequin had died must have triggered it.

"I'm going to sleep now." Rade put on his helmet and muted them. Then he lay down and closed his eyes, shutting out the world.

fifteen

The days passed slowly. The *Yarak* proceeded toward the nearest wormhole with the Hydra armada, heading back toward Bethesda's domain. The Argonauts were well-fed, and Rade had Tahoe lead them through calisthenics three times a day right there on the floor of the berthing area. Rade participated as well, glad to shift the burden of command onto someone else, if only momentarily, and for something rather inconsequential like PT.

Between those workout sessions, the team made ample use of their Implants for virtual reality purposes. Manic had downloaded and cached several new VR experiences before leaving behind human space all those weeks ago, and he doled them out to the group.

"Some of us spent time sending going away messages to our families," Fret said. "Instead, Manic, you used your last moments to download VR crap."

"Hey, it's not crap," Manic said. "And I sent my family messages. They were a bit short, I admit, but I sent them."

"Don't you have a little kid now or something?" Lui said. "From that stripper chick?"

"No," Manic said. "Well I mean, er... she says it's mine."

"Deadbeat dad," Tahoe muttered.

"I never claimed to be a model citizen," Manic said. "Besides, I send her money."

"So you admit it's yours, then?" Lui asked.

"Nope," Manic said. "I just send her the money because I'm generous like that. There wasn't a court order or anything."

"You're so full of it," Lui said. "I can see the bullshit pouring out of your ears."

"That's his brain," Bender said. He was taking a break from working on Harlequin. Lately he had started to alternate with TJ, and it was the latter's turn to help the Greens with the repair process that day.

"Yeah, my brain is so big it can't fit in my head," Manic said.

"No, it's oozing out like sludge because you never use it," Bender retorted. "Let this be a lesson to you all, boys and girls. This is what happens when you let your mind go."

"You must be talking from experience," Manic said. "Because yours oozed out years ago."

"Yeah?" Bender said. "How about I ooze my fist into your head and help you pound those brains back in there?"

"Go ahead and try," Manic said, standing up.

"I think I will," Bender replied.

"Easy, you two," Rade said. "Fight it out in a VR session if you have to. I don't want you knocking down all the curtains in here like last time. And need I remind you, you're salaries are already down four hundred each for the month. Don't make me dock you more."

"It's worth it," Bender said. But he lowered his fists, and flashed his golden grille at Manic. "We'll resume this conversation at a later date."

"Oh we will," Manic said.

In the succeeding days, Rade managed to scare up a bar of soap that Fret was hiding from everyone else; with the soap, and using his own helmet as a bucket, Rade finally succeeded in scouring himself clean. When finished, he dumped the cloudy water into the incinerator and air dried. Shaw borrowed the soap and their cleansing routine became a daily ritual, so that soon he and Shaw were having sex at least once a day again. They were careful to use the bar of soap sparingly, only in their most-needed regions, to make it last. That bar was more valuable than gold to them, at the moment.

Rade and Shaw had forgotten to activate a noise canceler during one particularly loud lovemaking session, a fact Manic alerted them to with an angry shout. Rade fumbled for his helmet and engaged the canceler, and then flopped back down atop Shaw, where he remained motionless, frozen with embarrassment. She broke the tension with that sweet laugh of hers, and soon they were both chortling uncontrollably. As the laughter subsided, the thrusting began anew.

A week into the return journey Bender returned from his repair work in the middle of the day.

Harlequin was with him.

The team members hugged the Artificial in turn.

"Well this is entirely unexpected," Harlequin said. "I feel so... loved."

"Ha!" Bender said. "You damn robot, that's not love they're showing you. It's gratitude. They're just happy your ass is still around to take the next round of incoming fire that comes our way. You're our shrapnel catcher, boy."

Harlequin seemed genuinely puzzled as he

addressed Bender. "You spent all this time repairing me with TJ and the Greens? Why? If I'm just another robot, it would have been easier to leave me deactivated, and then replace me with another unit, like a Centurion."

"It's his way of showing affection, Harlequin," Rade said.

"Affection, my ass," Bender said, moving toward his curtained off area. "I repaired my shrapnel catcher, and that's all there is to it. Now it's been a long week, and I'm going to crash if you bitches don't mind. So piss off."

"You calling the boss a bitch?" Fret said.

"No, just you," Bender said, ducking behind his curtain.

"How are you feeling?" Shaw asked Harlequin.

"The same as usual," Harlequin said. "All processes are running within expected operational parameters. Though I have no recollection of our last mission. I hope you did not have to restore my neural network from a backup."

"No," Rade said. "You're still you. Not a clone."

Harlequin slumped in relief, then instantly stood straight once more. "That is good."

"Yes it is," Rade said.

"You're terrified of that, aren't you, Harley?" Lui said. "Being cloned again."

"Wouldn't you be?" Harlequin said. "Dying, and then waking up as a clone? Actually, you wouldn't wake up at all. Only your clone would. Yes, I don't relish the thought."

They talked for a little while longer, mostly explaining what happened during the mission, and what Harlequin had done to get so much damage inflicted on himself, and then Surus took him to her curtained off area for "further discussion."

"What do you think they're talking about in there?" Lui asked.

"Dunno," Fret said. "Maybe they're having sex."

Manic pressed his lips together contemplatively. "It would suit them, I guess. Like attracts like, after all."

"Maybe Surus, in Phant form, transfers back and forth between them while they're doing it," TJ said. "That way she can experience the sex from both genders at the same time."

"You never know," Manic said. "At this point, it wouldn't surprise me. Those Phants are twisted beings when it comes to satisfying their carnal urges. That's what happens when you have no gender, I suppose. Because when someday you actually find yourself in a body that *has* a gender, you want to explore all facets of it. Or something."

"Yeah whatever man," Bender said, sticking his head out past his curtain. "You would know. You, the guy who uses female avatars for himself when engaging in immersive VR porn."

"I do not," Manic said. "Okay, maybe sometimes. But only to play with my pussy."

"I knew you had a pussy," Bender said, shutting the curtain.

Rade returned to the designated area he shared with Shaw, leaving the curtain open so he could watch for Harlequin when he emerged from his discussion with Surus.

Ten minutes later the Artificial came out and Rade beckoned Harlequin to join him. On cue, Shaw got up and went to grab a drink from the barrel in the airlock.

Rade activated the noise canceler in his helmet and extended it around himself and Harlequin, then set the helmet down.

"When Shaw asked how you were feeling earlier," Rade said. "She wasn't talking about your processes running within operational parameters. She was asking about you. How do *you* feel?"

"I'm not sure I understand the question," Harlequin said. "I feel fine."

"Okay," Rade said. "You're going with the canned response all AIs give when a human poses such a question. Let me rephrase it this way: when are you going to feel worthy of filling your predecessors shoes?"

"Ah," Harlequin said. He was quiet for a moment. "I don't think I'll ever feel worthy. It is unfortunately a notion engraved deep within my AI core. Despite my doubts, I am thankful that you brought me back, however. Better to be alive than merely a lifeless collection of bits in a memory core."

"I had to," Rade said. "I owed you that much, for what you did for me."

"I heard you almost got arrested for doing that," Harlequin said. "Bringing me back, I mean."

"Almost?" Rade said. "Yes, I was a red cunt hair away from jail. Stealing backup files of military combat robots or Artificials is a crime punishable by eight years in prison, at minimum."

"How did you avoid the sentence?"

"I had some help from two very good friends," Rade said. "You know them, in fact. TJ and Bender."

"Ah, the selfless hackers," Harlequin said. "Who pretend to have low intelligence quotients. Well, TJ, not so much. But Bender..."

"Forget about trying to prove yourself." Rade rested a hand on Harlequin's shoulder. "You're an Argonaut, now, my brother. If you were not worthy, you would not be here, trust me when I say this. Embrace who you are. Live with yourself. You are your own man. You don't have to live up to anything your predecessor has done. Give yourself permission to live."

Harlequin nodded slowly. "I will do my best, boss."

Rade grinned. "That's all I ask of you."

sixteen

The two weeks came to pass, and the *Yarak* assumed a geostationary orbit above Bethesda's colony world. The armada rejoined the other ships that remained in orbit, so that there were a total of fifty gathered warships. Rade wondered how many of them were itching to destroy the Phant ship. Probably quite a few. Bethesda had ordered several of her warships to remain in close proximity to the *Yarak*, "for their protection," as Azen put it.

Azen reported several shuttles departing from the Hydra ships and heading toward the surface. They were likely transporting Bethesda back to her court.

"She told me she will deliberate on whether or not to allow us Greens an audience," Azen said. "The fact that we have a free species allied with us—you humans—weighs heavily in our favor, she tells me. That and the part we played in her rescue. I suspect the deliberations are mostly for show, to appease those among her advisors and court who do not trust the Phants, Green or no."

Bethesda made them wait a full day in orbit. Finally, roughly thirty hours later, Azen came to the berthing area.

"She has decided to grant us an audience," Azen

said. "She says she will listen to what we have to say, but does not guarantee she will act. In fact, I have the distinct impression she won't. Though Bethesda is angered by the kidnapping attempt by the empress, it seems her advisors have counseled her into inaction. Even so, we have to try. She wants you all to come along, as she says our human allies will impress her court, and help convince them of our intentions."

"All of us?" Rade asked.

"All of you," Azen replied. "Or as many as you wish to bring. I should mention, we completed the repairs on Harlequin's Titan this very morning. So it is ready to go, should you desire his presence."

Rade glanced at Harlequin. "He's a member of this team like anyone else. He will come. When do we leave?"

"Immediately," Azen replied. "Before Bethesda changes her mind."

The Argonauts donned their helmets and followed Azen into the passageway beyond. Rade had gotten used to the undulating pipes in those bulkheads, and they no longer really bothered him.

"So Azen, only two Greens are coming?" Tahoe said. "You and Surus?"

"I am actually carrying five greens within the shell of this Artificial at the moment," Azen replied. "While only I am in control of the AI core, I don't have to tell you, it's a bit crowded in here."

They reached the mech holding area and loaded into their Titans.

"Feels like we're getting ready to fight," Lui said.

"Maybe we are," Tahoe replied.

"I'm afraid this isn't a fight that can be won with mechs alone," Azen said.

"Welcome aboard, boss," Electron told Rade when

the cockpit sealed.

"Hey El," Rade said. "You've kept the cockpit warm in my absence, I see."

"I always do," Electron replied. "What would I be good for, otherwise?"

Rade grinned. "Not much."

"So uh, when we get down there, you're going to translate the proceedings for us, Surus, or what?" Bender asked.

"Since the last mission, I've installed partial translations of the Hydra dialect within your AI subsystems," Surus replied. "There will be errors, but for the most part, you should be able to understand what the Hydra say, and our response to them. If Bethesda asks you any questions directly, relay your response to me and I will answer for you."

The Titans went to the hangar bay, where freshly fueled booster rockets were waiting. They launched the rockets first, then dropped shortly afterward, plunging toward the distant planet below.

Unlike the other world, this one was completely covered in an ocean of liquid methane. Everywhere Rade looked he saw that smooth, yellow sea. There were no clouds. It was essentially the perfect world for the Hydra as a species.

"Must be terraformed," Lui commented during the drop.

They splashed into the methane ocean one after the other and began the long descent. Another craft from the *Yarak* landed nearby and joined them. Basically a sphere with fins.

"The hell is that?" Bender said.

"Simply another vessel to convey more of us Greens to the audience," Azen replied.

The sun's rays penetrated only so far into the

depths, and darkness soon consumed the Titans. Robotic Hydra skirmishers met the team shortly thereafter and escorted them down.

Rade and the others transformed into submarine mode; they kept their LIDAR active in realtime, and it illuminated the seabed below them as they approached the undersea colony. The three dimensional wireframes depicted structures similar to those Rade had seen on the other world—arches, spires, and trees of coral, sometimes covered in platelets, other times spouting drifting streamers that reminded him of seaweed.

"Keep an eye out for any ambushes," Rade said. He constantly scanned those structures through his scope.

"I don't think they would ambush us now, after all of this," Azen said.

"Even so, we wouldn't be doing our jobs if we didn't watch for attacks," Rade said.

The coralline structures grew bigger the deeper into the colony the Titans traveled. Among them, Rade saw members of the Hydra race, essentially different versions of Bethesda. The organic sea creatures seemed to be mixtures of squids and jellyfish: they had pumping, bell-shaped bodies that swallowed liquid methane and pumped it out the back again for locomotive purposes, and long flagella-like tentacles that whipped the area directly behind them, apparently for steering. Smaller gripping appendages near the front were covered in suckers, and surrounded a beaklike maw that bore a striking similarity to that of an Earth octopus.

Some of the Hydras moved independently, but several more jetted past atop long, disk-like craft to view the odd spectacle of these alien visitors. From these bystanders came a steady series of pops and whines.

Electron translated some of those sounds, and he caught snippets such as "look at how ugly they are" and "I wonder if they're edible?"

"So this is what it feels like when *you're* the aliens," Fret said.

"Feels like we're part of a human menagerie or something," Bender said. "And we've been paraded out for show."

"Apparently we're allowed to turn on our headlamps, if we want," Azen said.

"Let's do it," Rade said.

Cones of light shot out, filling out a scene far more colorful than Rade had imagined, a veritable kaleidoscope of hues. Each platelet attached to the corals was a different color. The corals themselves reminded Rade of variegated marble, and when taken altogether covered the full gamut of the rainbow. The Hydra themselves were a mix of neon green, blue, and red.

"Psychedelic, man," TJ said.

The Hydra exhibited no apparent reaction to the light, and Rade wondered if they were even aware of it.

One of the creatures got close and jetted a cloud of black into Rade's path before a nearby skirmisher shoved the Hydra away.

"I think one of the aliens just spat at you, boss," Lui said.

"I guess we're well loved," Rade said.

Another creature, this one on a craft, sped by, dropping another cloud on Bender.

"These Hydra have no respect," Bender said as he emerged a moment later. "You save their monarch, and all they can do is shit on you in thanks."

The skirmishers escorted the team to an expansive reef. It was free of seaweed and other platelets. Above, Rade saw metal cylinders that could be only laser turrets. He guessed that the structure was the Hydra equivalent of a palace, with the defenses to match.

The Hydra robots led them toward an opening. More skirmishers waited by the entrance, and they moved aside to allow the group to pass. Rade and the others were sprayed with more black clouds by the onlookers before they made it inside.

The skirmishers led them through various tunnels until the group arrived at an open area within the massive coral reef; basically a small cavern. Two more skirmishers resided just inside the entrance, guarding.

Within, several Hydra floated, congregated around the walls of the cavern; none possessed those disk-like craft. One of them floated alone on the far side of the cavern, directly in front of the Argonauts. Two skirmishers resided on either side of her; the other aliens kept well clear of them.

Rade guessed the Hydra that floated apart from the others was Bethesda. Then again, she could be merely a stand-in, meant to draw fire in case things turned south. That was how Rade would have arranged it if he were in charge of providing security for the meeting.

"Lui, do we know if that's her?" Rade asked.

"Based on our previous encounter with her," Lui said. "Given the alien's size and shape, I'd say there's a good chance that it is. Or a lookalike, at least."

A modulating series of clicks emanated from that Hydra, followed by a long moan.

"Come forward," a female voice came from Rade's internal speakers.

Surus led the way in Swift, and the sphere-with-fins joined her. Rade and the others followed.

The Hydra's appendages squeezed together in front of her maw, and a single loud click came from her.

"Halt," came the translation.

The visitors obeyed. What followed was a series of pops, hisses and groans, as Azen and the alien conversed. Rade's AI translated everything that was spoken; given the contents of that conversation, Rade decided the alien was indeed Bethesda.

"I wish to thank you for your help in my rescue," Bethesda said. "You played a pivotal role. If you had not spotted those who attempted to carry me away when the diversion began, I may not have escaped. I also applaud your continuing efforts to retrieve me even when I fell over the continental shelf. You pursued, at great risk to yourselves. A risk that was borne mostly by your allies, these 'organics' as you call them. To have acquired such a brave species as allies shows me that you are entirely unlike your brethren. Though I knew this, of course, given my prior experience with you. But it is heartening to see that you have not changed. It also shows those doubters of my kind that not all Phants are to be hated, or mistrusted. I must ask, however: the metal one who came for me when all others would not, he survived, I hope?"

"He did," Azen replied. "In fact, he is with us now." Azen gestured toward Harlequin's Titan, which floated not far behind him.

"I am happy," Bethesda said. "I would employ that one's services if he were one of my kind. But tell me, who is in charge of the organics?"

"That would be me," Rade said, coming forward.

Surus translated.

"Do your Phant allies treat you well?" Bethesda said. "Or are they little more than your masters?"

"They treat us as equals," Rade said. "They have helped my race, too, against the other Phants. The Reds, Blacks, and Purples. The latter three came to conquer us, but Azen and the Greens repelled them, and saved my species. We're in their debt."

Another Hydra floated forward from a nearby wall. "We cannot trust the translation," it said. "Not when those so-called allies cannot speak directly to us, and must rely upon the Phants for communication. This alien may have said that they are all slaves to the Greens."

"I assure you, we are no slaves," Rade said.

"Again," the opposing Hydra said. "Putting words in the alien's mouth."

Bethesda opened up her appendages, spreading them wide. "I will be the judge of that. And I judge that no Green ordered the metal ones to come to my aid."

Another Hydra came forward. "I agree with Bethesda. You cannot order servants to their deaths like that. Such an action could have only been willing."

"Many a willing servant has chosen to die for its master," the opposing Hydra said. "How many here would die for Bethesda, for example?"

"But that is different," the other Hydra countered. "She is our monarch. We are happy to die in her service."

"Yes, but, we have seen those conquered by the Phants fight to the death for their masters," the opposing Hydra said. "All it will take is a simple review of the archives to confirm this. I say it cannot be proved that these so-called organics are allies and not slaves."

"Either way," Bethesda said. "This is twice the Greens have saved me now. First to help me escape the Phants during the original invasion, and now this. We owe them at least the courtesy of hearing what they have to say. Azen, if you will?"

"Thank you," Azen said. "My homeworld is under attack by your empress. We—"

Another Hydra shot forward and erupted in a loud series of clacks.

"She's not our empress," the Hydra said. "We do not recognize her authority here!"

"My apologies," Azen said. "My homeworld is under attack by she who has illegally claimed the title of empress. She has spread her forces throughout the atmosphere, scattering them among the different components of our hive. She is at her weakest. A well-timed attack now will catch her at unawares, causing her thinly-spread line to fight a war on two fronts. Their casualties will be severe, and the empress will be forced to retreat. Very likely, you will capture her in the confused rout that is sure to follow. If ever you sought to end the threat of this empress to your people, the time is now. Rightfully reclaim what is yours."

"I have no desire for the crown," Bethesda said.

"Even if you do not," Azen said. "It is in your best interests to attack Medea now. After she destroys our hive, what is to stop her from coming after you and your faction next?"

"That is why I am amassing an army," Bethesda said. "To protect myself against that very thing."

"Then why not take preventative measures now, while you still can?" Azen said. "Bring your armada. Strike while the advantage is yours."

"We will be outnumbered," Bethesda said.

"With our help, it won't matter," Azen said. "Make her fight a battle on two fronts. Together, we can defeat her."

A Hydra came forward. "If there is a chance we can make you empress, even a small one, we should take it, my queen."

Another Hydra spoke: "The best way to bring her down would be from the shadows, via the assassin's knife."

"We've tried," the first said. "She always ferrets out our assassins long before they reach her. She is far too experienced in that realm, having assassinated so many of our warlords."

Bethesda remained quiet for several moments. Then: "We will consider your request, Azen. Wait in the next room while we deliberate."

The team moved to the next room. Rade noticed that the sphere-with-wings had remained conspicuously silent during the exchange. He guessed that Azen was the spokesperson for the Greens, and they funneled all their questions to him.

An hour later Bethesda recalled them.

"We will fight," Bethesda announced. "But we believe that the combat won't be as easy as you describe. The empress will recall her fleet from the different parts of your homeworld when we enter the system, and she will engage us with the entirety of her forces."

"The Greens will continue to harry them from behind," Azen said. "They won't be able to regroup... they'll be forced to engage us."

"I'm not so certain," Bethesda said. "I believe they will regroup, despite your attempts."

"They'll still have to fight a war on two fronts," Azen insisted.

"Yes, but it will not be as easy as having their forces divided," Bethesda replied. "But we have a plan to ensure their immediate surrender."

"Oh?"

"We will target the flagship," Bethesda said. "With a covert penetrative force. We will concentrate all of our forces on that flagship, and create a defended channel for an elite team to board the ship and capture Medea. Once the rest of her fleet realizes she is our hostage, they will surrender."

"If it works," Azen agreed. "Then you will have won." He sounded cautious.

"Yes," Bethesda said. "Unfortunately, we are not equipped to handle such a mission. While boarding is sometimes attempted against enemies in Hydra space warfare, I dare not risk any of our skirmisher units this time. The empress has the ability to override any units we send aboard, via a universal hacking key. It is why we will have to rely upon you Greens to help us achieve this."

"We're not equipped at the moment, either," Azen said. "Very few of our units can operate effectively in liquid methane at the moment."

"What about your allies?" she said. "The metal ones seem readily capable of passing from the void of space and into liquid methane."

"Here it is, people," Liu said over a comm band that excluded Azen. "The regime change we were all talking about."

"I will have to ask them," Azen said. "Remember, they are not mine to command."

"Then do so," Bethesda said. "Tell them I will give them the blueprints to the flagship, and indicate where Medea will be holed up during the attack so they can plan their operation. I will also provide a life sustainment tank they can use for the capture of the empress. Finally, I will give them portable hacking units that will allow them to open any airlocks encountered along the way, once they breach the hull."

"When my team arrives, how will they know which one is her?" Rade said. "The Hydra all look the same to us."

"The empress produces a distinct pheromonal signaling chemical," Bethesda said. "I can provide a device to detect the presence of that chemical, and confirm which of them is her. So tell me, will the organics help?"

"Rade?" Azen said. "Do your Argonauts feel up to the task?"

"Wait wait wait," Bender said. "Let's talk about our pay, first. I want two years worth of salary for this."

"I'm sure Surus can accommodate your monetary demands," Azen said. "Rade? What say you?"

"We'll fight," Rade said.

seventeen

The armada departed the Hydra colony a few days thereafter. Bethesda had decided to gamble all of her ships in the attack; for her, this was obviously an all or nothing proposition.

From the Hydra planet, it would take two weeks and three wormhole jumps to reach the system containing the Green homeworld. The journey seemed long, and tense. No one was really looking forward to the mission. Rade didn't really see any other choice, however. The Greens had helped humanity; and now that they needed his aid in turn, he couldn't refuse them.

At one point near the end of the journey, during the designated night time, Rade sat up to rub his eyes in the dark. He couldn't sleep. Shaw's breathing beside him told him that she was awake, too.

"Does anyone still have nightmares about Gaul Prime?" Fret said from behind the curtains nearby.

"Every night," Rade said. He regretted the words instantly. He lay back down and rested his head on the pillow.

"Didn't know you were still up, boss," Fret said.

Rade didn't answer.

He felt Shaw's comforting hand around his.

Manic spoke into the darkness from behind another curtained off area. "I still see our brothers and sisters, getting pulled into the sand. I hear their screams. And I wish there was a way we could go back and change that day. I wish we could save all the good men and women who died. But we can't."

Rade never thought hearing, merely *hearing*, words would be so difficult. He could only imagine how difficult it must have been for Manic to say them.

"But there's no reversing the relentless, ravaging arrow of time," Manic continued. "I was scarred. *We* were scarred. And we deal with what happened in different ways. Some of us have nightmares. Others, well, we've compartmentalized it, I suppose. Buried it so deep that we never think about it ever again. That's the only way I can get through it. But sometimes during restless nights before battle, very much like this one, the memories surface again and take hold of me in their iron grip."

Rade had told himself that what had happened was hardest for him, because the men were his to command. But he realized he was badly mistaken. It was just as hard for his men, if not harder, by the sound of it.

"When are you going to forgive yourself?" Fret said.

"Never." Rade was surprised to hear his own voice answering. He was even more surprised when he continued. "To do so would serve only to tarnish the memory of those who died. Because it would mean they left this existence for nothing. If I forgive myself, it means I can allow myself to grow lax, and permit the same thing to happen all over again. I won't. I refuse. And as I told Shaw when she pulled me to the surface after I fired point-blank into the lionsquid, if ever I have a choice between saving my Argonauts and saving myself, I'm going to choose my Argonauts."

"But you're our boss," Bender said from his designated area nearby. "You can't take risks like that. In the military—"

"We're not in the military anymore," Rade interrupted. He felt drained. The effort of speaking those previous words had taxed him to the core. But he forced himself to continue. "While I demand strict discipline, I don't follow military rules to the letter. That one about always protecting the boss, I won't stand for it anymore. I'm not better than any of you. I'm your boss, yes, but I'm also an Argonaut first and foremost. You all mean more than anything in the galaxy to me. If I were back down on that seabed, getting dragged into the sediment by a lionsquid while three of you were in danger, I would make the same choice again. I would fire my rockets at point-blank range."

No one answered, respecting his position. Quiet descended once more upon the compartment.

After a few moments he found himself weeping softly. He quickly wiped his eyes, hoping Shaw didn't notice in the darkness. If she did, she left him alone, for which he was thankful.

In the days that followed, no one brought up the subject again.

WHEN THE *YARAK* emerged in the target system containing the besieged Green homeworld, Surus addressed the Argonauts.

"Azen tells me the fleet is withdrawing from its

positions in the atmosphere of the gas giant," Surus said. "And gathering around the flagship. It looks like Bethesda was right. The enemy will present a unified front by the time we arrive."

In three days the armada reached the outskirts of the gas giant that harbored the distributed hive of the Greens. The one hundred ships of Medea's fleet had assumed a defensive formation, creating a shield with their vessels around the flagship. Phants in golden mechs occasionally struck them from behind, making guerrilla attack runs from the surviving energy spheres in the atmosphere before returning.

"We're making our final approach," Surus said. "The armada is forming into a long cylinder: a sword to pierce their shield. We are to report to the mech bay immediately."

The Argonauts made their way to the compartment and loaded into their mechs. Azen met them, and took his place within the sphere Sprint carried over its passenger seat.

"I didn't think you'd be coming with us," Rade told the Green.

"Of course I'm coming with you," Azen said. "I plan to see this through to the end."

"You don't have any other Greens tagging along inside your host?" Rade asked.

"Only me," Azen replied.

The mechs made their way to the launch bay. The booster rockets were placed against the far bulkhead away from the egress, as the boosters would not be needed for the planned spacewalk.

The empty holding tank, which would be used to capture the empress, resided on the right-hand side of the bay doors. It was a little taller than a Titan, and three times as long. TJ and Manic were in charge of porting it. The Greens had installed one of those energetic membrane airlocks inside it, powered by a portable power source. That way the team could open the tank in void conditions if they had to, and any liquid methane they had stored within it wouldn't escape.

A few moments later the bay doors opened wide.

Beyond, Rade saw the planet looming in the distance below, a gas ball the size of a human torso. Around the *Yarak,* the ships of the armada had formed the protective cylinder Surus had told them about. It extended several kilometers in front of the Phant ship toward the planet. Also enclosed with the *Yarak* was a thick cloud of the smaller skirmishers, which would defend the team as they made their way to the target.

At the opening located at the head of the cylindrical array of ships, the vessels protecting Medea's flagship awaited. They formed a planar wall ten warships wide by ten tall. All of those warships essentially looked the same: massive monolithic shapes with three prongs emergent from the nose sections. There was little variance in ship design among them, save for size. A few of those vessels were departing the planar wall to intercept Bethesda's forces. It would be some time yet before those ships arrived.

The tension in the air was almost palpable. The waiting before any battle was always the worst part, at least for Rade.

"Hey Bender," Manic said suddenly. He had that tone of voice he used when he was up to no good.

Bender didn't reply.

"Bender," Manic tried again.

"*What?*" Bender answered.

"I used to need Viagra, until 1 met you," Manic told him.

"What the hell is Viagra, bitch?" Bender said.

"Ah, never mind," Manic said.

Fret was cracking up over the line.

"*What the hell is Viagra?*" Bender said.

"I just looked it up," Tahoe said. "It's an old trademark for an erectile dysfunction drug, popular over two hundred years ago before it was replaced by Virality and later male enhancements."

Bender was quiet for some time. Fret and Manic could be heard struggling to contain their laughter over the comm.

"That's right," Bender finally said. "Har har har. Let's laugh at how gay we are. The next time you claim to pick up a chick at the pleasure station, I'm going to remind you of this."

"Bender should make his own line of erectile dysfunction drugs," Fret said. "He could call it Mr. Penis. You ain't had a penis until you've tried Mr. Penis!"

Rade shook his head, smiling slightly. Then he said: "Can we get some quiet over the comm?"

While admittedly they could all use the distraction, Rade felt it was best if they concentrated on the launch, which could come any time now.

Rade saw flashes of light as explosions rocked that cylindrical envelope of ships protecting them. Enemy skirmishers pierced the lines and engaged Bethesda's units within. Invisible laser fire was exchange on both sides.

An enemy warship broke through and steered toward the *Yarak*. Three Hydra ships intercepted, shooting the intruder in half with their lasers. Five more of Medea's ships breached the cylinder before a dispatch from the armada arrived, and the intruders were dealt with in a similar manner.

The eight vessels composing the front portion of the cylinder accelerated, breaking away to ram into those of Medea's ships located near the center of her defensive planar. The hulls of the involved vessels disintegrated where the impacts occurred; meanwhile the frames of the attackers buckled and compressed at the same time, so that the colliding ships crumpled from the nose down. From the way the ships were swallowed up as they continued forward, it was almost like watching a bunch of vessels disappearing as their hulls crossed a hole in spacetime. But there were no wormholes here.

The full extent of the destruction was evident by the massive amount of debris left behind, distributed amid the broken enemy ships.

Rade stared in disbelief.

"Kamikazes," Bender said. "We're fighting on the side of friggin' Kamikazes."

"They're willing to give up everything to get us inside," Lui said. "Sacrificing all those lives to make us a path."

"Guess I should feel glad we're not the only ones doing the dying today," Fret said.

"None of you are going to die today," Rade said.

Other ships belonging to Medea's forces were scrambling to fill the hole formed by the attack, and to protect the flagship. Another eight vessels broke away from the forward portion of Bethesda's armada and made to intercept those ships.

"Now!" Azen said. "Launch."

eighteen

The Titans ran forward and leaped outside into the zero gravity of space. Rade ignored the nauseous feeling in his stomach and activated his jumpjets, thrusting forward. A friendly skirmisher latched onto him with its tentacles and carried him onward. Other skirmishers did the same for the other Titans.

The remaining swarm of Hydra robots formed a protective sphere around the group and shielded them as they made their way forward.

Rade couldn't see anything but that black envelope of shifting craft for several minutes. Occasionally there would be a flash and a clump of skirmishers would fall away at once. But always new friendly craft arrived to take their places.

He felt the G forces as the skirmisher that held him changed course, either to avoid the debris created by all the ships that had fallen, or to evade an incoming attack.

And then the swarm began parting. The skirmisher that held Rade released him, and he plunged toward the black hull of a Hydra ship that resided directly ahead. It had to be the flagship.

Rade engaged decelerating thrust for several

seconds, but still hit fairly hard, rattling his teeth. The surface caved around him slightly and he rebounded. He quickly activated the magnetic mounts in his feet and latched onto the surface.

Around him the hull was made of a smooth material, though covered in collections of pockmarks in places. Those marks were typical on the Whittle layers humans used to protect the inner armor of their starships from micrometeor impacts, layers that were typically offset a short distance from the actual hulls underneath. Those pockmarks, along with the slight depression caused by his impact, provided ample evidence to support the use of such a layer by the aliens.

Not so different after all, are we?

The other Titans smashed into the surface around him, creating similar hollows. TJ and Manic landed beside him. The large holding tank they ported created the biggest depression of them all.

Rade scanned the nearby hull for signs of any turrets pointing their way. Azen had assured him that the skirmisher swarm would drop them off at a safe area on the hull. Still, he never liked to place his fate in the assurances of aliens.

It seemed clear out there.

Rade focused instead on the void above him. He relied on the background light for target acquisition, not daring to use LIDAR or any other active sensor system that would give away his position. He did overlay the thermal band to make targeting easier.

He acquired a tango in his scope that was coming toward them. Bethesda's skirmishers intercepted the tango a moment later.

More attackers came from above, but always Bethesda's units were there to take them down. The golden mechs of the Greens occasionally joined the fray as well.

"According to the blueprints Bethesda gave me, the nearest external airlock is only a hundred meters away," Azen transmitted. "I'm transmitting the waypoint now."

Rade accepted the access request and the waypoint appeared on his overhead map.

"Tahoe, if you'll do the honors..." Rade said.

Tahoe organized them into a single file zig-zag formation, and they proceeded along the surface of the hull.

The magnetic mounts in Rade's sole assemblies loosened depending on the angle of his foot within the inner cocoon of the cockpit, allowing for an appropriate simulation of Earth gravity. It was a bit like walking in thick mud, in that it was easy for Rade to place each foot, but harder to lift it again.

"Keep your eyes on the void," Rade said.

Listening to his own advice, he held his scope toward the stars just in case one of the enemy skirmishers pierced the defenders to come down at them.

"We're here," Tahoe said.

"Surus, open it up," Rade ordered. In his scope he spotted a skirmisher break through the attackers and head toward them. Rade fired his cobra.

The skirmisher smashed into the hull nearby.

"Good shot," Bender said.

Surus applied a flat disk, the size of her Titan's fist, to the hull beside the airlock. That was a hacking device provided by Bethesda.

The hatch folded open a moment later and remnants of liquid methane that hadn't cleared the airlock in time misted outside, vaporizing and desublimating into a cloud of yellow crystals.

"Beautiful," Manic said.

"Reminds me of my piss," Bender said.

"Looks like we can fit four Titans at a time in the airlock," Surus said.

"I only want two for now," Rade said. "Tahoe, Lui, go. Assume a defensive position when you're inside."

"Roger that," Tahoe said.

The two of them went into the airlock and Surus used the disk to seal the outer hatch.

"We're in," Tahoe said in a few seconds. "Clear on the LIDAR band."

Rade hadn't been expecting that. Well, he'd take it.

"Do the provided blueprints mesh with the interior topography of your current position?" Rade asked. He didn't dare switch to Tahoe's viewpoint, not while he had to watch the void above.

"They do," Tahoe answered. "We're in a passageway that continues on for quite a ways in either direction. From the wireframe created by the LIDAR burst, I can see intersections branching out on either side every thirty meters or so, continuing on for quite a ways into the distance. There is gravity, though I can hardly notice it anymore because of the liquid methane. The pressure conditions aren't as intense as the seabeds of the two oceans we've visited, but it's still enough to crush our jumpsuits if we leave the cockpits of our Titans."

"Fret, Bender, join them," Rade said.

When they had successfully transferred inside, Rade turned toward TJ and Manic, who yet ported the glass container. "You two are up next."

The pair could barely fit the holding tank into the airlock.

"Going to have to leave it up to Tahoe's team to pull it inside," TJ said when it became obvious neither he nor Manic could squeeze in beside it.

"Tahoe, prepare to receive the holding tank," Rade sent.

Surus sealed the hatch, and when it reopened a moment later, the airlock was empty.

"Holding tank received," Tahoe sent.

Manic, TJ, Shaw and Rade went next.

Within the airlock, Rade felt the artificial gravity take over immediately. The outer hatch sealed, cloaking the compartment in darkness. Rade activated his headlamp in time to watch yellow liquid flooding inside. When the compartment was completely full, Rade released the magnetic mounts in his boots and floated upward. He almost couldn't tell there was gravity anymore because of the weightlessness induced by the methane, just as Tahoe had mentioned.

"Switch to LIDAR burst mode," Rade instructed the other three with him. Only Manic had turned his headlamp on when the hatch sealed, and he deactivated it at the same time as Rade. While there were probably sensor and camera systems aboard that would allow the aliens to track the positions of the intruders to a T, Rade preferred to err on the side of caution: he would stick with an active sensor method that was only moderately detectable.

The wireframe representation of the compartment appeared around them as the LIDAR burst engaged.

When the inner hatch opened Rade used his jumpjets to thrust through. He assumed a guard position just inside, as did the others. He aimed his scope down the rightmost passageway, which proved a series of white lines overlaid upon his vision in the darkness, forming the three-dimensional shape of the bulkheads, overhead and deck. The holding tank had been placed against the bulkhead and off to one side.

Entering the passageway with Harlequin, Surus carried the disk device in the hands of her mech; behind the Titans the inner hatch sealed.

"Harlequin, you have the honor of placing the first set of charges," Rade sent.

The storage compartment in the right leg of Harlequin's Titan opened, and he removed the large explosive charges he had placed within. Since the Argonauts couldn't simply exit their cockpits to apply the charges via their jumpsuits, due to the pressure, they had taped the individual explosives together four at a time to form bigger blocks the mechs could manipulate with their larger hands.

Harlequin affixed the taped blocks directly to the inner door.

"Will that be enough to blow the outer hatch, too?" Rade asked.

"Based on my materials analysis, yes," Harlequin said.

"Good, let's proceed," Rade said. "Surus, the next waypoint please."

The overhead map was completely filled out already, thanks to the blueprints Bethesda's faction had given Azen. Conveniently, the map showed where the team had made its point of entry. According to that map, the outer portion of the ship was mostly three decks of crisscrossing passageways connected by scuttles. Closer to the interior, the passageways gave way to larger compartments, or caverns really, connected by tunnels. The caverns were labeled with various names, such as hydroponics, engineering, hatchery, mess hall, and empress court. There was a secure bunker near the empress court where Medea would be evacuated in the case of a boarding situation, such as the one taking place at the moment. The mess hall was located adjacent to that bunker, and provided a place for the Argonauts to bypass most of the expected resistance awaiting in the court, and instead cut directly into the bunker. The team had to pass through a cavernous compartment labeled "exercise room" first to reach it.

The waypoint appeared. Rade and the others activated submarine mode and continued forward. They moved in single file, spread out in a zig-zag pattern so that the lead mechs didn't block the view forward of those that followed.

Staying close to the left bulkhead, Manic and TJ resumed their portage of the holding tank, carrying it parallel with respect to the passageway. At the front, Manic had shoved his feet beneath the grips in the forward portion of the tank, while the head of TJ's Titan was situated under the rearmost grip. They couldn't use their hands because the fins containing the turbines necessary for locomotion in submarine mode required the arms to be spreadeagled.

"Good neck workout," TJ commented.

"Calves, for me," Manic said.

On point, Bender and Tahoe paused at every intersection to clear the passageways on either side. They would activate walker mode, descend to the deck, then move outward with shields in one hand and cobras the other to "pie" the areas beyond. Nothing ever was lying in wait. When they determined it was clear, they switched back to submarine mode and continued.

The Argonauts proceeded past several of the intersections in that manner, continuing straight ahead for the most part, though occasionally taking the indicated turns and scuttles of the route Surus had stenciled onto the blueprint. Breach seals sometimes blocked their path, but Surus used her hacking device to get through them. Rade had his Argonauts place charges at all of those seals, as the hatches closed behind the party after they passed, and Rade wasn't big on that.

As they neared the compartment labeled "exercise room" on the map, Bender announced: "Got some tangos incoming. Skirmishers."

"Take them down," Rade said. He glanced at his overhead map and saw the three red dots that had appeared in the distance.

Azen had replenished their missile inventory with suitable replacements, and the Titans on point fired.

"I just took a laser impact," Tahoe announced. "My head armor held up, but I can't take another."

"Fret, assume his position," Rade said. "Tahoe, fall back. Walker mode, people. Deploy shields."

A flash came from ahead, followed by a shockwave transmitted through the liquid methane.

"A laser just detonated one of the rockets," Lui said. "The remaining two are continuing toward their targets."

Rade finished transforming into walker mode and deployed the shield in his right hand, taking cover behind it so he could aim the cobra in his left at the tangos.

Two more flashes appeared ahead, followed by another shockwave. "Two of the skirmishers are down."

Rade aligned his targeting reticle over the last known position of the remaining tango. He zoomed out slightly, and said: "Electron, switch to realtime LIDAR."

The wireframe of the tango snapped forward. Rade immediately swung the crosshairs over the incoming skirmisher's center of mass and fired. He wasn't the only one who shot, apparently, because a moment later the thing ceased all motion and simply drifted in space.

The party approached the fallen tangos on foot, bounding slowly across the deck through the liquid, the artificial gravity, and the liquid itself, fighting them the whole way. Bender reached the area where the closest skirmisher had drifted to the deck.

"Hmm," Bender said. "Permission to switch to headlamps? I'm detecting a foreign substance in the liquid. Seems to be organic. I think it's blood."

"Do it," Rade said. He switched to Bender's point of view.

The LIDAR wireframe vanished as the cone of light from Bender's headlamp appeared, illuminating the fallen skirmisher. A dark cloud misted from the metal side of the dead tango. Bender waved his hand through it a few times, dispersing the cloud in swirls.

Below, a panel had been blown aside on the hull of the skirmisher, partially revealing the organic occupant within. Rade saw skin that was a neon blue; it matched up with the coloration of the central bulb region found on Hydra bodies.

"I always thought these things were robots," TJ said, continuing to carry the holding tank with Manic on foot.

"So did I," Lui said. "Guess we've been fighting the Hydra equivalent of mechs all this time."

"I did say these were weaponized battle suits at one point," Surus said.

"Maybe you did," Lui said. "But it's only really hit home now."

Bender deactivated his headlamp. The party gradually bounded forward to the next two downed skirmishers, which had also drifted to the bottom of the passageway. The bulkheads nearby exhibited signs of concussive damage, the planar surfaces dented into rounder shapes where the missiles had detonated. Bender momentarily shone his headlamp down at the lifeless tangos; these also misted clouds of blood.

"Activate submarine mode," Rade said. "Bender, Fret, stay on point. Utilize LIDAR bursts and thermal vision only. We change back into walker mode the instant any new tangos are detected."

The party continued forward in submarine mode through the lightless passageway.

"Something strange going on here," Fret said from his position near the front. "The viscosity seems to have doubled. I'm at half speed, and quickly slowing."

"Same thing here," Bender said.

"Full stop," Rade said.

Those just behind Bender and Fret were similarly slowed by that invisible force, and had piled up so that they resided in nearly the same position. Rade and the others managed to stop before hitting them.

"Light check," Rade said. He activated his headlamp. Ahead, the way was blocked by an oily, black substance. Four mechs were in the thick of it.

"Looks like we accelerated straight into a trap," Lui said.

"Switch to walker mode," Rade told the four who were inside that oil. "And backtrack. Get out of there. Surus, we'll have to take another way around."

With difficulty, Bender, Fret and the other two were able to wade through the viscid substance, and finally emerged.

"Well that was fun," Fret said.

"Got four more tangos incoming behind us," Lui announced.

nineteen

"Get behind your shields!" Rade quickly deactivated his headlamp and switched to walker mode, placing his shield in front of him. He lifted his cobra overtop the edge of the shield and switched to the viewpoint of the scope. He zoomed in on the wireframe targets and saw the outline of four Hydras with strange rectangular blocks held in front of them. Did they have shields, too?

"Take them out," Rade said.

He centered his cobra above the rectangular block and squeezed the trigger; the Hydra shifted at the same time and Rade hit the rectangular block instead.

"I got one," Bender said. "No wait, it's still moving."

"Don't think these are skirmishers," Manic said.

Rade aligned his targeting reticle with the head area of his target, aiming above the rectangular block once again.

"No," Lui said. "It appears these are Hydras in the flesh. They've forgone their usual battle suits."

"So the bugs are weaponless?" Bender said, sounding hopeful.

Rade fired again, scoring a hit, he thought, but the target didn't stop. He decided to fire a rocket instead.

Others were doing the same beside him.

"I didn't say that," Lui replied. "It looks like they've wrapped their forward appendages around some sort of portable weapon arrays. You see those rectangle blocks they're holding in front of themselves? Those are the weapons. And they're assailing us with laser blasts at this very moment."

"So that's why my AI is going nuts about my shield integrity," Manic said.

"Uh, yeah," Lui said.

Rade fired his cobra again and the missile struck at the same time. A flash came, followed by a shockwave. The tango ceased its advance.

"Bugs bugs bugs," Bender sung. "Gonna cook me some bugs."

"Why do you call these ones bugs anyway?" Fret said. "They're in an ocean. Lobster is a better term. Lobsters are the bugs of the sea, after all."

"Fine," Bender said. "I'm going to cook me some lobster tonight."

"They don't even look remotely like lobsters," Manic said.

Rade aimed at another tango, but it too had stopped. He fired anyway, then checked the other two. Those Hydras were motionless as well.

"Looks like we got them all," Rade said. "Shoot them with your cobras again, just to be sure. Meanwhile, Surus, can we get that new path?"

"Done," Surus said.

A dashed line appeared on the overhead map, indicating the new route.

"I'm picking up another four tangos on the rear quarter," Lui said. "Blocking the way."

The team launched missiles and fired lasers, and took them out in a similar manner.

"More," Lui said.

Rade glanced at the overhead map. Five more red dots had appeared in the passageway, overlapping the route Surus had created.

"They just keep coming," Fret said. "We're trapped."

"We'll have to force our way through that oily substance," Rade said. "Keep your shields held behind you, and proceed into the blockage! Liberally activate your jumpjets for speed boosts."

Rade turned around and, holding his shield behind him, slowly but steadily bounded toward the area filled with black oil. He couldn't see the substance on the LIDAR band, but he knew immediately when he was inside because his speed became a crawl. It was like trudging through the thickest marsh in existence. His servomotors strained against the repulsive forces with each step. He concentrated on placing each of his feet. Left foot. The other. Left. Right. He fired an aft burst from his jumpjets; it helped a little.

"Electron, take over control of my legs and jumpjets," he instructed the AI. "Get us through.

Rade fired a missile, but it took several sluggish moments for it to clear the viscid area before continuing on at full speed toward the targets. He squeezed his trigger as more enemies appeared.

TJ, at the rear of the holding tank, couldn't contribute to the fight, because he used his free hand to shield his body and the tank. Manic, at the front of it, couldn't play a part either, as none of his weapons reached past the broad edge of the container.

"Got more ahead of us," Bender said.

"Bender, Fret, Lui, Surus," Rade said. "Cover our front. Shaw, Tahoe, Harlequin, and I will take the rear. Manic and TJ, keep moving forward. Remain behind your shields at all times, Argonauts."

Shaw, Tahoe, Harlequin and Rade joined their shields, and they retreated in unison behind their shared cover.

Rade released a few more rockets, and targeted other enemies through the scope of his cobra. Meanwhile, Electron carried him ever forward through the viscid substance.

And then Rade's feet began to move faster.

"We're through," Electron said.

"Retain control for the moment," Rade instructed the AI. "I'm going to keep tracking the tangos at our rear."

"There's a side passageway up ahead," Surus said. "I'm marking it on your maps. It should allow us to circumvent the forward attackers, and continue on toward the target."

Several tense moments passed. Bender, Fret, and Surus reached the side passage; they "pied" the corridor in unison, slowly increasing their angle of exposure to any attackers awaiting within.

"It's clear!" Surus said.

Bender remained near the opening to the passageway; he faced the forward tangos, keeping both shields deployed to protect the Argonauts behind him. When everyone had maneuvered within, Bender followed Tahoe inside on drag.

Twenty meters ahead, another breach seal blocked their way forward. Surus moved to the door and placed her hacking device.

"It's not opening," Surus said. "It looks like their AI finally inoculated their software against the hack. Should I install the variant?" That was a different cyberattack that would firmly lock all hatches ship-wide. Rade guessed that secondary hack would only work for a short while as well before the AI found a way to circumvent, and he wanted to save the cyberattack until they really needed it, as in: trapping the empress in her bunker.

"Not yet," Rade said. "Lui, place a charge."

Lui used his jumpjets to hurry to the seal; once there he attached two of the taped explosives. "Set!"

"Get back, Argonauts," Rade said.

They retreated to the intersection behind them; Bender and Tahoe aimed their cobras past the edges on either side, firing to keep the incoming aliens at bay. They launched a few rockets as well.

"Now, Lui!" Rade said.

The charges detonated. The shockwave knocked Rade backward slightly, but he quickly recovered. Ahead, on the LIDAR band, the breach door had peeled inward, forming a gap wide enough for two Titans to jet past. There were no tangos beyond.

"Go go go!" Rade said. "Submarine mode, let's put some distance between ourselves and the pursuers!"

The Titans transformed and accelerated rapidly through the liquid, the turbines beneath their arms spinning at full speed.

Far ahead, more skirmishers and armed Hydra appeared in the darkness, courtesy of the LIDAR bursts.

"Walker mode!" Rade said.

They switched back and landed on the deck, deploying their shields and continuing slowly forward. The party members were running out of rockets and relying more and more on their cobras.

"Kinda wish we had some frag grenades right about now," Fret said.

"Wrong mech model, bro," Lui replied.

"Tangos on drag again," Bender said.

"Let's get some shields on the rear, people!" Rade said.

The Argonauts continued forward through the darkness, struggling to take down the enemies that were coming at them from both sides. Always there was a new alien to replace any that fell. Rade kept an eye on the vitals of his teammates—so far everyone remained in the green.

"Friendly reminder, take the left passageway," Surus said.

She didn't have to remind him. Rade glanced often at his overhead map as he advanced, continually judging the distance to the corridor as indicated by the route she had stenciled in. He had no doubt that every other member of the party was doing the same.

The point men, Tahoe and Fret, finally reached the area where the corridor branched both ways, and they paused near the edges. According to the map, the "exercise room" awaited a hundred and fifty meters down the leftmost side.

"Watch for the defensive lasers on the left," Surus said. "The turrets should have deployed close to the entrance of the adjoining compartment."

"*What* defensive lasers?" Tahoe said.

"They're marked on the map," Surus said.

"Oh."

Tahoe and Fret stood back to back, holding their shields toward the forward attackers while they pied the passageways to the left and right with their cobras at the same time.

Tahoe fired his cobra twice in rapid succession. Then he halted in place for a few moments, ostensibly to allow the cobra to recharge to full strength; Fret remained motionless with him. Then Tahoe continued the pieing motion and fired the cobra twice more.

"Clear!" Tahoe said. "Four defensive lasers, out of action."

"Clear on the right side as well!" Fret said.

"Then go!" Rade said.

Tahoe moved into the left passageway, while Fret halted to stand guard in front of it, deploying both of his shields to cover the party against the forward aggressors.

"How are your shields holding up?" Lui asked as he passed inside.

"Down to about forty percent," Fret replied.

Rade piled inside with the remainder of the party, and Fret followed on drag behind Bender.

Ahead, the passageway continued directly toward the "exercise room" compartment—there were no other branches for the entire one hundred and fifty meters. No enemies resided in their path, either. The LIDAR burst reported a breach seal blocking the way into the destination compartment.

"Transform!" Rade said.

They switched to submarine mode and accelerated toward the seal.

When they arrived, once more Surus moved forward, changing back to walker mode. "This probably won't work, but I might as well try." She placed her hacking disk.

"Wait," Rade said. "What are the chances we'll find more tangos waiting for us on the other side?"

"Very high," Surus said. "I admit I'm a little surprised they weren't waiting for us here already."

"Of course they weren't waiting," Manic said. "They assumed their defensive lasers would readily protect the entrance. Or at least slow us down."

"If that's true," Lui said. "Everything lurking in the compartment beyond is probably rushing toward this entrance as we speak."

"Don't even bother trying to open it, Surus," Rade said. "Shaw, place your charges."

Nemesis moved past Swift as Shaw directed the mech to attach the explosive blocks retrieved from storage.

"Charges placed!" Shaw announced.

"All right, let's give the door some clearance, Argonauts!" Rade said, engaging submarine mode.

As they retreated, Tahoe said: "The breach seal is opening!"

Rade glanced at the feed from the rear view camera. Sure enough, the white wireframes of tangos were revealed as the seal slid upward.

"Switch to walkers!" Rade said. "Defend!"

Rade transformed, swiveling around in time to watch as the charges sloughed right off the door. The taped explosives were swatted about as skirmishers poured through.

Rade placed his shield in time, blocking the incoming laser strikes, and returned fire.

"Tangos have reached our rear as well," Fret announced.

"Form up!" Rade said. "Defend both flanks! TJ, open up the holding tank. Deactivate the energy membrane and fill her up."

A moment later TJ said: "Holding tank is full and secured!"

"Retreat a bit further," Rade sent.

The group backed away from the onslaught, firing at the wave after wave of skirmishers and armed Hydras that swam into the tunnel.

"My shields are reaching critical levels," Tahoe said from his position on point.

"As are mine," Fret said, on drag.

Rade's own shield was getting fairly chewed up. He could already see circular bite marks along the edges where enemy lasers had bored through.

He glanced at the overhead map. The charges they had placed at the seals along the way were portrayed as flashing purple dots. Up ahead, the charges Shaw had recently placed had drifted a little more toward the party, thanks to the incoming waves. Rade decided it was safest to withdraw further.

"Just a bit more..." Rade said.

When he had judged the distance sufficient, he said: "Blow all the charges we've placed, people! From here to the outer hull! And attach yourselves to the forward bulkhead!"

Keeping his shield pointed toward the incoming attackers, Rade fired his jumpjets to hurl himself against the bulkhead and then activated his magnetic mounts to cling to the metal.

Everyone else did the same. TJ and Manic flung the holding tank against that bulkhead, and secured it via the magnets embedded in its own rim.

Rade saw the flash in the darkness, heard the muted detonation, and felt the shockwave as the explosive forces ripped past. Skirmishers and Hydras smashed into the bulkheads, and into the shields of the Titans themselves.

twenty

Rade waited for the inexorable pull of explosive decompression, but it did not come. He worried for a moment that some of the aliens had found the previous charges and repositioned or disarmed them, preventing the breaches from reaching all the way to the hull.

But then the whoosh came. Rade felt the incredible suction as the liquid methane was drawn out toward the distant hull breach. Thanks to the charges the party had placed at every seal between their current location and the entry point, they had effectively created a penetrative rupture all the way to the adjacent compartment; it was essentially equivalent to firing a super-powerful laser completely through the otherwise heavily-armored hull.

Aliens continued to sweep past, sometimes rebounding from his shield. Worried about the tank, Rade glanced at the feed from TJ's camera: TJ had extended his shield beside him, over the glass, protecting as much of the glass from impacts as possible.

Rade dismissed the feed and fought against the flow to aim his cobra toward the breached entrance; he switched on his headlamp, as the LIDAR bursts didn't update his display fast enough to target any of the incoming aliens, and then he shot at the flailing bodies as they were sucked past. He didn't want to risk the chance any of them might shoot him first. He wasn't the only one, apparently:

"Wooyah!" Bender said. "It's like a shooting gallery."

"Fish in a barrel!" Manic agreed.

"Electrons traveling through a wire?" Harlequin tried.

"Don't think that analogy fits, Harley boy," Bender said.

Rade had to occasionally pull his cobra back to avoid having it crushed against his shield when Hydras or skirmishers struck, but a moment later he always replaced the weapon and fired away. He didn't expect that all of the aliens waiting in the cavernous compartment beyond would be drawn out by the decompressing liquid, of course... because of the bottleneck created by the relatively tiny exit to the compartment, not all of the aliens would be able to pass through at the same time, and would instead crash into each other and partially clog the opening; Rade expected that just inside the entrance he would find a lot of beached aliens.

The flow ended as quickly as it began. The lifeless bodies of Hydras and skirmishers rolled to the deck beside the Titans as the supporting liquid receded, their bodies glued in place by the artificial gravity still active in the atmosphereless passageway. Rade quickly deactivated his headlamp, as did others around him.

"What happened?" Fret said. "Did we empty out all the methane?"

Rade glanced toward the entrance to the adjacent compartment. The LIDAR burst reported a complete seal.

"Don't think so," Tahoe said.

"Let's worry about that later," Rade said. "I want kill shots applied to these skirmishers."

Rade and the others released their magnetic mounts and fell to the deck. Free of the drag caused by the liquid methane, the Argonauts moved easily in the vacuum environment; they fired at the few skirmishers lying about, not wanting to take the chance that any of them had escaped the team's initial laser onslaught. Azen had earlier explained that while the skirmishers could function both in the zero G of deep space and the buoyant environment of the ship, they would be useless without the liquid methane, as the artificial gravity would pin them to the deck. Indeed, the targets made no move to defend themselves as the team fired at each of them in turn. Of course, that could be merely because the team's cobras had already shot every last one of them as they had emerged.

None of Rade's companions bothered to shoot any of the unsuited Hydras, however. Rade momentarily switched on his headlamp and saw that the formerly neon-bright skin of the aliens had turned completely black where the liquid had boiled away and seared their flesh. Crystals formed a thin icy layer over their bodies. It was obvious they were dead.

Actually, scratch that part about none of the Argonauts bothering to shoot the Hydras: Bender walked right up to one of the dead things and fired his cobra into its frozen maw at point-blank range.

Rade deactivated his headlamp as the gore burst forth.

"Lobster bisque time, baby!" Bender said. "Not bad for some Tech Class III humans, huh?"

"Are these aliens really Tech Class IV?" Lui said.

"They seem closer to our level of technology more than anything else."

"You forget I modified the armor of your Titans to withstand their powerful lasers," Surus said. "But you are correct, the best definition of the Hydra would be to call them an early Tech Class IV race. A mid to late Tech Class IV would have issued a disarming pulse to disable your explosives. If that was what we were facing, I would have modified the plan accordingly. Every Tech Class has its weaknesses, even races of the highest class. Trust me, we Phants have learned to find and exploit those weaknesses."

"Just as you've found and exploited my weaknesses, Surus my girl?" Bender said. "Let's grab dinner tonight. Your treat? Or we can eat in. Lobster's on me!"

"TJ, how is the tank?" Rade glanced at the wide object on the LIDAR band.

"Held up just fine," TJ said. "No thanks to my efforts."

"So about that liquid methane..." Tahoe said. "Did we empty it all, or not?"

"According to my calculations," Harlequin said. "Given the size of the adjacent compartment as depicted on our maps, we only drained half of the liquid contents before the hatch resealed."

"The hatch *resealed?*" Lui's mech pivoted toward the passageway up ahead.

"Not entirely," Azen said from the spherical chamber on the back of Surus' mech. "The explosion caused severe damage to the hatch. If you zoom in on the LIDAR band, you can see that it was in the process of sealing when the charges detonated. The force caused the hatch to peel outward, creating a gap three-quarters the width of the opening. It was still wide enough for most of the Hydras and skirmishers to pass through, but I believe enough of them must have smashed into the gap at the same time to clog it. Either that, or something bigger... something that was never meant to travel these outer passageways."

Rade zoomed in on the blockage as Azen spoke, and saw where the actual hatch ended and the blockage began—it almost looked embossed where the hatch stood out in relief against whatever had lodged against it from the inside, plugging the hole.

"Bender, check it out," Rade said.

Bender approached, then momentarily switched on his headlamp. "Hmm. Looks like we're going to have to go with the 'something bigger' option Azen mentioned. I think this is actually one of those lionsquids we encountered on the original colony. But whatever the hell it is, it's certainly not going to harm us now."

"All right, get back Bender," Rade said. "We're going to clear that blockage!"

Bender retreated.

"Target the plug and fire at will, Argonauts," Rade said.

Rade centered his targeting reticle over the gap and switched to headlamp mode to illuminate the black, frozen skin that resided past the metal of the hatch.

As the lasers impacted, blood gushed forth, vaporizing and desublimating into a crystal mist almost instantaneously. At the back of his mind, Rade considered just how narrow the conditions were for life to exist in this universe. In the deep space that composed ninety-nine point nine nine percent of the universe, life couldn't survive. Not even alien life. And as for himself and his Argonauts, the only thing keeping them from the cold death of the void were the hulls of their Titans and the pressurized suits the men wore underneath; all it would take was a penetration shot to any of their cockpits, and the operator within would suffer a fate similar to the dead creature they now bled.

"This isn't going to work," Tahoe said. "We'll be here all day."

"Cease firing," Bender said.

"Do it," Rade ordered his men.

"Allow me." Bender casually walked his mech forward, and when he reached the hatch he shoved his fingers into the torn skin of the blocking creature. He pressed, hard, slowly ripping the alien equivalent of tendons and cartilage or whatever the hell was inside those things, until the forearms of his mech were embedded to the elbows. Then he shifted slightly, as if digging around with his hands inside, and then he pulled his arms out. A huge glob of gore came with them, along with what looked like chunks of organs. They turned black and released mist when they were exposed to the vacuum, and soundlessly dropped to the deck below the Titan. Crystals formed on the surface of the disgusting mess.

Bender shoved his arms and repeated the process again and again; each time he buried his arms inside a little deeper, and shoveled out more of the innards.

"Like being a midwife," Bender said.

"I was actually thinking, it's like cleaning a freshly plucked chicken," Lui commented.

"Good ol' chicken!" Bender said.

The organs began to ooze forth of their own accord from the large hole Bender had carved as the innards of the creature were forced outward by the pressure of the liquid methane on the other side of its body.

And then, just like that the creature turned inside out, its viscera gushing onto Bender as the disemboweled creature could no longer counter the weight of the methane pressing down on it. The liquid itself followed shortly after, a tidal wave whose front edge was a frothy mass of vaporizing mist.

"Attach!" Rade said. "TJ, protect the tank!"

Rade and the others leaped onto the bulkhead and activated their magnetic mounts. Bender was swept by as the liquid engulfed them all once more. His Titan rebounded from TJ's shield, which was extended over the tank; Rade glanced at his overhead map and saw Bender's blue dot stop near the intersection behind them, where he had finally latched on, thankfully.

More skirmishers and armed Hydra were sucked past, sometimes slamming into the Titans and their shields. Rade and the others fired at the aliens with their cobras.

"It's open season again!" Manic said.

Finally the flow subsided and the remaining liquid misted from the surfaces and dispersed.

Rade realized he had his headlamp still active and he quickly turned it off. He glanced toward the entrance. There was no longer anything blocking it on the other side. He did see what appeared to be part of a skirmisher lying next to it. Rade quickly aimed his cobra at it and fired.

"Dismount from the bulkheads and apply kill shots," Rade ordered.

Once more they moved among the bodies, killing the new skirmishers that had been beached in the passageway.

"Whew!" Bender said when they were done. "Going back to the midwife analogy: I'd have to say, her water *really* broke."

"I almost feel kind of bad," Manic said. "We obviously have the advantage here."

"Do we?" Fret said. "Just because we have a map showing where all their defenses are, and just because we've been lucky so far, doesn't mean the playing field is level. Not at all. We're still nine Titans against a whole crew of angry aliens."

"Try not to be a morale drag," Bender said. "Besides, I wouldn't have it any other way, bitch."

"Don't call me a bitch," Fret said.

"I meant Shaw," Bender quipped.

"Don't call me a bitch either," Shaw said.

"Fine. I was talking about Surus," Bender said. "And keep your pie hole shut, you alien. You don't get to retort."

"I'm fine being called a bitch," Surus said.

"You... you are?" Bender acted stunned. "I think I'm in love."

"TJ, the tank?" Rade asked.

"Intact," TJ said.

"Good," Rade said. "Tahoe, Bender, clear the entrance. Apply kill shots to skirmishers you find lying on the deck inside. Watch for the tracking turrets embedded in the distant bulkheads. The defenses will still function without the methane, correct, Azen?"

"That is correct," Azen replied. "I'm overlaying the expected positions on your HUDs, so they stand out."

Tahoe and Bender carefully approached the opening in their Titans. Their shields were deployed in their right hands, the cobras their left.

twenty-one

Rade waited tensely as the pair neared the entrance.

"Hold," Tahoe said. His laser swiveled upward slightly, and he fired. On the overhead map, one of the red dots marking the location of a defensive turret turned black. Located on the far bulkhead inside the compartment beyond, it would have been directly in Tahoe's line of sight.

Tahoe pied as much of the righthand side of the entrance as he could without stepping through, firing as he did so. On the overhead map, Rade watched as more turret indicators on the distant bulkheads winked out. The red dots of skirmishers appeared on the deck in the compartment as well as they came into Tahoe's line of sight, and they also turned black. Rade pulled up Tahoe's status display, and realized the Titan's shield integrity was decreasing—it was taking several laser hits.

Tahoe repeated the maneuver for the lefthand side of the entrance, and then he paused to let his cobra cool down for a moment. When he was ready, Tahoe and Bender proceeded through the gap, easily fitting through the half-closed seal. Tahoe went high, Bender low—Bender held his shield horizontally in front to achieve the lower posture. The two Titans swiveled in place, firing as they did so.

Several shots later, Tahoe reported in: "Clear."

On the map, all of the turrets marked on the surrounding bulkheads had turned black. As had the indicators of the skirmishers piled around within the entrance.

"Inside!" Rade said.

The Titans entered, forming a defensive half-circle in front of the opening as TJ and Manic ported in the heavy tank that was now filled with liquid methane. Fret brought up the rear, watching their drag quarter.

Around Rade, the entrance was crowded by dead Hydras and skirmishers. He switched to headlamp mode to survey the bodies; any Hydra residing outside a skirmisher suit was dead, its flesh blackened and covered in methane crystals.

"This is creepy as hell," Shaw said.

"You know, if these Hydras were smart, they would have cut the artificial gravity in this section," Lui said. "That way their skirmishers could have continued to attack us."

"I don't think it works that way," Tahoe said. "They'd have to cut it for the whole ship."

"Then maybe they should," Lui said.

"Don't give them any ideas," Tahoe said.

Rade scanned the cavernous compartment. Colored the black of death, coral shapes covered the deck, clotting the way forward. Rade saw the familiar branching tree structures and arches, as well as a few long ridges coated in platelets. There were many places for an ambush out there.

"So this is the lobster exercise room," Fret said.

"Not much of an exercise room is it?" Bender said. "Though I suppose all these undersea bugs can do for exercise is swim around in circles all day. That and masturbate."

"Like you?" Manic said.

"Yep," Bender said. "Why do you think my grip strength is so strong?"

"That's a bit disturbing..." Lui said.

Rade deactivated his headlamps and switched to LIDAR burst mode.

"We move forward," Rade said. The entrance to their next destination, the "mess hall," lay at the far side of the cavernous compartment. "Tahoe, there's enough room in here for traveling overwatch. Take us forward."

Tahoe divided the squad into two fire teams and they proceeded forward, breaking through the coral structures or traveling around them as necessary. Rade was part of the second team, located fifty meters behind the first, and he scanned the cavern around them, providing the necessary overwatch. TJ and Manic were with him, porting the tank.

There were several sealed hatches at different heights that provided means of egress; Rade feared the doors might open at any time, allowing attackers to flood inside. Then again, unless those hatches formed airlocks, such an attack wouldn't be all that feasible unless the aliens desired to vent the atmosphere of the adjacent passageways.

The dead corals were so thick in some places that the party members had to use their jumpjets to thrust over them. They occasionally opened fire at skirmishers that had become lodged behind the structures during the explosive decompression, and the spent targets offered little resistance.

There were also a few more beached Hydras, their corpses covered in methane crystals. There was one particular formation of corals—a series of arches—that had caught at least six of them, their bodies entwined in death.

TJ and Manic continued to hoist the heavy holding tank. Despite the added weight of the liquid methane within, they seemed to have no problem carrying the container; Rade wondered if having a struggling empress trapped inside would change that.

They reached the area that led to the adjacent compartment labeled "mess hall" on the map. A breach seal had activated, sealing it off from the current area. The seal resided about twelve meters above the deck, obviously designed to be accessed while liquid was in place.

"They're going to realize what we're up to very soon now," Lui said.

"True enough," Rade said. "Surus, get up there and install the variant." That was the alternate hack that would lock all hatches ship-wide, and trap the empress in her bunker. "Unless you can install it from where you are, of course."

"No, I'll need to get up there." Surus activated the jumpjets of her mech, Swift, and ascended to the hatch, using her magnetic mounts to secure herself in place. She applied the disk-like hack device.

"It's done," Surus replied. "I've locked all hatches ship-wide. When the empress realizes our plan and tries to leave her bunker, it will be too late."

"Unless the AI manages to inoculate against the hack before then, like it did the other," TJ said.

"Let's hope not," Manic said.

"Surus, place charges while you're up there," Rade said.

Surus opened the storage compartment of her mech and attached a block of four explosives to the hatch. Then she dropped away, firing her jumpjets to cushion her impact with the deck below.

"Line the bulkhead on either side underneath," Rade said.

The Titans hurried forward, taking their places on the bulkhead beneath the hatch.

"Headlamps on," Rade said. The LIDAR bursts would update the displays far too slowly for what was to come. "And Surus? Blow it."

The explosion came, spreading superheated gases outward in the void. Liquid methane surged forth immediately afterward; it came tumbling down in the artificial gravity like a waterfall. The foaming front expanded across the deck, smashing across the coral structures; the liquid expelled mist all along its length, boiling away so that none of it reached the exit passageway on the far side.

Hydras and skirmishers were embedded within those falls, and came pouring out with the flow.

The waiting Titans picked them off. Most of the aliens seemed to be Hydras in organic form, some armed, some not, with a few skirmishers in the mix, as well as a few lionsquids and other smaller, worm-like creatures Rade hadn't seen before. Perhaps food sources.

There were too many to shoot them all.

As the flow receded, those organisms that Rade and the party had failed to terminate were left squirming on the deck under the illumination of their headlamps. His attention was drawn to a bunch of white worms, the size of human arms, that had landed nearby. They lethargically wiggled back and forth, like dying caterpillars caught in slow motion, their skin smoking and blackening as the liquid methane boiled away. In moments they ceased moving entirely, their bodies crystalizing.

"What a way to go," Lui said. "I almost feel sorry for these things."

Bender aimed his cobra at one of the frozen worms and fired. It shattered into a thousand fragments that spread across the deck.

"I don't," Bender quipped.

"Let's get some kill shots on the skirmishers," Rade said. "Tahoe and Bender, get up there and clear the entrance to the mess hall. Return to LIDAR burst mode."

Headlamps went out across the squad and darkness descended once more, though it was soon replaced by the wireframes of LIDAR. While Tahoe and Bender jetted up to the newly opened compartment, Rade and the others moved among the fresh enemy units scattered about the deck below and executed the surviving skirmishers.

In moments, they had cleared the murk of all tangos.

"We've taken out a few skirmishers that were caught up here," Tahoe said. "It was mostly dead lionsquids and Hydras. We also eliminated the defensive turrets in the bulkheads already."

Rade glanced at his overhead map. In the "mess hall" compartment, the enemy laser indicators had all gone black.

"Good job," Rade sent. "Let's get up there, people."

"Wait," Bender said. "I see some skirmishers you guys missed from my vantage up here."

He aimed his cobra down from his position at the hatch above and eliminated two more red dots that had shown up on the overhead map: a pair of skirmishers that had lodged behind some coral reefs near the middle of the cavernous compartment, and were otherwise hidden from Rade's view.

Rade and the others jetted up to the opening and proceeded inside, assuming a defensive semi-circle around the tank. Fret once more guarded the rear.

Within, Rade found himself in another cavernous compartment similar to the last, though the coral formations on the deck seemed thicker. Nearby, there were several more of those small dead worms on the deck, distributed between the bodies of dead Hydras and lionsquids.

"Looks like we're late to the buffet," Lui said.

"Ain't never been late to no buffet," Bender said. "In fact, as far as I'm concerned, the buffet is just starting."

Rade surveyed the steep bulkhead beside them. Midway up resided the area they were to blast through to reach the empress.

"Tahoe, Bender, Lui, Fret," Rade said. "Spread out and comb through these corals. Make sure we don't have any skirmishers hidden in there, lying in wait. Meanwhile, the rest of you, start climbing."

Rade led the way up the smooth wall, followed by Shaw and Surus. TJ and Manic followed thereafter, holding the glass container horizontally between them, obviously struggling to carry it up. Harlequin brought up the rear underneath them.

Rade alternately activated and deactivated the magnetic mounts in his arms and legs; he would position the hand and foot on one side of his body, turn on the magnets, then release the mounts of the opposite limbs, pressing down on the leg that remained secured so that he was able to reach up with his free hand. Then he would reattach and repeat the process with the other side, slowly pulling himself up in that manner.

Rade paused every now and then to carefully scan the deck below, in case some previously hidden skirmishers had come within his line of sight. He never picked out anything.

However Lui, on the deck, soon spotted a skirmisher behind a set of platelets and terminated it. But so far no one else down there had found anything.

Rade reached the designated spot in the bulkhead that Azen had marked on the map. His HUD portrayed it as a flat, green rectangle overlaying the surface in front of him.

"Okay, people," Rade said. "Our target lies on the other side of this wall. I'm attaching the charges." He opened his storage compartment and found the bundled bricks, then secured them to the bulkhead.

"TJ, Manic, place the tank directly underneath, please," Rade said.

Surus and Shaw moved out of the way, allowing TJ and Manic to position the tank as requested.

"Secure it," Rade said.

TJ and Manic shoved the container against the bulkhead and activated its mounting magnets.

"Secure," TJ said.

"Azen, how much time will we have once the liquid drains before she dies?" Rade asked.

"About three minutes," Azen said. "She will suffer severe burns to her epidermal layer within the first ten seconds, and will lose consciousness in another twenty. But she will survive if we get to her before the sixty second mark."

"Set timers to sixty seconds," Rade said. "Surus, prepare the detection device."

Surus produced a small cylindrical device. Bethesda had given that to the team; when pressed directly against the skin, the device would detect the unique chemical markers identifying the empress.

"All right," Rade said. "Assume positions for the detonation. Headlamps on. Remember, no shooting of any targets. Not even skirmisher units."

"You really think the empress is going to be inside a skirmisher battle suit?" Tahoe asked.

"Anything is possible at this point," Rade said.

Rade and Harlequin took their places on the left side of the bulkhead, away from the charges. Shaw moved to the right side, and Surus joined her. TJ and Manic remained on either flank of the tank underneath.

On the deck below, Tahoe, Lui, Bender and Fret had assumed attack positions, weapons aimed up toward the charges. Headlamps provided realtime illumination.

"Fire in the hole," Rade said.

He detonated the charges.

twenty-two

There was a bright flash, but no sound in the void; the liquid methane gushed outside instantly, pouring onto the tank and cascading over the edge before crystallizing into mist.

An armed Hydra flowed out and bounced off the top of the tank; Rade resisted the urge to shoot it, in case it was the empress. Two more Hydras, also carrying weapon bars, were sucked outside and then the torrent ceased. The wet surfaces misted as the liquid vaporized and desublimated.

"Start timers." Rade detached his right arm from the bulkhead and alternated the magnets in the rest of his body to edge his way toward the gap the charges had torn. He switched to the point of view of his scope, activated the weaponlight, and placed his cobra through the opening.

Before he could get his bearings, Electron reported: "We're taking laser fire."

Rade quickly withdrew his hand.

"Damage?"

"The cobra is intact," Electron said. "We lost two fingers on the hand below, however."

"Do you see anything from down there?" Rade asked Tahoe.

"We can't get a bead on the inside, not from this angle, no," Tahoe replied.

"Shit, we have to get in there," Rade said. "Time's ticking."

He released all of his magnetic mountings and jetted toward the holding tank, which was yet secured to the bulkhead. He unfolded his shield in midair, and placed it firmly in front of himself as he landed. The gap he had blown was right in front of him, beginning at chest height and extending upward.

"Our shield is taking fire," Electron said.

Rade extended his cobra above the tip of the shield and aimed it through the gap. He saw two skirmishers on the deck immediately within. They'd braced their tentacles against the bulkhead near the opening, preventing themselves from being sucked outside, and had their weapons trained on the entrance.

Rade fired several shots, silencing both skirmishers. Then he ran his scope from left to right across the remainder of the chamber. The hatch on the far side was closed tightly. He spotted several lifeless Hydras on the deck. From the illumination provided by the weaponlight, he saw that their skin had already blackened.

He hoped the team wasn't too late.

"Surus, get in there and find our empress!" Rade sent.

Surus released the bulkhead and jetted onto Rade's shielding, leaping off it to vault inside.

He watched as she moved from body to body, kneeling to apply the small cylindrical detection device Bethesda had provided.

Beside one Hydra, which seemed little different than the others, Surus said: "Here!"

She hoisted the body into the air with her mech.

Rade cleared the tank, leaping onto the bulkhead nearby and activating his magnets.

"Open her up, TJ!" Rade said. "And ensure the membrane is engaged!"

The top of the tank slid open; the liquid methane didn't flow out thanks to the energetic membrane tech the Greens had imbued the container with. When Surus reached the gap in the bulkhead, she unceremoniously dumped the body of the empress inside. The energy membrane gave way where the organic flesh touched, resealing behind it to ensure only a small amount of the methane leached.

"How is she?" Rade asked. "Alive?"

"I can't tell," Surus said.

Rade gazed at the blackened form behind the glass. It wasn't moving.

"Either way, time to go!" Rade said. "Leap down, Argonauts!"

Rade deactivated his magnets and applied his jumpjets to cushion his descent. He broke a small coral arch as he landed. TJ and Manic impacted noiselessly beside him. The container they held slammed into the deck, breaking through a reef. Within, the dark form of the empress stirred slightly.

"I think she's alive after all," TJ said.

Rade continued to scan the coral structures around him as he, Tahoe, Lui and the others joined up with them. The Argonauts headed toward the entrance.

"Taking fire!" Lui said.

Rade and the others dropped behind their shields. A red dot had appeared on the overhead map, near the far side of the compartment.

"Looks like you missed one of the skirmishers, Bender..." Manic said.

"Wasn't me!" Bender said. "That was Fret's area to

cover."

Rade's lifted his scope past the edge of his shield and aimed toward the distant target. It was currently hidden from view behind a reef-like structure.

"Harlequin, Bender," Rade said. "Low-crawl to its flanks and take it out."

Rade kept his scope aimed at the reef, and continually moved the targeting reticle back and forth, but spotted nothing.

A minute later Harlequin reported in. "I have the target in my sights. It's a skirmisher. It's struggling to pull itself along the deck with its tentacles."

"Take it out," Rade said.

The red dot winked out on the overhead map.

"Skirmisher eliminated," Harlequin reported.

"Let's move, Argonauts!" Rade said.

The party hurried toward the exit.

By then the empress had fully roused inside the tank. She would flail about frantically for several moments, slightly pulling TJ and Manic to and fro at their positions on the outside of the container, and then she would rest for several moments, only to start her struggles anew.

Rade and Tahoe paused by the exit to survey the "exercise room" below. Nothing moved down there.

Rade stepped back. "Bender, Fret, go."

The two Titans leaped past. Rade and the others followed, smashing into the coral below, and assuming a defensive semicircle at the bottom. TJ and Manic landed behind them, and then the boarding party continued the retreat.

With their headlamps active, they made their way through the cavernous compartment; passing the dead bodies at the exit, they hurried onward into the passageway beyond. They followed the previously explored route, using the overhead map for guidance. They came across the occasional dead Hydra along the way, as well as a few skirmishers, which were attempting to crawl their way across the deck. Tahoe and Bender promptly terminated those latter units.

They were about three hundred meters from the exit when yellow fumes began to fill the passageway.

"The hell is that?" Manic said.

"Methane gas," Lui replied.

Condensation formed on the bulkheads.

"Looks like they managed to affect emergency repairs to the hull," TJ said.

"Hurry up, Argonauts!" Rade sent.

That condensation began to trickle down the bulkheads as the atmosphere attained critical pressure, and in moments liquid methane was flooding the deck from hidden vents.

The Titans waded through the rising liquid, struggling against the viscosity.

The empress had stopped struggling a while ago; she had realized the futility of it all—to break free would only mean her instant death. But with the liquid methane on the rise outside, she began fighting anew. She flailed about, and repeatedly rammed into the glass walls of the container, striking so hard that Rade could hear the thuds transmitting through the liquid around him. Small cracks began to form in the glass where she impacted.

"Damn it," Rade said. "Hurry!"

The liquid was past their waists by then. High enough to transform.

"Submarine mode, people!" Rade said.

He transformed and the turbines propelled him forward faster through the liquid. "Headlamps off. LIDAR burst mode!"

Darkness enveloped them, the surfaces around them replaced by the white wireframes of LIDAR. The liquid methane level was represented by a slowly rising horizontal plane, colored yellow.

They had closed to twenty-five meters of the exit when Lui announced: "I got multiple tangos up ahead."

"Back to walkers!" Rade said. "And defend!"

Rade switched back and lifted his shield in front of him. While the liquid methane hadn't completely filled the passageway yet, by then it was high enough to completely submerse the Titans.

Rade could hear the repeated thudding of the empress behind him as she battered the tank. She hadn't broken through the glass yet. But she seemed close, judging from the spreading cracks.

"Got tangos behind us, too," Fret said.

"Form two lines," Rade had his scope aimed in the forward direction. "Defend the front and rear quarters."

Rade joined his shield to the mechs of Tahoe and Shaw beside him, with Bender abutting Shaw on the right. Behind him, Harlequin, Surus, Lui and Fret formed a similar defensive bulwark in the rear quarter, protecting TJ, Manic and their precious cargo.

Rade lifted his scope over the top, and when the LIDAR burst updated, he fired. The others fired at the same time, and in moments the tangos had fallen. He glanced at his overhead map. The red dots behind them had been taken care of by Harlequin and the others.

But more tangos replaced them on both sides.

"Press on!" Rade said.

They slowly made their way forward, continually under fire.

Pieces occasionally broke off from the edges of his shield, forcing him to tighten his formation with the others who defended beside him.

The squad members stepped past the floating bodies of those they had defeated moments before, and reached the exit. The external hatch had indeed been repaired, though the inner was still damaged, forming a small alcove.

"TJ, put down your load and place some charges!" Rade sent.

"Aye boss," TJ replied.

Rade continued to take down the incoming attackers. He glanced at the overhead map and saw the blue dot representing TJ move into the alcove of the airlock behind him.

"Charges are placed," TJ sent.

"Get back to the tank!" Rade said. He waited until TJ was in position, then: "Argonauts, backtrack! Clear the airlock!"

The group retreated from the opening.

When Rade judged the distance sufficient he called a halt.

"TJ, prepare to blow the charges," Rade said. "Argonauts, do not engage your magnetic mounts. We *want* to get sucked out."

"Now we're talkin'!" Bender said.

"TJ, blow the charges," Rade instructed.

A flash came from ahead; the explosive shockwave followed, along with the muted noise of the explosion; Rade stumbled backward.

Then he was inexorably sucked toward the puncture. He slid forward, and was swept upward into the airlock and out into space. While there was no gravity out there, he still felt the slight G forces of his acceleration.

Rade deactivated LIDAR mode, as there was sufficient light to see outside the ship. Around him, the liquid methane vaporized into a thin mist of yellow crystals. The alien hull rapidly receded behind.

Above, the two fleets were still heavily engaged, as far as he could tell, with skirmisher swarms on either side flowing among the warships both near and far.

He surveyed his Titans; everyone had emerged intact, and their vitals were green.

But then the enemy skirmishers began to get sucked out; as the liquid desublimated, they shook off the methane crystals and accelerated toward Rade and the others.

"Time to defend," Rade said.

He switched to the electrolaser in his right hand and opened fire. A stream of lightning erupted from the weapon, tearing through his target.

Allied skirmishers swooped in, wrapping their tentacles around Rade and the others and carrying them into the main defensive swarm, which headed back toward Bethesda's fleet. Those allies defended constantly against the enemy skirmishers; more and more were coming in from other warships, so that the attack was relentless, with Medea's forces refusing to let their empress go without a fight.

But additional members of the allied swarm were always joining in the defense, and it soon became clear that the enemy was not going to reach their precious empress.

"How's the tank?" Rade sent Manic.

"Still intact," Manic replied. "The empress had kept smashing into it after we were sucked into the void, and for a while there I thought she preferred death or something to capture. But she's decided to play docile for the time being."

"Maybe she knocked herself out," Bender suggested.

"It's certainly possible," TJ replied.

"Hey, empress, knock yourself out, bitch!" Bender sent.

"Don't think she can hear you," Manic replied.

Bethesda's warship loomed ahead. Just underneath the bottommost of the three prongs, a hangar bay opened to receive the Argonauts. It had been evacuated of all liquid.

The escorting skirmishers fell to the deck inside as they entered the artificial gravity of the hangar environment, and they released Rade and his Argonauts.

Rade activated his headlamp and turned around to watch the bay doors shut behind him. He glanced at the holding tank. The black form of the empress lurked within, seeming lifeless. The only indication he had that she was still alive was the fact her appendages occasionally opened and closed near her maw.

"We did it," Bender said, sounding like he didn't believe it.

Rade felt strangely lightheaded. He turned toward Nemesis and unconsciously reached out toward Shaw's mech; she stepped forward and slammed the metal body against his own, giving him a Titan hug.

Rade couldn't help but laugh then. It was a laugh of utter relief, utter joy. He heard other unrestrained guffaws echoing over the comm, and he knew he wasn't alone in his feelings.

"We fucking did it," Bender said. It sounded like he was choking up.

"You humans are strange beasts," Harlequin said.

twenty-three

The hangar began to fill with liquid methane and in moments the skirmishers were back on their feet, as it were, and they swam to and fro between the cones of the light produced by the headlamps of the Titans while waiting for the bay to fill.

Rade and the others remained firmly rooted to the deck, thanks to the gravity.

When the liquid methane reached the top of the hangar, a nearby skirmisher wrapped its tentacles around Rade, hoisting him into the air. Those segmented tentacles pinned the arms of his mech to the body, and prevented him from using his weapon mounts. Other skirmishers did the same to his companions. While their shoulder launchers were exposed, none of them had any rockets left, so they were essentially disarmed.

"Well that was rude," Manic said.

Two skirmishers lifted the tank TJ and Manic had ported.

A clacking sound emerged from one of the skirmishers, followed by a whiny moan.

"We will escort you to Bethesda," came the translation. "She wishes to personally thank you for the part you have all played."

"How about an update on the battle effort?" Rade said.

"Bethesda will reveal all," came the response.

And so the Argonauts and their important cargo were carried deeper into the ship. Rade would have preferred to proceed forward on his own in submarine mode, but he could understand why Bethesda had them carried. If he had aliens aboard his own ship, he would keep them on a tight leash himself. Especially given the hacking technology Surus had on her person—well, her mech, to be exact.

They were carried through a series of passageways that reminded Rade of the layout he had seen aboard the vessel of the empress. Those passageways soon gave way to cavernous compartments as the skirmishers made their way deeper into the vessel. The compartments seemed smaller than those the empress had on her ship; the bottoms were covered with coral reefs, and lionsquids and Hydras swam from place to place, alongside skirmishers. The aliens were all strangely silent. Perhaps Bethesda had warned them that the intruders could understand their language?

Finally the escorted Titans reached a central cavern, which Rade guessed served as Bethesda's court while aboard. A score of aliens resided on the opposite side of the expansive compartment, barely visible within the dense liquid: the light from the mech headlamps had difficulty penetrating that far.

When they had traveled only a short distance inside, a loud click came from one of the aliens as it squeezed its appendages together.

"Halt," came the translation.

The skirmishers stopped. Rade found it puzzling that Bethesda would want them so far away from her.

It was as if she was afraid of them. Assuming that this was Bethesda, of course.

More clacks and hisses and whines.

"Bring me the prisoner," the AI translated.

The skirmishers carried forward the glass tank containing the empress, and halted twenty meters from the speaker.

"Engage the live transmission," the speaker said. "I want all of my forces, and Medea's, to watch."

Rade wondered what she meant by "watch," considering that it would have been completely dark in there if it weren't for the headlamps of Rade and his Argonauts. Likely, the echolocation and sound data would be transmitted.

"It has been done," a nearby servant said.

"Empress Medea, you stand before me, Queen Bethesda of Polyp VI, Birth Dome 52," the speaker said. So it was Bethesda after all. "I charge you with high treason against your people. You have assassinated the warlords of those who came to pledge allegiance and fight at your side, so that they would forfeit their lands and vassals to you. You have razed defenseless colonies, and attacked their fleeing citizens, cloaking your actions in the guise of uniting us against a common foe. This ends today."

The tank opened. The empress floated free. With that blackened skin, and those uncertain movements, she looked a beaten, defeated creature before Bethesda.

"Lest you all believe that this is not the empress," Bethesda said. "I bring forth two witnesses, captured from one of your fallen warships. The viscount breeeeeeee-zzzzzzzzzzzz-vaaaaaaaga and High General pffffft-dooooooo-zeeeeeee." The translator didn't have a word for the strange hissing and moaning sounds Bethesda used for their names.

Bender was laughing over the comm. "Jeez, and Manic says I come up with bad names. Viscount Breezy Vagina and High General Puff-Dee-Do, together again like you've never seen them before!"

A pair of skirmishers near Bethesda brought forth two Hydra that were obviously prisoners—their rear tentacles and their frontal appendages were tied together, so that they could move only by pumping their bell-shaped bodies.

"Identify her," Bethesda commanded.

"My empress, forgive me," one of the prisoners said.

"It is she," the second prisoner said. "Though she is a shadow of her former self. I recognize her only because of the pheromones she releases into the environment."

"Release them," Bethesda said.

The skirmishers cut the cords that bound the Hydra prisoners.

The pair seemed surprised, judging from the way they turned toward one another, as if exchanging a glance.

"Go to her," Bethesda instructed.

The pair whipped their rear tentacles like flagella, and pumped their bodies, moving toward the empress, who simply drifted in place lifelessly, apparently no longer caring what happened to her.

When the pair reached her, they turned around to face Bethesda.

"Execute them," Bethesda said.

The skirmishers opened fire. The two servants flailed about as the lasers drilled holes into their bodies; Empress Medea remained motionless the whole time, either resigned to her fate or too exhausted to care.

In moments all movement ceased among the three of them, and the black clouds of their blood spread outward from the bodies.

Rade could only shake his head. All that work to retrieve the empress alive, for *this?*

"Now I am the empress," Bethesda said. "Members of the fleet, hear me: those of you who still follow Medea, I expect your submission within the hour. You have a blank slate going forward. Your transgressions against me will be forgotten from this moment forward, but only if you yield to me. Once all of you have come to my side, we will continue the attack against the Green homeworld, and destroy our enemies. End the live transmission."

She turned her attention toward Rade and the others, who were still held firmly by the skirmishers.

"What treachery is this?" Azen said. "You must withdraw! We had a deal!"

"I must do no such thing," Bethesda said. "Be forewarned, Green... stay inside your host, as you value the lives of your organic allies. If you emerge, I will have my skirmishers strike them all down."

"But... why?" Azen said.

"I would have withdrawn from your homeworld as we originally agreed," Bethesda said. "Until my doctors detected the bioengineered retrovirus you infected me with. A virus that would have altered my brain structure and chemistry, allowing you to control me. My doctors have removed the virus and cured me, of course. But that doesn't forgive the act. It is you have betrayed *me*, Azen. For the last time."

"It wasn't us!" Azen said. "It was Medea!"

"Nice try," Bethesda responded. "But we saw genetic markers in the virus characteristic of Phant bioengineering techniques. The Hydra do not use the engram masking gene, for example."

"We humans didn't know about this," Rade said. "Surus, tell her."

Surus did.

"Perhaps that is true," Bethesda responded. "Which only shows you why you must never trust a Phant. You organics will have to evaluate very carefully the alliance you have made with these Greens. Just as I have reevaluated my alliance with them. I had thought the Greens were our friends. I was wrong. And now I will destroy their homeworld, and eliminate the threat they pose to my people in this region of space once and for all. As for all of you, I am as yet undecided on your fates. You have helped me, yet betrayed me at the same time. I must confer with my councilors. I am raising a noise canceler."

Rade had grown accustomed to the background din of whines and hisses so that when the complete silence followed, it was slightly unnerving. Still, it gave him time to gather his thoughts, and the foremost on his mind formulated into an angry question.

"What the hell happened, Azen?" Rade said. "You infested Bethesda with a retrovirus? Why?"

"A precautionary measure," Azen said. "Or an 'insurance policy,' as you humans say. I needed to be absolutely certain she would withdraw from the Green homeworld if we helped her become empress. I feared she would use our planet as political pawn to convince the remaining warlords to follow her. So I did the unthinkable: I infected her with a communicable retrovirus my kind had used against her race during the previous war. What I didn't expect was for the plan to backfire so spectacularly. If only I had had the time to alter the virus protein signature ..."

"How did you even get it in her bloodstream?" Fret asked. "I didn't see you touch her even once!"

"I didn't have to," Azen said. "This sphere I've attached to Surus' Titan is equipped with hidden spray nozzles. I simply dispersed the virus into the liquid methane when the empress returned from her trip over the continental shelf. When she ingested the liquid as part of her locomotive process, it infected her."

"I can see why she's keeping us so far back," Manic said.

"She's probably also afraid of the Greens directly," Fret said. "She did threaten to strike us all down if either of the Phants flowed from their hosts. I'm assuming your touch is as fatal to them as it is to humans, Azen?"

"It is," Azen replied. "But do you see that belt wrapped around her body, and the bodies of her court members? Those are essentially equivalent to the EM emitters you humans designed—repelling us so that we can't get close enough to touch them in our natural form."

"So why would she threaten to shoot us all down?" Fret said.

"Would you want Phants snooping around inside your ship?" Azen asked.

"Good point," Fret replied.

"Spray nozzles," Surus said. "I didn't know you installed spray nozzles in my passenger seat."

"I purposely did not reveal that to you," Azen said. "Nor to our human allies. I wasn't sure I could trust any of you to follow through with the plan when it became necessary to use the retrovirus."

"A good decision on your part," Surus said. "Because I certainly would not have allowed it."

"Nor would've I," Rade said.

"Then I chose wisely," Azen said.

"Given our current predicament," Bender said. "I think not."

"It's all a matter of perspective," Azen said. "If I had succeeded, we would not be having this discussion right now."

"You said the retrovirus was communicable?" Lui asked.

"Yes," Azen said. "She would have spread it to her staff, closest advisers, and family members. I would have had control of the entire ruling family if they ever attempted to attack us. But unfortunately, it sounds like her doctors caught it in time. And by the way, the control genes are latent. If Bethesda ended up not betraying us, and withdrew from our homeworld, I would have never activated the modified genes. It would have been as if she was never infected."

"And yet you and your kind would still have the option to take control whenever you pleased," Rade said. "At some point in the future, as suited your whims. Would you ever do this to us, Azen? Infect the commander-in-chiefs of all human governments and their staffs in secret, so you had absolute control over us?"

"How do we know he hasn't already?" Manic said. "Or infected *us*, personally? If these retroviral genes are latent, like he claims, then he could take control of us at any time."

"I assure you I have not infected any humans," Azen said. "You have not given me reason to. But if one day you ever attack the Greens, I will not hesitate to do whatever is necessary to save my people. I will use retroviruses, bioweapons, everything in my power. Wouldn't you do the same for your species?"

"But what you did here was wrong," Rade said. "You betrayed a race that agreed to help you. Just because you weren't sure you could trust them. I would never do that, personally. But there are others in my government who would, I admit."

"There you go," Azen said. "You humans are not so different from us Phants."

"Speak for yourself," Surus said. "I'm with Rade on this. You shouldn't have infected Bethesda, at least not until you were absolutely certain she would turn on us. Instead, by doing so you forced her hand—you could be single-handedly responsible for the fall of our current homeworld, and the irrecoverable loss of hundreds of millions of Green lives."

"Damn Phants," Bender said. "Always want to take control of us. Having one host isn't enough. Oh no, they want control of the whole race. Mark my words, when we're on the cusp of Tech Class IV, they're going to infect us all. As a *precautionary* measure, of course, as Azen calls it."

The noise canceler must have lifted then, because Rade heard the background shrieks and clacks once more.

"I have decided your fates," Bethesda said. "The Phants are parasites, and I want them off my vessel. Most of the organics will go with them. My skirmishers will bring you to the hangar and throw you into the void, allowing you to proceed to your ship unharmed. You may leave this place and never return. Consider it repayment for bringing me the empress. I would rather not give you anything for the treachery you have inflicted, but if it allows me to be free of the two Greens aboard, then so be it. But if the Greens attempt to leave their metal bodies at any time while my skirmishers are bringing you to the hangar, or if the organics attempt to escape and return here, you will all die. But if you cooperate, and the Greens remain inside their robot shells, you may go in peace. That is my offer to you. Disarm them."

While the original aliens held them, more skirmishers came forward; the metal tentacles that gripped the Titans shifted, allowing the newcomers to rip away the weapon mounts on the mechs. The aliens opened up the Titan storage compartments, and emptied all the extra gear and explosive charges. One of the skirmishers took the hacking disk from Surus.

"Two of the organics and their metal suits will stay behind for my people to study, so that we are ready, should one day we ever face your kind. Bring me that one." A tentacle pointed toward them. Rade wasn't sure who she was indicating. "And that one."

Two skirmishers moved forward. One of them held Shaw's mech, the other Harlequin's.

"Well that's not going to work," Rade said.

"What exactly do they mean by study?" Harlequin said.

"Dissection, most likely," Shaw said. "In my case, anyway. In yours, dismantlement, and the unraveling of your AI core."

"I see," Harlequin said. "Uh, Rade? You're not going to allow this to stand, are you?"

"Tell them they can't have any prisoners," Rade said. "Do it, Surus. Tell her we'll fight our way back here with our bare hands if we have to."

Surus converted Rade's words into a chain of hisses, moans, and pops.

Rade listened to the translation. Surus had ignored his request, making her own plea.

"Take me and the other Green," Surus said. "It is we who did this. We deserve whatever punishment you wish to inflict. Let the organics go. They are innocent in this matter."

"I have made my decision," Bethesda responded. "I will carry no Greens aboard. Take them from my presence!"

Rade and the others were dragged unceremoniously toward the entrance, while the mechs of Shaw and Harlequin were hauled toward the opposite side of the room.

Rade struggled against his binds. He fired his jumpjets, pulling the skirmisher that held him into the overhead. It gripped him tighter than ever.

A loud clacking and hissing sound came from an unsuited Hydra nearby. It had trained its weapon bar on Rade's Titan.

"Cease!" came the translation. "Or we will shoot you all down."

Rade stopped his struggles, and allowed the skirmisher to continue carrying him away. He realized a few of the others had activated their jets as well, but none of them had gotten very far, and they all followed Rade's example and surrendered.

"We're going to come back for you," Rade sent Shaw and Harlequin. "You know that, right? No matter what happens."

"I know," Shaw said.

twenty-four

"Surus," Rade said as he was led into the adjacent cavern. "How long would it take you to flow from the Titan and into the skirmisher that holds you? Could you do so unnoticed, and take control of its AI?"

"I wish I could," Surus said. "But their battle suits are shielded, as are the bulkheads of these passageways. And the armed Hydras with them are wearing anti-Phant belts. I'm afraid we are useless."

A breach seal opened and the Argonauts were led into a smaller adjoining passageway, carried by the robot skirmishers; several unsuited Hydras that wielded weapon bars in their forward appendages also escorted them.

"Shaw, update me," Rade said. He tried her point of view and saw that she was being carried through a passageway similar to his own, near the outskirts of the hull. The signal distorted digitally so that he wasn't sure how much longer he would remain in contact with her.

"I see you accessing my video feed," Shaw said. "Not much else to report other than what you picked up."

He glanced at the overhead map. The blue dots of

her and Harlequin were being carried into the outer passageways on the farther side of the ship.

More seals opened and closed as Rade and the others were led toward the hangar.

"How are we going to open those doors behind us?" Fret said. "Without a hacking device? Because even if we escape, which is doubtful—given that we have no weapons—we'll never get past those doors."

"Surus, can you flow into them in your natural form somehow and manually hack them?" Rade asked.

"No," Surus said. "When I said I couldn't flow into any of the bulkheads, I meant it."

"What about the weapons on some of these armed Hydras that are escorting us?" Rade said. "The ones without battle suits? Can we use those as laser drills maybe, to cut through the doors?"

"They will have biometric lockouts," Surus said. "It won't be so simple as pressing a trigger, assuming the fingers of your Titans could even fit around them. Which they can't."

Rade was growing desperate.

He tried breaking free from the binds that enwrapped his arms once more, but the metal tentacles held him tight. He considered firing his jumpjets, but that would only bring on an enemy attack. It wouldn't do if they were all mowed down before they could escape.

"Once they throw us out the hangar," Rade said. "If we jet back to the hull, how easy will it be to get back inside?"

"Assuming these skirmishers don't escort us part of the way, and that we don't come within the line of fire of any nearby hull turrets, once we return to the hull it will be impossible to enter without any cutting weapons," Surus said. "Given that they have taken away the hacking device. And the surgical lasers in your jumpsuits are far to weak to make a dent in their armor, if that's what you're thinking."

"What about if we return to the *Yarak* as Bethesda claims she will allow us to do," Rade said. "We can grab laser rifles and come back? Or grab another hacking device. I'm assuming you made a duplicate?"

"I suspect skirmishers will intercept long before we reach the hull," Surus said.

"Then escort us in with those golden mechs of yours!" Rade said.

"There aren't any aboard the *Yarak*," Azen said. "And those in the hives below are occupied at the moment, to say the least."

"There has to be a way. Come on guys, ideas."

"I'm out," TJ said.

"Nothing here," Lui said.

"Tahoe?" Rade tried.

"Sorry, boss," Tahoe replied.

Rade slumped in his jumpsuit. He switched to Shaw's point of view. The video feed froze and pixelated intermittently, but he saw that she was being carried through a hatch and into a wider compartment.

"Shaw, it looks like you and Harlequin are on your own for the moment," Rade sent. "Can you get away?"

"Not sure," her distorted voice came back. "Harlequin and I have been tossing ideas back and forth. We're planning on using our jumpjets at some point to catch the skirmishers off guard. But even if we can escape and disable our captors, we're basically trapped by all these breach seals that have closed behind us."

Rade shut his eyes. "Damn it to hell."

"We're nearing the hangar, according to the map," Lui said. "If we're going to escape, now's the time."

Something Shaw said tickled away at his subconscious. Jumpjets... catch the skirmishers off guard... a hint of an idea formed. It was a small hope, but a hope nonetheless.

"What if we fire our jumpjets strategically?" Rade said. "Say, to smash the skirmishers that hold us into the unsuited Hydras escorting us? I don't expect the skirmishers to release us, but at least we'll stun the escorts."

"We wouldn't get them all," Surus said. "Not in the first volley. There are too many of them."

"We could instruct our mechs to immediately fire subsequent thrusts in an attempt to stun the remainder," Rade said.

"We could try, yes," Surus said. "But even if we succeed, some of the Hydras will fire at us, either before or after we stun them. And even if we somehow miraculously manage to stun all the Hydras without taking losses, what then? We'll still be held by the skirmishers."

"Then we begin smashing the skirmishers against each other until they release us, too," Rade said. "And in between we continue bashing the Hydras until they stop moving."

"It just seems, mmm, too brute force, if you get my meaning," Surus said. "Strategic thinking beats brute force every time."

"I'm as much for strategic thinking as the next man," Rade said. "But this is all I have right now."

"And what about the breach seals?" Surus said. "There's still the small problem of not being able to open them once we're free."

"One step at a time, Surus," Rade said.

"It's too risky," Surus said. "Better to let the Hydra eject us from the ship, and then try to enter another way."

"No," Rade said. "If we allow them to throw us from the ship and into the waiting swarm of skirmishers outside, we're not coming back. We have to fight here. My Argonauts are aware of the risks."

"We're well aware," Bender said. "We live for this shit."

"I say we do it," Manic chimed in. "I'd rather have a slim chance than no chance at all. And I'd definitely rather go down fighting than leaving Shaw and Harlequin to die here."

"The rest of you, are you with me?" Rade asked.

"We're with you," came the chorus of replies.

Rade nodded to himself.

Of course I didn't have to ask.

"By the way, did anyone else notice that the new empress forgot to have our shields removed?" Manic pointed out.

"That will be useful once we break free of the skirmishers," Rade said. "But until then... Electron, coordinate with the other Titan AIs to fire the necessary jumpjets—aim to hit as many of the escorting Hydras as possible with each thrust."

"The jumpjet nozzles on some mechs are covered by the enwrapping tentacles," Electron said. "But I will account accordingly."

"Good," Rade said. "Let me know when you're ready."

"Ready," Electron replied a moment later.

"On my mark," Rade said.

"Wait," Azen said.

"Azen, we don't have time to wait." Rade glanced at the overhead map. They had reached the hanger bay area.

"Let me explain—" Azen said.

"Then explain!" Rade said. "Quickly!"

The outer hatch of the airlock leading to the hangar was opening.

"The virus," Azen said. "I mentioned it was communicable, didn't I?" He sounded gleeful.

"Yes..." Rade said.

"It appears the new empress neglected to inoculate all of her guards," Azen said. "One of those who escorts us is now under my control."

The inner hatch to the hangar opened as Rade processed the latest news.

"Well that makes things slightly easier," Rade said. "Okay. Slight modification to the plan."

He quickly explained it as they were brought into the hangar.

The last of the Titans was carried into the large compartment. Around them, inactive skirmishers floated close to the deck, secured in place with docking clamps, waiting for Hydras to board them and join the fray outside.

Most of the escort followed the prisoners into the bay, except for the one Hydra Azen had under his control. It lingered just beyond the outer hatch of the airlock, its weapon bar pointed ominously inside.

A member of the escorting Hydras pumped its bulbous body to turn back toward the airlock, apparently wondering why the other had not followed. It made a hissing and clacking sound.

"You there, what are you doing?" came the translation.

"Now, Electron," Rade said.

twenty-five

Rade relinquished control of the mech to the local AI.

Electron jetted the Titan sideways at full burn, traveling through the liquid methane to ram into the closest unsuited Hydra. Electron immediately fired its lateral jets after impact, crashing into a second Hydra just in front a moment later.

Around Rade, all of the other Titans were firing their jumpjets and ramming into Hydras.

"Go, Azen!" Rade said.

The alien convert by the door opened fire with its weapons bar. Invisible lasers targeted the Hydras stunned by the Titans one at a time. In moments, all ten had been hit.

"Pivot!" Rade ordered the Titans. "Get your backs toward the airlock." He didn't want any of the Titans to be facing the wrong way when the incoming lasers came.

Lateral jets fired throughout the squad, turning them around.

The convert turned its weapons on the skirmishers. Rade felt the grip loosen around his Titan when his captor was struck by one of those beams.

He heard a thud behind him; glancing in the

rearview camera feed he realized the airlock had sealed. Someone had decided to eject the Titans from the hangar bay, it seemed.

"Mount!" Rade said. He activated the magnetic mounts in his feet, gluing himself to the deck. The other Titans did the same.

The bay doors began to open.

Immediately the liquid methane gushed outside, drawing the floating corpses of the unsuited Hydras with it into the void.

The damaged skirmisher was partially drawn away from Rade's mech: it had only two tentacles wrapped around the Titan when the explosive decompression ended a moment later. The skirmisher slammed into the deck under the influence of the artificial gravity.

Rade shucked off the tentacles and stepped free.

"Azen, see if our friend can reseal the doors and depressurize the bay," Rade said.

The others sloughed off the damaged skirmishers. Bender unfolded his shield and used it as a bludgeon to repeatedly strike down on the particular skirmisher that had held him, until he had cracked open the outer shell and began to pummel the already dead Hydra pilot within.

"Help," Tahoe said.

Rade glanced at his friend's mech; one skirmisher had survived relatively unscathed, and remained tightly gripping Tahoe's Titan. It was bringing its laser turrets to bear on Bender...

"Bender!" Rade warned.

Bender noticed the threat in time and swiveled his shield toward the skirmisher, defending against the laser attack.

The skirmisher shifted its tentacles slightly to push itself off of Tahoe's Titan, and then it aimed its weapons directly down on Tahoe's mech.

Rade was only two meters away; he fired Electron's jumpjets and closed the gap, ramming into the two of them. As all three of them fell to the floor, Rade wrapped his large steel hands around the turrets and bent them backwards.

When he struck the deck, Bender and Fret joined in, and together they managed to wrench the skirmisher off of Tahoe's Titan. Those tentacles flailed about frantically, striking each of them in turn.

The bay doors closed, and the methane began misting into the compartment, thanks to Azen's convert outside. The mist condensed on the bulkheads as the atmospheric pressure increased, and as critical mass was reached, the mist became a flood.

The liquid levels rose, and the combatants splashed about the deck.

The skirmisher abruptly ceased all motion and toppled backwards. Behind it stood Sprint. The shield edge of Surus' mech was held outward like a blade, the tip coated in black blood where it had penetrated the skirmisher's outer shell.

"To the airlock," Rade said as the liquid methane reached the waist of his mech.

He waded toward the inner hatch.

"My convert friend is going to lose his access privileges soon, I think," Azen said. "We must hurry."

"Can't he fill this bucket up any faster?" Bender said as the liquid reached their necks.

"Unfortunately, no," Azen replied.

Finally the compartment filled entirely, and the inner and outer airlocks opened. The convert was waiting patiently outside.

Rade heard a simpering whine then, and was reminded of a begging dog.

"Hello, masters," came the translation. "Tell me what I must do to please you."

Rade shuddered, remembering his own words and behavior when a Black had a taken over his mind once before. Phants didn't mess around when they took control of a subject.

Rade had kept his headlamps active all that time, but it was time to go dark.

"Headlamps off, Argonauts," Rade said. "LIDAR burst mode. We're coming for you, Shaw."

His view went dark as the familiar white wireframes overlaid his vision.

He momentarily switched to Shaw's point of view. Her headlamp was still on. Skirmishers were strapping her to a large operating table.

"We tried to use our jumpjets," Shaw said, her voice distorting. "Like you. We smashed our captors into the bulkheads, and we fought, really fought. But it didn't matter... more of them swarmed us, and they managed to strap our mechs into these giant hospital beds. Skirmishers have come in... they've surrounded Harlequin."

"They're attempting to cut me out of the Titan with their lasers," Harlequin said.

"Don't they understand the pressure of their liquid methane environment will crush your jumpsuit?" Rade said.

"Obviously not," Harlequin said. "Either that, or they don't care."

"It's probably better this way," Shaw said. "I'd prefer not to be dissected alive."

"They're not going to dissect you," Rade said. "We're coming, damn it. You have to last a little longer."

"We'll do what we can," Shaw said.

"I won't let them harm her," Harlequin said. "I promise you, Rade."

"Thank you, Harlequin," Rade said. But considering that they were drilling through Harlequin's mech at that very moment, Rade didn't have much faith in his ability to uphold that promise.

He glanced at the overhead map and saw Shaw's position in relation to their own. She was close to the outer hull, on the far side of the ship. Some areas between here and there were not filled out, but if the layout was the same as the previous Hydra vessel they had boarded, likely Rade and the others would be able to stay within the outer hull region, and the relative safety of the passageways there, which would help to funnel the alien attacks into something manageable.

"Submarine mode," Rade said. "Until we make contact."

"That will be shortly," Azen said. "The convert still has access to the ship's AI for the time being. I'm able to see the locations of all the other units. I'll translate that to your own overhead maps."

On the HUD map, Rade saw red dots approaching from the passageways on either side. Hundreds of them.

"Damn," Rade said.

"How do we know it's real?" Fret said. "Maybe the AI is purposely feeding the convert misinformation, just to scare us."

Rade considered that. "No, I think it's real. There's no need to scare: the Empress has an army to throw against us, remember. Let's move!"

Rade activated the turbines in his fins and accelerated forward. He let Bender and Tahoe pull ahead in the passageway. The converted Hydra stayed just behind him, in the middle of the group, and was followed by the remaining Titans.

It didn't take long until first contact.

"Tangos spotted," Bender said.

"Walker mode!" Rade said. "Deploy shields. Let's protect our only weapon."

Rade, Tahoe, Lui and Bender placed the shields they held in both hands side by side, forming a protective barrier in the front. The outermost edges of those shields were frayed from previous damage, but hopefully the material would last a little longer.

Fret, Manic, Surus, and TJ handled the rear. The Hydra convert remained sandwiched between them.

"We're taking laser fire on our shields," Lui said.

"Azen, get our friend to take out the tangos," Rade said. "And make sure it remains behind the cover we're providing."

Rade felt the Hydra partially press against the back side of his mech—the inner actuators of his cocoon translated the feeling by pressing against his jumpsuit. He glanced up, and saw that the alien kept most of its body hidden behind the shield. It seemed to be carefully lifting that horizontal weapons bar it carried in its appendages over the top edge; as it did so, Rade felt the pressure shift against him as it placed more of its weight against his Titan.

"Feels like it's humping us," Bender said.

"I think it's opening fire," Lui said. "The tangos are ceasing their approach ahead, and drifting down toward the deck."

Rade zoomed in. When the LIDAR updated, the four wireframes of the tangos indeed seemed on a downward trend.

"Got tangos on drag," Fret announced.

The Hydra swiveled around and moved behind Fret and the others instead, and fired once more.

"Tangos down," Fret said.

"Hmm," Manic said. "This is working surprisingly well. Methinks that these Hydra are going to start incorporating shields into their arsenals very soon."

The Titans switched back to submarine mode and continued forward, making their way toward the positions where Shaw and Harlequin were taken, as indicated on the overhead maps. Shaw told him the skirmishers had already broken through the outer shell of Harlequin's mech, and that he had ceased transmitting.

Rade and the others kept encountering more tangos, and their advance was delayed longer and longer as more of the Hydras successively came at them.

They finally reached a breach seal; according to the map, on the other side the passageway was filled to the brim with tangos. At least a hundred, spread out in a long line. Behind the Titans, a similar number of tangos was coming at them from the rear.

"What do we do?" Fret asked.

"All we can do," Rade said. "We open it and continue forward. Assuming the convert still has access. Azen?"

The Hydra moved toward the seal; the hatch opened, but a moment later a lucky shot smashed into the weapon bar it held. The creature went limp, drifting toward the deck. Its maw appendages moved slowly, and it emitted a weak siren sound.

"I'm sorry... masters," came the translation, and then it died.

"Now what?" Fret said.

twenty-six

Rade and the others stooped behind their diminishing shields, the borders slowly becoming smaller as the lasers ate away at the edges. The Titans closed ranks, tightening their formation as their protection shrank.

"We can't do this all day, you know that right?" Fret said.

"Update me, Shaw..." Rade said.

"They've completely cut Harlequin from the mech," Shaw said. "His jumpsuit has caved from the pressure. He's definitely offline."

"Damn it," Bender said. "These bitches are going to pay."

"Harlequin survived the immense pressure before," Manic said. "He'll survive again."

"If he's lucky," Fret said.

"He'll be lucky," Bender said.

"On a more positive note," Shaw said. "Your attack has drawn the skirmishers away. They've left me here alone. I'm trying to escape."

"Keep me updated," Rade said.

He moved lower as a large upper portion of his left shield broke away.

"More guards are coming under my control," Azen

said.

"How far away are they?" Rade asked.

"Some of them are in the midst of the enemy," Azen said. "I'm turning them against their brethren now."

"The incoming fire just ceased," Lui said.

Rade glanced at the white wireframes in the distance, and momentarily switched to full LIDAR mode. Chaos and confusion seemed to be sowing through the ranks as Hydras and skirmishers turned upon one another. But then the dissenters seemed to have fallen, and the remainder aimed their lasers at Rade and the others once more.

He switched back to LIDAR burst mode and took cover.

"Azen, will any more of them be joining us?" Rade asked. He had forgotten the qualms he had with the Greens controlling the Hydra. Now he *wanted* them all under Azen's command. With Shaw and his brothers in danger, the morality of the situation was thrown to the side. She and the Argonauts were more important than the freedom of any alien race. It was wrong to feel that way, he knew, but he couldn't help it.

It was a terrible thought, knowing he would subjugate an entire race if it meant saving her. And yet there it was.

Rade dismissed the notion. The guilt didn't matter. Freeing her and Harlequin was the only thing he cared about at the moment.

"I believe more of them will be converted, yes," Azen replied. "And I take back my earlier comment about Bethesda neglecting to inoculate all of her soldiers. I'm starting to believe that the new empress did in fact do so. She wouldn't have been that incompetent."

"Then how are you able to control more of them?" Fret said.

"The retrovirus is mutating," Azen said.

"Mutating?" Fret asked.

"Yes," Azen replied. "I created it to be highly-communicable, remember. I believe it mutated as it was shared among her staff and closest advisors. They thought they could inoculate against it. They were wrong. It could have several variants by now. They'll have to create new vaccines, and cure those with the existing infections. It will be too late by then."

Rade and the others hid behind their ever-diminishing shields, waiting. It wasn't long before Azen announced that more had joined their side. Azen had the tangos turn amongst themselves once more, and this time the converts proved the survivors. There were only three of them left standing in the front quarter, and four the rear quarter. That was enough to provide the escort Rade and the others needed.

"I'm getting similar ratios all across the ship," Azen said. "The uprising is spreading. I don't think we'll be facing too much resistance, going forward."

"I'm out," Shaw announced. "A Hydra just came up to me and freed me. I've loaded up Harlequin into my passenger seat. I abandoned his Titan: the mech's AI core was sliced in half when the skirmishers penetrated the cockpit. It's gone." She paused. "We just met up with more Hydras... they were waiting outside to escort me. This is so strange."

"We'll rendezvous with you shortly," Rade said. He glanced at Sprint. "Thank you, Azen."

The party switched into submarine mode and proceeded forward. They encountered further resistance of course, but the Hydra converts dealt with the tangos readily. It helped that more Hydras often switched to their side in the middle of the battle.

The Hydras with them readily opened any breach seals along the way. Some of them had begun to lose access to the hatches, so Azen simply cycled through them until they found a Hydra that still could open them.

"One of the ship's main officers just fell under my control," Azen said. "The chief engineer, I believe. I've had it lock out most of the crew from the AI, except himself, and those with us. We should have no more problems opening the breach seals."

It took about ten minutes and three more short clashes to reach Shaw and her escort, which had grown to eight Hydras; the combined group then turned around to head back the way they had come. In total they now had an escort of twenty Hydras: five skirmishers, and fifteen unsuited Hydras.

There seemed only token resistance on the return trip, prompting Rade to ask: "How much of the ship do you have under control?"

"Only twenty-five percent," Azen said. "But the new empress has recalled most of her skirmishers to defend the throne room. Hydras have been converting throughout the ship, and I've been sending as many of them as I can against her. A little diversion to aid in our escape."

"Good," Rade said.

Traveling in submarine mode, Manic was on point for the Titans, following the ten Hydras that led the way.

"Hey Bender," Manic said.

Bender ignored him.

"Bender," Manic pressed.

"*What?*" Bender said.

"See the way the Hydras are whipping their

tentacles and pumping their bodies?" Manic said.

"So, bitch?" Bender said.

"That's what I'm going to do to your ass when we get back," Manic said. He sounded like he was struggling to contain a chortle.

"Really," Bender said. His voice was the epitome of annoyance. "You're going to pump my ass. And whip me." It wasn't a question, but a statement.

"Oh yeah," Manic said. "You're going to be my new bitch."

"Boss, do I really have to wait until we get back before I can mess up this mofo?" Bender asked.

"Manic, cut the shit," Rade said.

"Sorry," Manic said. "But come on Bender, you have to admit, you're looking forward to it."

"See," Bender said. "This is what I was saying. Manic claims he likes women. But we all know where his true inclinations lie."

"Hey, I admit it, I'm gay," Manic said. "But I like to eat pussy."

"*What?*" Bender said. "That makes no sense. Goddamn, Manic, if you don't shut your pie hole, I swear I'm going to—"

Twin explosions rocked the passageway, coming from both the forward and rear vectors.

The shockwaves sent Rade's Titan reeling. He spun three times before coming to a halt against a nearby bulkhead, hitting hard. When he recovered, he saw that portions of the passageway ahead and behind had widened into craters, with the deck, overhead, and bulkheads compressed outward from the explosive forces.

The ranks of the Hydras had been devastated: Rade spotted eight of them drifting lifelessly in the passageway, clouds of blood oozing from their flanks.

There were body parts everywhere: mangled appendages, severed tentacles...

"It seems the AI found a way to overload the power cores in the skirmisher units," Azen said. "To use them as bombs. They've blown up all the skirmishers with us. I'm pulling back the remaining skirmisher units in our path to give us the necessary space."

"Check in, people," Rade said. He glanced at the team's vitals. Everyone was green. No, wait.

One of the Argonauts was edging toward red.

"Manic," Rade said. "Are you all right? Manic!"

Rade accelerated toward him, but Bender beat him to the Titan. On the LIDAR band, Rade saw several twisted pieces of metal protruding from the front portion of the cockpit.

"Manic—" Rade tried again.

"Got shrapnel in my chest," Manic replied, sounding strained. "The fragments sealed both the breaches in my suit, and the perforations in my cockpit, apparently, so I still have pressure... but... man, it hurts."

"Can you move your Titan?" Rade asked.

"That's a negative with a big N," Manic said. "The AI core is fried. My Titan is useless. Sorry, brothers. You're going to have to leave me."

"Don't get melodramatic," Rade said. "No one's leaving you."

"I'll carry him." Tahoe came forward.

"Get the *fuck* back!" Bender said. "I got him!" Softer: "You're going to be all right Manic." He positioned his Titan on top and activated the magnetic mounts in his chest to secure Manic's mech. "Well let's go! We have to get him out of here to give him treatment."

"Azen," Rade said. "Get the surviving Hydras back in the middle. We have to protect them. Bender, you and Manic join them."

The three surviving Hydras assumed positions in the middle of the group, and Fret led the way forward. The party members passed by the dead bodies in the cratered area and continued toward the hangar.

They were nearly there when Fret announced: "Tangos blocking our path."

"Walker mode," Rade said. The group transformed and placed their shields together.

"We just lost two Hydras," Azen said. "Lucky shots."

"Damn it, protect the last one!" Rade said. "*Carefully* fire back at the attackers from cover!"

"They're right in front of the hangar," Fret said. "Damn our bad luck."

"It's not bad luck," Shaw said. "The empress obviously planned this. She wanted to lull us into a false sense of security, make us believe we could actually escape, and then close the noose just when freedom seemed ours."

"And I thought I was the pessimistic one," Fret commented.

"Tangos on the rear," TJ said.

The last Hydra was able to take down a few of the attackers, but they kept coming. A long, endless stream of them. Shields were beginning to fail across the group, forcing members to retreat to the center area with Bender and the Hydra.

"I want the bodies of those two Hydras placed on point and drag!" Rade said. "We need to augment our shields before it's too late!"

And so the Titans moved one of the bodies to the front, and another to the rear, and they used them to add to their shielding. Unfortunately, the corpses didn't decrease the intensity of the lasers all that much. The beams mostly just passed through the bodies.

"Why aren't the attackers converting, Azen?" Rade said after the team had dug in for at least a minute.

"I don't know," Azen said. "Perhaps the doctors found a new vaccine already. Or the mutated strain doesn't effect these."

"Well it's pretty obvious the empress sent units that weren't affected by the retrovirus!" TJ said.

"Gah!" Shaw said.

"What is it?" Rade asked. His heart had leaped to his throat with fear for her.

"I have a big hole in the center of my shield," Shaw said. "The laser nearly drilled completely through my cockpit. I have to drop out."

Rade was relieved she wasn't injured.

She retreated, leaving him to defend the front rank alone. Everyone else had rearranged to stand in single-file behind him, with TJ the only one guarding the rear quarter.

His own shield couldn't take much more of this.

"Wait, one of them just turned," Azen said. "He pilots a skirmisher. I think I've found the secret the AI uses to overload their power sources. I believe I can detonate the unit."

"Do it!" Rade said.

The shockwave came a moment later.

Ahead, all of the tangos had been eliminated. For the moment.

"Let's go!" Rade said.

He switched to submarine mode and accelerated toward the hanger. Everyone else followed his example, save for TJ on drag, who bounded forward in walker mode so that he could use his shields to protect the party from the rear tangos. He used his jumpjets to increase his bounding speed.

Rade plowed through the cratered section. The airlock leading to the hangar had been blown completely open—both the inner and outer hatches had caved.

"Well, at least we don't have to worry about whether the Hydra convert with us still has access to the hangar," Fret said.

"But we do have to worry," Surus said. "Because what if it can't open the external bay doors?"

"Then we shoot *through* them." Rade transformed into walker mode as he arrived. He and Shaw careful entered behind the remnants of their shields. There were still a few skirmisher units lying inactive on the deck, but otherwise the area proved clear.

Rade regarded the offline skirmishers warily. "Stay back, people. They could blow at any time. Azen, does the Hydra convert have access?"

"Negative," Azen replied.

"Then tell it to start shooting at the doors," Rade replied.

It had only just started shooting when the skirmishers detonated.

Rade spun backwards, slamming into a nearby bulkhead. An alarm sounded in his cockpit.

"Warning," Electron said. "Hull integrity fifteen percent. Warning."

He was already being sucked outward. The explosions had torn open the hangar bay doors.

Rade plunged into space and switched back to the visual light band as the zero gravity made his stomach do flips. Around him the liquid methane boiled away into a dissipating mist. Behind, the outflow continued from the hull, forming a spreading yellow fog. From it emerged his fellow Titans.

"Warning," Electron repeated. "Hull integrity fifteen percent."

"Are we close to a hull breach?" Rade asked.

"No," Electron replied.

"Then stop the warnings!" Rade said.

The Hydra convert floated near him, a black, lifeless husk.

Rade glanced at the team's vitals, starting with Shaw. Everyone was still in the green, thankfully. Excluding Manic.

Flashes came from deep space around him. The other Hydra ships were out there, some of them still fighting.

"I have some good news," Azen transmitted. "Incredibly, the new empress has yet to destroy the *Yarak*. I'm marking its position on your overhead maps."

Rade accepted the mark request. A waypoint appeared.

"Use your Jumpjets, Argonauts!" Rade said. "We make for the *Yarak!*"

Rade thrust toward the faraway ship, which was a mere dot among the countless points of light out there. The other Titans followed his lead. The gas giant floated below them in the distance. Its influence made their mechs respond sluggishly even at that range.

"Got skirmishers coming on our tails," TJ said.

twenty-seven

"Azen, do you have control of anything out here?" Rade asked.

"There are a few skirmishers, yes," Azen said. "I've called out to them, but they're too far away to be of much help at the moment. They were engaged in quelling those warlords who refused to fall in line and follow Bethesda, and as such the closest is about five minutes distant."

"Argonauts, form a straight line," Rade said. "TJ's shields are the only thing protecting most of us at the moment."

"Uh," TJ said from his drag position. "My shields aren't going to last much longer."

Rade spotted a debris field up ahead, where a Hydra warship had been destroyed.

"Electron," Rade said. "Coordinate with the other Titan AIs. Alter our course to bring us safely to that debris field."

"By safely," Electron said. "You mean so that TJ's shields provide optimal coverage to the rest of the group during the journey there?"

"Yes, that's what I mean," Rade said.

The Titans jetted toward the debris. Clumps of pebble-sized fragments struck Electron's hull. It sounded like hail: while there was no atmosphere in the cockpit itself at the moment, while operating in deep space environments the mech was set up to transmit external vibrations directly to his helmet speakers.

"Argonauts, look for Titan-sized fragments to use as shields," Rade said. "Preferably from the hull, where the armor is thickest."

As Rade entered deeper into the debris, he spotted the blackened corpses of Hydras floating among the wreckage. The metal pieces were particularly big here.

"That one," Rade said, eyeing a potential candidate. "Analyze, Electron."

"It appears to be a hull fragment," Electron said. "It should provide the shielding you are after."

"Take me to it," Rade said.

Electron carried Rade to the large fragment. The other Titans remained close behind, so that TJ could continue to shield him and the others.

Rade placed his hands behind the material and activated the magnets, securing himself.

"Electron, place me beside TJ," Rade said. "We'll help shield the others as they grab fragments."

Rade moved into placed beside TJ; the collective shield grew as more and more of the Titans found appropriate hull pieces and joined Rade and TJ. The surrounding debris also helped provide cover against the lasers of the incoming skirmishers.

When everyone had grabbed a piece of the wreckage, including TJ, Rade gave the order to proceed from the debris field, and the group made their way toward the *Yarak* once more. They kept their shields placed between themselves and the enemy. Rade glanced often at his overhead map to gauge the enemy distance; he didn't want to allow the pursuing skirmishers too near lest the units explode.

It was at that point Manic's vitals flatlined.

"Manic?" Bender said. "Manic!"

Their injured brother didn't answer.

"I'm leaving my cockpit to issue emergency resuscitation," Bender said. "Juggernaut is taking over for me."

Rade pressed his lips together—he wanted to be the one to help Manic. But Bender was the closest—he *was* carrying Manic's mech, after all. And he did have corpsman training, like Rade, and so was just as qualified to revive him as anyone.

"I'll shield them," Tahoe said.

Rade momentarily switched to Bender's viewpoint and watched Juggernaut release the debris fragment while continuing to hold onto Manic's Titan. Tahoe jetted beside them and grabbed the fragment, placing it alongside his own to provide protection for Bender and Manic.

Bender repositioned Manic's Titan, swiveling the mech around. Via Juggernaut, he pulled at the damaged cockpit hatch for several moments before at last prying it open—Rade was worried that releasing the cockpit would dislodge some of the shrapnel embedded in Manic's jumpsuit and depressurize it. But according to Rade's HUD, Manic's internal suit pressure remained stable. That was a good sign.

Bender opened his own cockpit and jetted out in his jumpsuit, grabbing Manic. Then he thrust back to Juggernaut and carried the motionless Argonaut inside, sealing the cockpit behind him. The inner actuators wouldn't activate, not with two people inside the cockpit, Rade knew; Juggernaut would remain in control until Manic was well enough to climb into the external passenger seat. Bender began flooding the compartment with atmosphere so that he could begin the delicate task of removing the jumpsuit and stabilizing Manic.

Rade returned to his own point of view. There was nothing more he could do for them at the moment.

We have to get back to the ship.

"Some of the skirmishers under my control are finally coming into range," Azen said. "I'm dispatching them toward the pursuers. That should buy us some more time."

Rade overlaid the thermal band over the visual spectrum to see better, and saw red forms all around him. Several of those forms were coming in from the righthand side of his vision: he realized those were the skirmishers Azen was referring to. They began decelerating as they closed to intercept the pursuers. Flashes erupted as laser fire was exchanged. One of the enemies detonated, taking down two of the newcomers.

"They really like that new exploding trick they've learned," Shaw said.

"I don't think the skirmishers have any choice over the matter," Azen said. "Bethesda has sent specific instructions to the AIs of the battle suits, instructing them to explode when they are in range of enemy units, whether the actual Hydra pilots within like it or not."

"I wouldn't want to serve in her ranks," Fret commented.

As they approached the *Yarak*, Lui reported: "I'm detecting a massive amount of laser fire directed toward the Phant ship. Looks like several Hydra vessels are attacking her. I suggest breaking off our approach, boss. Unless you want to be hit in the crossfire!"

Rade hesitated, but when he saw the profusion of beams appearing on the overhead map, lasers that were invisible on the visual spectrum, he made up his mind. "Break off the approach."

"Apparently Bethesda changed her mind about allowing us to return to the *Yarak*," Lui said.

"Guess she wasn't too happy that we took her prisoners," TJ said.

"I think she was more pissed off that Azen's retrovirus mutated," Tahoe said.

"Wouldn't you be?" Shaw said.

"Ohhhh shit," Lui said.

"What is—" But Tahoe cut off mid sentence.

Rade's gaze drifted toward the Phant ship above him. Or rather, where the skull-shaped vessel used to reside. In its place was an expanding globe of debris, composed of countless dispersing streaks similar to an exploding firework.

Rade couldn't help the sinking feeling in his stomach.

"There goes our way out of this," Fret said.

The skirmishers continued to pursue behind them. They had broken ahead of Azen's converts, it seemed; either that, or destroyed them all.

"What now?" Tahoe said.

"Maybe more of them will be converted to Azen's control?" Fret asked hopefully.

"Eventually, yes," Azen said. "But who can say how many, or when? With the *Yarak* lost, we must proceed toward the homeworld, and make our way toward one of the sub-hives!"

"Are you nuts?" Tahoe said. "You want us to pilot mechs into a gas giant? If you think the controls are sluggish now, wait until we're irreparably caught by the gravity field. We won't have enough thrust to change our descent worth a damn."

"It's our only choice," Azen said. "I'm instructing one of the sub-hives to alter orbit to intercept us. I'm asking my brothers to send a few of the golden mechs in aid. I believe they will help, given everything we have done for them. In the meantime, I'm relaying the necessary velocity vectors, and the trajectory we must join for the best possible chance of reaching the sub-hive."

Rade accepted the coordinates. "Switch to the new trajectory, Argonauts. I'm not big on flying into a gas giant, either, but this is the best option we have at the moment."

Rade had Electron engage the thrusters to accelerate on the appropriate velocity vector; the Titan descended toward the gas giant, and the others fell in behind him. He held the debris toward the pursuing skirmishers and their lasers the whole time.

He glanced at Manic's vitals. Bender had managed to stabilize him. Rade was relieved.

"Good work, Bender," Rade said.

"Thank you," Bender replied.

"Is he conscious?" Tahoe asked.

"Hey guys," Manic said, sounding weak.

"Don't know why you're congratulating Bender," Fret said. "All he's done is awakened Manic to die with the rest of us."

"I wouldn't have it any other way," Manic said. "I proudly die with my brothers."

"We're not going to die," Rade said. "Not if I can help it."

"Come on, Argonauts," Shaw said. "Where's your famous fighting spirit? You were MOTHs, once. You still are, at heart. So fight to the bitter end, like you all taught me to do. Fight, goddamnit!"

Rade was never prouder of her than in that moment.

"We must make directional changes," Azen said. "Link the thrust of your units to Sprint. Surus will guide us in."

In moments, everyone had done so.

"Not sure how much guiding you can do at this point," Lui said. "We're fairly close to the giant right now. Our jumpjets will only shift our orbits by minuscule amounts."

"Minuscule is all I need," Azen said. "As I told you, I'm instructing the nearest sub-hive to intercept, energy sphere and all. We will make it."

"Unless one of Bethesda's ships manages to shoot it down before we arrive," Fret said.

"*We'll make it*," Shaw insisted, repeating Azen's words.

"Seems Bethesda is worried about that very thing," Lui said. "Check out our six. There are more skirmishers than ever on our tail. And we've got no way to fire back. It's a good thing Rade stopped to pick up that debris. But it's not going to last for much longer. Not for all of us, anyway. Those of us in the rearmost sections are taking the most heat. If we could somehow spread out the damage, we could make it last for forty-five minutes. Or an hour maybe."

"I don't understand it, this is their hull armor, what the hell!" Fret said. "Supposed to be Tech Class IV!"

"Keep in mind, the hull pieces were already fairly damaged from the original explosion that created them," TJ said. "That happens when a ship blows up."

"Azen," Rade said. "Redirect us into a line as part of your trajectory updates. Single file. I want our mechs essentially touching. I want the piece of debris held by the Titan on drag capable of shielding us all."

Azen did so, and they slowly moved into place as they continued the descent toward the giant red and orange ball below.

When everyone had formed a tight, long line, as per Rade's instructions, with Fret bringing up the rear, Rade said: "Fret, we're going to rotate out that piece of debris you're using to protect us all. When its integrity gets low, let it drift away directly behind you. Then the next person in line will pass his or her debris fragment forward. We will continue doing that as each hull piece loses its effectiveness."

And so they did.

"You know, I'm kind of wondering why Bethesda hasn't targeted us with the heavy lasers aboard her starship," Tahoe said.

"Even Tech Class IV technology has limits when targeting objects as small as mechs," Azen said. "Especially early Tech Class IV. Besides, it looks like she has her hands full defending against the warlords who refused to accept her. Not to mention the little uprising we've created aboard her own ship."

Half an hour passed. The team went through nearly half of those hull pieces. Meanwhile below, the gas giant consumed almost everything. Azen issued the occasional burst of thrust from the mechs, but it had little change on the trajectory as far as Rade could tell. Propellant levels were low squad-wide.

"Sky diving into a gas giant in a mech," Fret said. "I can scratch that off my bucket list."

"Never been on mine," Tahoe said.

"Electron, how are we doing on the heat and radiation levels?" Rade asked.

"This gas giant is on the lower end of the spectrum, in terms of mass and therefore radiation emission," Electron replied. "So heat and radiation levels are well within hull tolerances. The levels will remain so during the duration of our descent. However, pressure levels are what we really have to worry about."

"I don't think we're going to fall that far," Rade said. "Have a look at what just arrived."

Below, from the whirling clouds, a Phant sub-hive emerged. The spherical energy field parted the red and orange gases; the bottom portion of the sphere was covered in that series of tall parallel plates composing the main city, and around the lower rim of the energy field were the wind turbines and lightning rods that generated power from the never-ending storm that roiled within the planet's atmosphere.

The sub-hive was moving very slowly, however... obviously struggling against the immense gravitational forces to reach a higher orbit. It was definitely moving in the same direction as the Argonauts, and close to the same speed, because though the team continued the descent, they didn't appear to be getting any closer to it.

"I just made a quick calculation," Lui said. "Our trajectory doesn't line up. If they don't slow down, we're not going to make it."

"And if they *do* slow down, they'll drop into the atmosphere," Azen said.

"Then I don't see how we're going to dock with them," Lui said.

"Have some faith," Azen said.

"At this point, I'm all faithed out," Lui replied.

"As are we all," Fret added.

Rade saw them first. "What are those dots?"

twenty-eight

Rade zoomed in on the sub-hive. He saw skirmishers flitting to and fro within the energy sphere, leaping between the internal grav channels that provided transportation throughout the interior. In the midst of the alien units were golden mechs; some of the latter had emerged from the energy field and were headed slowly toward the party. Two skirmishers were with them—obviously converts.

"Finally," Tahoe said. "The Greens have come."

It took another ten minutes for the golden mechs to reach them. There were only four. The two skirmisher converts continued past the Argonauts to engage the pursuers.

"The Greens say we are to link together completely," Azen transmitted.

"Activate magnetic mounts," Rade ordered. "Secure yourself to the Titan in front of you."

When that was done, the four golden mechs grabbed the long chain of Titans and guided them in. Meanwhile, they released particle beams at the pursuing skirmishers behind them, and intermittently activated energy shields to provide what protection they could to the descending party, though for the most part the latest debris fragment Fret's Titan held was enough. Rade was familiar with the weaponry aboard those mechs, as he had once had the opportunity to pilot them, with Surus in fact.

"Ah, my golden mechs, I've missed you in the long time we've been parted," Lui said.

"It seems like so long ago when we last got a chance to fly them," Tahoe said.

"It was *long ago*," Fret said. "The First Alien War. The war that introduced us to the Phants. Sometimes I think it would have been for the best if we never traveled through that Slipstream."

"You can't change history, my friend," Lui said. "What's done is done."

Rade thought of the time travel device Surus had captured in their last mission, from the destroyed homeworld of the Xaranth, the "gatorbeetles." He wasn't so sure that history could not be changed anymore. Of course, the device was currently unusable as it needed a matching Acceptor unit.

Not that any of that was relevant to their current situation, of course. Still, Lui's words made him think. If they ever found the matching Acceptor, could he save the brothers who had fallen at Gaul Prime, and in other missions? And more importantly, would he actually go through with the act of saving them, given the potentially disastrous impact on the timeline?

He hoped he never faced such a choice.

The golden mechs deposited them safely inside the energy sphere; as the squad passed through, Rade felt the artificial gravity take hold immediately.

The mechs dropped them ten meters above one of the larger floating platforms, capable of fitting all of the Titans. They were in a grav channel that pulled them toward the platform, so the Argonauts released their magnetic mounts to separate from the chain they'd formed, and fired their jumpjets to cushion their fall.

After Rade landed, he glanced up to watch the golden mechs leap between grav channels; the units appeared to be making their way toward the ceiling of the energy sphere.

"Where are they going?" Tahoe asked.

"To intercept the skirmishers that were on our tail," Azen replied.

The four mechs penetrated the sphere and proceeded away from the sub-hive. A swarm of black shapes streaked through the sky toward them.

"I don't remember the jumpjets on those golden units being so powerful," Lui said. "I seem to recall something about a charged-based system that allowed for ten second jumps, with thirty seconds downtime required between each use."

"We've made some modifications in the fifteen years since you last used them," Azen said. "In any case, forget them. We must make our way to the Acceptor and evacuate before the sub-hive falls. Already the new empress has brought more of the enemy warships to bear."

Overhead, it seemed to Rade that more of those pronged-shaped warships had indeed maneuvered into position, apparently intent on destroying this one sub-hive that had so brazenly chosen to expose itself by flying above the clouds.

"Wish we could help in the defense," Rade said.

"I do, too," Azen said. "It's unfortunate that the new empress decided to strip away our weapons. This way. Follow Surus, she will lead you onto the appropriate grav channels."

And so they followed Surus as she moved from channel to channel; the shifting gravity conduits carried them on the different paths leading through the interior of the sphere. Everyone had low propellant levels, but thankfully the small spurts required to jet between grav channels didn't use too much of their precious fuel.

Above, skirmishers breached the energy dome, and began firing at the plates that composed the hive. More golden mechs intercepted.

"So this is how it feels when a homeworld is about to fall," Lui said.

"Not good," Tahoe replied.

"What's going to happen once we leave?" Shaw asked. "And all the hives fall?"

"The surviving Greens will come back to this world eventually," Azen said. "And find a way to save those of our kind who have become trapped on the surface of the gas giant. We'll find a way. If it means spending a millennium blasting away the gases from the atmosphere, we'll do it."

"But you'll lose all that geronium..." TJ said.

"There comes a point when the lives of your comrades matter more than your food source," Azen said.

"I can agree with that," TJ said.

Surus led them between two of the resinous plates, and the Titans passed by the hundreds of decagonal cells contained within them. Rade didn't see any of the jellyfish-like creatures, nor the green mists of the Phants, as were typical to those cells. The place was a ghost town.

Surus jetted forward, landing inside one of the cells. The other Titans landed in cells nearby.

Surus pointed down. "The Acceptor is on that platform below."

Rade looked down. He saw a massive globe of

green mist floating between the two plates. It had to be thousands of Phants grouped together.

"I don't see a platform," Tahoe said. "All I see is Phants."

"It's there, buried by the Greens," Surus said. "They're evacuating, you see. Every Acceptor in this hive will look the same."

"So what do we do?" TJ said.

"We could force our way past," Fret suggested. "The EM emitters in our jumpsuits will shove them aside."

"If you do that, you'll force some of them into gravity channels that will take them well away from the Acceptor," Surus replied. "They could have difficulty returning."

"No," Tahoe said. "We should wait in line like the rest of them."

"What line?" TJ said. "There's no line down there. It's just a chaotic mass of Greens."

"I say to hell with the Green bitches," Bender said. "Manic needs immediate attention. As does Harlequin. I say we shove our way past."

"Azen, ask the Phants if they'll be gracious enough to let us pass," Rade said. "Considering everything we've done for them."

Azen replied several moments later. "I asked. You can see the results below."

"None of them moved out of the way..." Rade said.

"I know."

"They steered their hive here to help us and now they won't let us through?" Rade pressed.

"The senior command steered the hive," Azen said. "Not the common citizens, who you see below. Needless to say, none of the senior command have evacuated their posts. Whereas the common citizens..."

Rade glanced upward. More of the skirmishers were penetrating the energy sphere.

"Well boss?" Fret said. "You have to make a choice. Disperse a couple of Phants to make room for our passage, keeping in mind that most of them probably won't evacuate in time anyway, or we wait here until the Acceptor clears. The hive will probably fall before then, killing us all."

Before Rade could decide, one of the skirmishers flew between the pair of plates the party currently resided within, distracting him as it tore its way downward, ripping huge gashes in the resinous structures with its tentacles; the skirmisher passed fifty meters away to the right. A golden mech pursued it.

Rade made up his mind. He wasn't going to risk losing more of his Argonauts. "We're going to shove our way through the Phants. If it means some of them have to die, then so be it. I'm sorry, Azen."

"Hell yeah!" Bender said. "That's my boss."

"Then I can't go with you, I'm afraid," Surus said.

"That's your choice, Surus," Rade said. "I'm sorry to see us part ways like this."

"As am I," Surus replied. "If I survive, I'll meet you on the other side. Though I fear our relationship won't be the same."

"Wait," Azen said.

Now that he had made up his mind, Rade's found his patience levels had become extremely low. "Why?"

"They're withdrawing," Lui said. His Titan was peering skyward.

Rade followed his gaze. Sure enough, the remaining skirmishers within the energy sphere were selecting those grav channels that took them closer to the outskirts. Beyond them, the dark shapes of the warships were visibly shrinking in size with each passing moment.

"The skirmishers will never make it back to their motherships," TJ said.

"I know," Azen said. "That's my doing."

"You're doing?" Rade asked.

"The empress reacquired the mutated version of the retrovirus. I was able to assume control of her mind before her doctors could detect it. Through her, I ordered the unconditional withdrawal of all warships, with a general recall of the skirmishers—but none of the latter will actually escape the gravity of the gas giant, as TJ mentioned, not with the warships withdrawing like that."

"So it's over, then," Rade said. "We've repelled the invasion force against your planet."

"We have," Azen agreed.

"We don't have to flee," Rade continued.

"We don't," Azen said.

"What about the disobedient warlords?" Rade said.

"They're withdrawing, too," Azen said. "They don't want to be left behind to wage war against the Greens alone. Plus if they wish to continue harrying the ships of the new empress, they have to follow the main fleet."

"What about her doctors?" Tahoe said. "Won't they cure her, like they did before? And then she'll just steer the fleet back?"

"The first thing I did when I gained control was order all of her medical staff killed," Azen said. "They won't be of any help to her now.

"Nice!" Bender said. "Very, very nice. Lobster fricassee, on the house. I like your style, Azen. For a bug, you're not bad."

"You know that *you* are a bug to me, right?" Azen said.

"Whatever," Bender said. "My bug to your amoeba."

"Amoeba's infect bugs," Lui said.

"And our immune systems fight them off," Bender said.

"You're actually going to let Azen get away with calling you a bug, Bender?" Manic said, his words sounding forced. "I wouldn't stand for that."

"What am I supposed to do?" Bender said. "He's a Phant."

The Greens below seemed to have realized that the threat had passed, and many of them were hesitantly dispersing. An insistent few remained on the platform, and took turns teleporting from the disk in groups of ten.

"Are there any Weavers here that can help Manic?" Rade asked.

"Human-style Weavers?" Azen said. "No. Not in this particular hive. We will change the destination of the Acceptor below when it becomes clear, and use it to return to Surus' base in human territory. Her facilities are much better equipped at the moment."

Rade and the others used their jumpjets to land on the free space that had cleared up along the edge of the platform, and then they waited another minute for the final throng of Greens to take the Acceptor.

When it had cleared, Surus said: "I've changed the coordinates to point to my base. Since the destination disk can only fit two Titans at a time, only two of you may step onto the disk at once. Shaw, Bender, you both carry the injured. You should be the ones to go first. Please, step onto the disk."

Nemesis and Juggernaut moved onto the

Acceptor.

"Please reposition," Surus said. "You need to be in the center."

The two Titans did so.

"Tell Noctua I will be arriving shortly," Surus said. "Tell her to send for the Weavers."

And then the two Titans winked out.

The others moved onto the disk in pairs, and Rade watched his companions vanish in turn.

He almost couldn't believe that the mission was done. And that they had survived, and actually won.

Though the cost was high. An entire alien race, subjugated.

"Rade?" Surus moved onto the disk. "It's time."

Rade joined her Titan on the Acceptor. "Azen isn't staying here?"

"I will come for a day or so," Azen said. "Surus has promised me a tour of this base of hers."

The Green homeworld winked out, replaced by the circular chamber containing the destination disk. Centurion combat robots stood along the walls, their rifles lowered. The Titans were crowded between them along the outskirts of the Acceptor.

"Welcome back, sweet master." Noctua flew down from her T-shaped perch to land on Sprint's shoulder. "I missed you."

"And I missed you, as always, Noctua," Surus said.

"I hope your mission wasn't too trying," the golden owl said.

"It was... difficult," Surus said.

twenty-nine

Rade watched Shaw and Bender deliver Harlequin and Manic to the Weavers that had come to the Acceptor room, and when that was done, he and the others returned their mechs to the appropriate building.

As soon as he climbed out of the cockpit, he removed his helmet and breathed the fresh air of the base. He missed that evergreen smell. Others were doing the same around him, attaching their helmets to their harnesses.

"The base guest house is yours," Surus said. "I've marked it on your maps. I'll leave it up to you to divide the rooms as you see fit. There is clothing of different sizes available in the closets."

Rade led his Argonauts to the guest house, chose the first available quarters for himself and Shaw, and then went inside and locked the door. He stripped out of his jumpsuit and selected a shirt and cargo pants in his size from the closet. He donned the items wearily.

Shaw had undressed as well, but she ignored the articles of clothing, instead attempting to wrap her naked body around him.

Rade slid from her grasp.

"Not now, babe, I'm exhausted." He flopped

down on the bed. He felt a little bad about denying her, but the guilt faded as he fell fast asleep.

Rade woke up to the smell of Shaw's famous coffee.

He sneaked up behind her and wrapped his arms around her waist from behind.

"How's my favorite warrior this morning?" Shaw asked.

"How's my favorite astrogator?" He kissed her on the neck from behind. The smell of her hair... so clean. She had obviously taken a fresh shower. With soap. Unlike him.

"Mmm, I've missed your touch," Shaw said. "It feels like we've been locked inside those jumpsuits for ages. But, hun... you stink."

Rade released her. "Right then." He took the proffered cup of coffee, drank a long sip and then gave it back to her before proceeding to the head.

He had only just turned on the hot water in the hydro-recycle container when he saw her disrobing in front of him, just outside.

"Well, don't stand out there freezing," Rade opened the glass sliding door.

"I'm your astrogator," Shaw said as she entered and wrapped her hands around his neck. "Where should I set a course?"

"Where do you think?" Rade said. He shoved her against the wall of the container and took her.

When they had both orgasmed, she took the soap and bathed him. He was turned on all over again by the time she was done, and he had her again.

After the second time, she said: "You know, I'm not sure I feel like leaving our quarters today. Or in fact, even leaving the hydro container. Can't we just stay here all day?"

Rade smiled sadly. "Wish we could. But we have a few very important people we have to check up on."

"True enough," Shaw said.

"Besides, we're wasting water," Rade said.

"It's recycled," Shaw reminded him.

They left the head, dried up, and dressed. Rade sat down to eat the quick breakfast of chicken and vegetables the suite's robot chef had prepared.

Shaw joined him, and together they downed the meal in silence.

"I'm going to have to have a talk with the Argonauts at some point," Rade announced.

Shaw nodded. "You're not sure about staying on with this client."

"You hit on it," Rade said. "I'm still putting together what I want to say. I think I'll bring it up on liberty in a few days, once we've all had a chance to relax and reflect."

"Let's hear what you have so far," Shaw said.

Rade grinned sheepishly. "I actually haven't started. But it'll be about rights and wrongs, and the dangers inherit to this profession."

"I look forward to hearing what you come up with," Shaw said.

When finished their meal, they made their way outside to check up on their friends.

They found Tahoe and Bender on their way down the hallway steps already.

"Hey guys," Shaw said.

"Hey, come with us," Bender said. "We're visiting Manic."

Tahoe stopped the first Artificial that walked by, an Emilia Bounty clone, and asked where they could find their friends.

"Manic is in the base sickbay," the Artificial said.

"While Harlequin is in the repair shop. I'm marking both locations on your maps. You'll be pleased to hear that the two are on the mend, and are trending toward a complete recovery."

Rade accepted the Artificial's connection request, and saw the two waypoints appear.

"That's great news," Bender said. "Hey, what are you doing later by the way? Would you like to grab some chicken?"

"I'm afraid not," the Artificial said.

When they had walked out of earshot, Bender said: "Damn duplicate Artificials. Guess I hoped they hadn't cloned her cold-ass personality, too."

When they arrived at the sickbay, Manic was already sitting up on the hospital bed. Lui and Fret were there. "Hey guys."

"Manic!" Bender said, grinning widely. Then he realized everyone else was looking at him, and he quickly dropped the smile. "I mean, you bitch. What the hell is wrong with you? Stepping into a bomb blast the way you did."

"Good to see you, too, Bender," Manic said. He extended a hand. "Thank you for everything. What you did back there... stabilizing me like that... I don't think I would have made it."

"Ah shut the hell up," Bender said. His lips were starting to twitch and he blinked rapidly. "I only did what anyone else would have done. You're a goddamn brother. That's all that needs to be said. Besides, what the hell would I do if you were gone? Need someone whose ass I can kick."

Rade stayed and bantered for a while, then he left with Shaw to check on Harlequin.

When he reached the repair house, he found Surus inside, standing next to Harlequin. The latter was on his feet as well, while a third Artificial worked on an open panel in his back.

"Hello, Rade, Shaw," Harlequin said. "Apparently my AI core wasn't as severely damaged as the last time my suit integrity failed. The robots are repairing minor damage to the surrounding circuits... it looks like I'll be out of here in a few hours."

"That's great news," Rade said.

"I hear we had quite an adventure back there," Harlequin said. "I only wish I had been awake to see it with my own eyes. Surus transferred the necessary video archives for my perusal, and I have watched some of it. Near the end, the intensity levels were off the charts. To use a human expression."

"I'm sure Shaw has more archival video she can share with you to fill in some of the blanks," Surus said.

Harlequin glanced at Shaw. "Yes, I would appreciate that."

Surus turned toward Rade. "I will let you three converse."

With that, she departed, leaving Rade and Shaw alone with Harlequin and the repair robot.

"So this is the second time I've cheated death, apparently," Harlequin said. "My only regret is that I couldn't save Shaw. We tried to get away, we did, but—"

Rade raised a hand. "It's okay, Harlequin. I understand. Trust me. Sometimes, there's just nothing you can do."

"You're not mad at me?" Harlequin said. "After the promise I made?"

Rade felt his expression sour. "Of course not. You're a brother, just like every other Argonaut."

"Then how come Surus is the only one who visited

me so far?" Harlequin said.

"Bender will be here shortly, and Tahoe, I'm sure," Rade said. "They're just having a quick visit with Manic at the moment."

Harlequin's expression seemed to sadden slightly. "I see."

Shaw spoke up. "You're upset because they chose to visit a human first?"

Harlequin nodded. "Yes. I suppose it will always be my lot in life to come second to human beings. No matter how much of a brother I ever become. You and Shaw visited Manic first as well, didn't you?"

"Well yes," Rade said. "But only because the sickbay was closer to the guest house." It was a lie—the repair shop and the sickbay were about the same distance away, but he couldn't bring himself to tell Harlequin the truth.

"Oh," Harlequin said, his expressing brightening slightly. "That makes sense, then. I was sorry to hear about Manic, by the way. I want to visit him as well. He will recover?"

"That's what we've heard," Rade said. "He seems fine. Like you."

Harlequin nodded. "That is good." He opened his mouth, then closed it again, seeming hesitant.

"What is it?" Rade asked.

"I, well," Harlequin paused once more. "I have a question."

"Ask anything," Rade said.

"How did my predecessor die?" Harlequin said. "I know it was bravely. I've inferred as much: you told me he gave his life for you. But what were the exact circumstances?"

Rade smiled sadly. "It happened near the end of the Second Alien War. We were making a run for an escape shuttle. Being shot all to hell by a bunch of robot aliens. Me and another Marine were shot down. There was no way we were going to make it to the shuttle. Your predecessor turned back into the fray, took several laser hits, and threw us into the retreating shuttle. He was too shot up to save himself. We left him there on the surface."

Harlequin nodded slowly. "Thank you."

RADE JOINED SURUS in the Acceptor room that evening to bid Azen farewell. Shaw and Harlequin had come as well. The rest of the Argonauts had elected to remain in their quarters. "We've seen enough of the Greens to last until the next century," was TJ's comment.

Azen resided within his usual Sino-Korean Artificial host. He shook the hands of Rade, Shaw, and Harlequin in turn.

"Thank you for everything you have done," Azen said. "Without your help, I could not have saved my homeworld."

"Sure," Rade said. "I just wish you had let us in on your plans. So we could have stopped you."

"From infecting the new empress with a virus that allowed me to control her?" Azen asked. "But if you did that, none of you would have ever returned. We would have met our doom on Bethesda's warship."

"Actually, we wouldn't have," Rade said. "Because she wouldn't have turned against us in the first place. She only did so because her doctors found out about the virus you secretly infected her with."

"You don't know that," Azen said.

Rade sighed. "No, I suppose I don't. Still, I'd like to believe she would have kept her word."

"If only I shared your lofty ideals regarding other races," Azen said. "While that may have been the second time I saved her life, there was no guarantee she would have kept her word. Politics can override integrity for even the most honorable of species. The Phants have conquered a hundred races. We know what treachery is firsthand."

"You make it sound like you were part of that conquering," Rade said.

"The Greens were, at first," Azen said. "Until we decided to turn our back on the evil ways of the others. We were responsible for the fall of so many planets, converting them to geronium factories, poisoning neighboring stars in the process... thousands of suns in the galactic core have gone nova because of us. It is not something I am proud of."

"When we visited the Xaranth world with Surus, its sun hadn't gone nova," Rade said.

"No," Surus told him. "But its lifespan has been greatly shortened. It will die far earlier than it should have. Which is why I fear the Xaranth will never achieve their former Tech Class."

"So what happens to the Hydra as a species now?" Rade said. "The virus will spread, I'm sure. The Greens will have complete control over every last one of them."

"We will use this power wisely," Azen said. "Once the Hydra have left our space, we will relinquish control and allow the virus to lie dormant within them. But should they ever return, we will exert control once again, and send them away."

"You won't use it to wipe them out?" Shaw asked.

"Why would we?" Azen said. "We left them alone

all these years. We seek only peace with them."

"But isn't there a chance that her doctors will cure her again, when she regains control and realizes what you've done?" Shaw said.

"There is a chance, yes," Azen said. "Though I am confident the virus will simply mutate once more, and lie dormant, undetected."

"What you've done still bothers me to the core," Rade said. "I'm still not convinced you haven't infected us in some way. Humans with senior positions in the world governments, I mean."

"Even if we had, you would be safe as long as you left us Greens alone," Azen said. "Surus, you will change the Acceptor destination to point to a different world once I return, I presume? As a safeguard?"

"Of course," Surus said. "None shall reach the Green homeworld from here. Unless someday I need to change the destination back, of course."

"Thank you," Azen said. "Farewell, humans. As always, it has been a... well, quite the trip."

He stepped onto the Acceptor and vanished.

When he was gone Surus turned toward Rade.

"I would like you to know that Azen's beliefs are not representative of all Greens," Surus said.

"That's exactly what I'm afraid of," Rade said.

"What do you mean?" Surus said.

Shaw answered for him. "Azen says he would never use that retroviral technology against humanity. But that doesn't mean other Greens wouldn't. Or other Phant factions."

THE NEXT DAY the team returned to the *Argonaut*

waiting in orbit. Rade had Shaw direct the ship toward a nearby base, two days away in the Taurus system. When they arrived, Rade set his crew loose to mess shit up. It seemed like an eternity since they'd had their last liberty.

He gathered the crew for a special dinner that evening in one of the more expensive restaurants in the station. Surus wasn't invited.

Rade called for silence when everyone was finished their meals, and he instructed the Argonauts to raise their noise cancelers to isolate the table from the rest of the restaurant. Then he spoke.

"What happened in that last mission, well, it didn't sit right with my morals," Rade said. "We've basically given the Greens the power to subjugate an entire alien race. Sure, they claim they'll only use that ability when in absolute need, but still, it seems wrong. It reeks of the power-hungry behavior we've seen in other Phants. Those factions who wouldn't hesitate to conquer humanity, and the hundreds of other species before us.

"But there's something else that's been on my mind as well, bothering me lately. We've been coming too close to death ever since taking on this new client. I've almost lost Shaw three times now. Last mission, Manic was severely injured, and Harlequin damaged almost beyond repair. I'm not sure I've set us on the right path.

"So I've gathered you here today to make a vote. While I like hunting Phants as much as every one of you, I don't like abetting morally-questionable behavior, nor risking my life while doing so. Surus claims she had no idea what Azen had planned, and says she is just as angry about what he did as the rest of us. I believe her, I think. But the rest of you need to make up your own minds. So my question to you is, do we continue retaining Surus as a client? Do we continue to risk our lives hunting Phants for her? Or do we let her go and set out on our own, and go back to the way things were before?"

There was silence around the table for several moments.

"I say we stay with her," Bender said.

"You would," Manic quipped.

"I don't mean that just because she's hot," Bender said. "Okay, well, maybe I do. But seriously, we're doing what we do best right now. Hunting bugs. There ain't no better life than this, mark my words. It was what we were meant to do. Can any of you really even consider going back to an ordinary life now, after everything we've seen and done? Can we go back to providing 'security services' to ordinary clients? Protecting their rich-ass daughters from being kidnapped while they go on their shopping sprees? Securing the smuggling lines of some low-life warlord? Come on, seriously? We can't."

"Bender has a point," Manic said. "We have something good here. There are risks, yes. And sometimes our client might ask us to do things that go against our morals. But I say we stay, and decide for ourselves during each and every mission whether something we are about to do goes against our collective belief system. And we adjust our course of action accordingly."

"I think what the boss is trying to say here," Tahoe interjected. "Is that we didn't know our actions were morally wrong. We only learned after the fact. So the question is more like, should we stay with a client who does things that go against our moral codes, and only tells us about it after the fact?"

"But like the boss said, Surus didn't actually know about those actions," Fret said.

"Which only goes to show," Tahoe said. "That the Greens do have the ability to deceive. They're not the morally pure beings we thought they were."

"No species is perfect," TJ said. "Not even humanity. In Azen, I can easily see half a dozen generals and admirals from the United Systems military. And we worked for them for fifteen years."

"Yeah, but that's different," Tahoe said. "We were forced to obey their orders to the letter, as required by the terms of our enlistment. We fought for different reasons, some of us to gain our citizenship, some of us because we had nothing else to do in life. And yes, we had to take on missions that were morally questionable all the time. But we're free now to make up our own minds on what is right and wrong. We don't have to follow Surus. I say we make our own way."

Rade nodded. "All who want to keep Surus as a client, with the caveat that we will only obey her if it fits our moral code, raise your hands."

Nearly everyone raised their hands. Tahoe did not. Nor did Harlequin, surprisingly.

"Then it's settled," Rade said. "We go with her. Tahoe and Harlequin, I'm not going to make you continue with the Argonauts if this isn't what you want. I can buy you out right here if—"

"We're coming of course," Harlequin said. "While we might not always agree with the policies and politics of whatever employers we take on, our place is at your side."

Tahoe nodded. "He speaks for me."

"Thank you," Rade said. "Thank you all." He raised his glass. "So here's to an amazing liberty. When we leave this place behind a week from now, I fully expect that I'll have to break half of you out of prison, and the other half out of the infirmary."

Rade watched them enjoy their after dinner drinks. The manager came over a few times and asked if they could quiet down, and Rade always agreed, but as soon as the robot had gone off, they reverted to their rowdy selves.

Ah well. Argonauts will be Argonauts.

He wondered what Surus was doing at that very moment. Likely conversing with some Green in another part of human space. Conversing... or plotting. He wasn't sure how comfortable he was with the network of "friendly" Phants she had with her in their part of the galaxy.

Even though the crew had voted to retain her as a client, he decided he would have to watch her very closely in the months to come.

Beware of Greens bearing gifts.

Thank you for reading.

Acknowledgments

THANK YOU to my knowledgeable beta readers and advanced reviewers who helped smooth out the rough edges of the prerelease manuscript: Nicole P., Lisa A. G., Gregg C., Jeff K., Mark C., Jeremy G., Doug B., Jenny O., Amy B., Bryan O., Lezza M., Gene A., Larry J., Allen M., Gary F., Eric, Robine, Noel, Anton, Spencer, Norman, Trudi, Corey, Erol, Terje, David, Charles, Walter, Lisa, Ramon, Chris, Scott, Michael, Chris, Bob, Jim, Maureen, Zane, Chuck, Shayne, Anna, Dave, Roger, Nick, Gerry, Charles, Annie, Patrick, Mike, Jeff, Lisa, Jason, Bryant, Janna, Tom, Jerry, Chris, Jim, Brandon, Kathy, Norm, Jonathan, Derek, Shawn, Judi, Eric, Rick, Bryan, Barry, Sherman, Jim, Bob, Ralph, Darren, Michael, Chris, Michael, Julie, Glenn, Rickie, Rhonda, Neil, Claude, Ski, Joe, Paul, Larry, John, Norma, Jeff, David, Brennan, Phyllis, Robert, Darren, Daniel, Montzalee, Robert, Dave, Diane, Peter, Skip, Louise, Dave, Brent, Erin, Paul, Jeremy, Dan, Garland, Sharon, Dave, Pat, Nathan, Max, Martin, Greg, David, Myles, Nancy, Ed, David, Karen, Becky, Jacob, Ben, Don, Carl, Gene, Bob, Luke, Teri, Gerald, Lee, Rich, Ken, Daniel, Chris, Al, Andy, Tim, Robert, Fred, David, Mitch, Don, Tony, Dian, Tony, John, Sandy, James, David, Pat, Jean, Bryan, William, Roy, Dave, Vincent, Tim, Richard, Kevin, George, Andrew, John, Richard, Robin, Sue, Mark, Jerry, Rodger, Rob, Byron, Ty,

Mike, Gerry, Steve, Benjamin, Anna, Keith, Jeff, Josh, Herb, Bev, Simon, John, David, Greg, Larry, Timothy, Tony, Ian, Niraj, Maureen, Jim, Len, Bryan, Todd, Maria, Angela, Gerhard, Renee, Pete, Hemantkumar, Tim, Joseph, Will, David, Suzanne, Steve, Derek, Valerie, Laurence, James, Andy, Mark, Tarzy, Christina, Rick, Mike, Paula, Tim, Jim, Gal, Anthony, Ron, Dietrich, Mindy, Ben, Steve, Paddy & Penny, Troy, Marti, Herb, Jim, David, Alan, Leslie, Chuck, Dan, Perry, Chris, Rich, Rod, Trevor, Rick, Michael, Tim, Mark, Alex, John, William, Doug, Tony, David, Sam, Derek, John, Jay, Tom, Bryant, Larry, Anjanette, Gary, Travis, Jennifer, Henry, Drew, Michelle, Bob, Gregg, Billy, Jack, Lance, Sandra, Libby, Jonathan, Karl, Bruce, Clay, Gary, Sarge, Andrew, Deborah, Steve, and Curtis.

Without you all, this novel would have typos, continuity errors, and excessive lapses in realism. Thank you for helping me make this the best military science fiction novel it could possibly be, and thank you for leaving the early reviews that help new readers find my books.

And of course I'd be remiss if I didn't thank my mother, father, and brothers, whose untiring wisdom and thought-provoking insights have always guided me through the untamed warrens of life.

— Isaac Hooke

ALIEN EMPRESS (ARGONAUTS BOOK 3)

www.isaachooke.com